THE HYBRID HEIR

The Paranormals of Ahl Book 3.5

ML CONKLIN

The Hybrid Heir (The Paranormals of Ahl Book 3.5)

For information contact :

MLConklin@MLConklin.com

Sign up for the newsletter for updates and information on new releases:

http://www.mlconklin.com

Cover design by Getcovers.com

ISBN E-book:979-8-9900731-8-0

ISBN Paperback : 979-8-9900731-9-7

First Edition: February 2025

A Note from the Author

Thank you for reading this series. I really appreciate it. The Hybrid Heir is the book 3.5 in the Paranormals of Ahl series. It is the second book featuring Lily as the main character. If you haven't read the first four books in the series (Book 2.5 is also from Lily's perspective), I suggest you start with The Dragon Problem (Book 1) and read the series in order, or you'll be lost.

Trigger warnings and heads-up:

- A reference to past child abuse.
- References to torture.
- Violence and death throughout the book.
- Lily's a vampire. Blood drinking is referenced several times.
- The gnome won't stop cussing, and other profanity.
- I'm not a spicy writer. Though there are some sexual innuendos and one slightly spicy scene.
- The romance has an age gap.

Chapter One

A loud creak came from the cheap plastic chair as my weight shifted. I stared across a worn table at a rat-faced woman and fought to focus on her face instead of the pulse. A difficult task, considering how fast her heart was beating. My vampire side is great. It's a deeply integrated part of my life. Being extra strong and super fast is fun. Claws and fangs are handy. Shadow blending and enhanced senses are the best. But they had no place in a bland interview room.

I'd gone my entire life thinking I didn't need blood, only to learn I'd hobbled myself. After my new sister and grandfather forced it on me to save my life, I became stronger and faster. My already excellent hearing sharpened. Since that awful day, I couldn't live without it. The cravings were like a drug addiction. They consumed me and made me feel urges I'd never imagined. Like the urge to dive across the desk and drain the woman interviewing me.

"It says here you worked as a data analyst in your last job."

I clenched my fists and pasted on a smile. "Yes."

Her already too-small face pinched. "Then why apply for a job in retail?"

"I needed a change of pace." My lie hung in the air, though the human woman wouldn't notice. I had no desire to work in retail so much as to find a toxic workplace. The big chain stores were notorious for having a ton of work drama, and I wanted nothing more than to score a job in one to soak it up.

"Hmm." She leaned back and crossed her arms, ignoring the goosebumps my predatory nature gave her. "Can I be honest?"

Here we go. "Please."

"You're overqualified for this position, and you won't fit in culturally."

Dang it! I heard they cut hours when the employee needed extra money and forced them to work past the end of their shift without pay. I wanted in on the action. "How do you know if you don't give me the chance?"

Her eyes narrowed. "I know."

I stood and clutched the chair to stop myself from launching at her. "Thanks for your time." My chest puffed out at how polite I sounded as I left the store.

The stabbing sensation I always felt when a blood relative was close started before I reached my new van, and I stifled a groan. I paused and texted my brother to tell him I failed yet another interview. He responded with 'good.' Whatever that meant. I groaned as I hopped inside. "Hey, Gramps. What are you doing here?"

"Lily. I am here to train you," his voice sounded extra dry.

My head twisted toward him. Dull navy-blue eyes met mine without a single spark of expression in them. A common trait in older vampires. "I'm a little busy."

"Yes. Seeking unneeded employment is a wise use of your time."

I adored Quin. His sarcasm was first-class. "What exactly is it you consider worth my time?"

"Training."

I sighed and pushed the start button. "Why would you bother when Roman has already tried and failed?"

"My methods are more suited for your unique personality."

I loosened my grip on the steering wheel when it creaked. Gramps wasn't the cause of my irritation. The frustration stemmed from interviewing at five toxic workplaces and not finding a job. Though he was a close second. My blood relatives not only encroached on my life but ripped up my boundaries, stomped on them, and served seven-course meals with a smile on their faces while doing it.

My new sister put an entire magical realm in my backyard. And Gramps spent the weeks before the recent battle insisting I physically train like a soldier. Then he followed me around the fight and critiqued my skills as we slaughtered demons and Bellicose minions. I had to admit that part was fascinating, and I learned a lot from it. But since that awful day, he still hung around. "Oh?"

"You will see."

I bet. "Why aren't you bothering Jen?" My sister was much more interesting than me. Especially since she started becoming the queen we desperately needed.

"Jen is gone."

My heart ached as my head twisted toward him. I already lost my new brother, and if Jen was gone, too, then no one was running the coalition. Besides, we became closer every time she stormed into my life, and I liked her. "What do you mean, she's gone?"

"Let us engage in conversation as if the road were not full of other vehicles."

I refocused on driving. Not because of his comment, but because the van was brand new, and I didn't want to wreck it. "Is she okay?"

"The First took her to an undisclosed location."

So Jen was getting her freak on with her man. Nice. I'd love to find someone to scratch that itch. The face of a sexy blond god floated through my mind, and I brushed it away. "And you decided to bother me while she's gone?"

"Yes."

I sighed and tapped the steering wheel. I was trying to get back to my life, and it wasn't going to happen with gramps hanging around.

Luckily, he disappeared as soon as I pulled through my wards and parked. Probably going to the strange, unwanted pocket in my back field. I slogged into the kitchen, opened the fridge, and spotted the blood bags. The grinding sound, followed by the loud clang, didn't register at first. I blinked when I realized the refrigerator door was off its hinges, laying on the cracked tile.

"Great. Now we'll have to eat all the food today," my brother said from his seat at the table.

I grabbed a blood pack and chugged it. "You can eat it. I'm going for a run."

Alex set his spoon down. "You've been off since the prince died."

A dull ache flared at the mention of the brother I'd barely known, and I rubbed my chest. "No, I haven't. It's because I can't find a job, and my new family members keep blocking me from moving on with my life." I threw the empty bag in the magic contraption Jen's witch friend Tracy installed. I smacked my lips and resisted gagging at how tasty I found blood. "Maybe I'll brush my teeth before I run."

Alex shrugged. "Deny it all you want. But it bothers you."

I dismissed him with a wave and raced up the stairs. It wasn't until I reached the top that I noticed the thrum in my veins from the only blood bond I held. Elsie, the vampire my grandmother insisted I take, had arrived and was inside the room beside mine. I whizzed past and slammed my bedroom door. Elsie was okay for a vampire, but I didn't need another encroachment.

After changing clothes, I went fluid to avoid Elsie and Alex. As I zipped out of the house and down a trail, I gave the gate to the weird new pocket a wide berth.

Two tiny figures blocked my path as I slowed to a human jog. "What the fuck are you doing, Lily?"

I stopped. "Hey, Flemming. Matilda. You better not let Jen hear you cussing." Flemming had lost his wife and kids when I found him. He made the mistake of cussing at my sister when she came to heal me after a car accident. Being the most powerful person on the planet, she could have destroyed him for the disrespect. Our mother would have. Instead, she made an agreement. She'd find his family if he stopped cussing. Jen completed her end of the deal when we found them in a garden center. And Flemming had cut back, but still slipped a lot.

"I understand the limits of the damn agreement."

My gnome's match, Matilda, elbowed him. "The foul-mouthed scallywag better stop using that fucking language in my presence!"

"Erm. Sure. What do you need?"

Flemming threw his arms in the air. "What the fuck do you think?" He stabbed a finger toward a new road opposite the gate. The mages and elves worked together to build it, allowing hybrids access to the pocket. "It's a damn travesty to have this piece of shit cutting through my territory."

I examined the new road for a long moment and then nodded. "Yeah. It was either make a road in the side field or let them cut through the driveway and trample the lawn." I turned my attention back to the gnomes. "Do you like that option better?"

Flemming ripped his hat off, thought better of it, then shoved it back on his head. "Hell no, I don't like it fucking better! I don't like this damn thing here at all!"

I pressed my lips together to suppress a laugh. When I had it under control, I spoke. "I hate it, too. But here we are."

"Just make sure none of those assholes ruin the maze or my lawn."

"I'll do my best."

The two gnomes disappeared into the field.

I gave the road one more considering look before continuing my run. It wasn't like anyone used it since there were two other gates. Most hybrids used the one at Dale's bar or another near my parent's place. Though, occasionally, a stray would trot up the road and disappear inside the pocket.

Three laps around the fields and through the maze later, I slowed to a walk to think. The road reminded me my anger wasn't about the blood but all the changes. So much had changed in such a short time I hadn't processed it.

Not only did I meet my biological family, but they'd established themselves as permanent fixtures in my life. And I felt conflicted about Mat's death. I liked the guy and looked forward to pushing his buttons. It hurt because now I'd never have a chance to know him. But his funeral wasn't as sad for me as it was for the people I stood with that day.

I plopped onto a chair on the back deck and eyed Cavil's house. He was another new fixture. The guy saved my ass more than once during the battle and often checked on me. I didn't mind, aside from how, whenever he showed up, my stomach became an Olympic gymnast. He brought light to my darkness and made me long to dive into it, even though I'd probably burn myself. And that, more than anything else, scared the shit out of me. I had to leash those emotions because I cherished his friendship and refused to ruin it by sleeping with him.

Alex came out the sliding door, scanned my face, and slumped into a chair. "Talk it out, Lily."

My lips turned up. "You sound like Dad."

"Thank you. Now, talk."

I let out a long sigh. "None of this makes sense. Why was my birth family so nice to me from the start?"

"Because they're good people?"

"But they're not. Well, except for Jen. Sort of. But people called Mat the bloody prince because he was a stone-cold killer. And I once read a story about how Ara kidnapped a woman and tortured her with a thousand cuts simply because she flirted with Quin. And have you heard those brutal vampire stories the humans tell? Well, most of them are based on Gramps, and they're not even close to as brutal as the actual incidents. According to the history books, my entire family is a gaggle of violent assholes."

"Yet they embraced you."

"Exactly. I show up, and Mat's all like, 'Welcome, sis. Here's special permission to enter our neighborhood. Wanna fight at my side?' And

Ara starts baking cookies and serving delicious tea. Quin…okay, maybe he didn't go out of his way to make me feel welcome, but he's still hanging around."

"Yeah. I get it. Have you ever read up on Mom and Dad's history?"

"What's that got to do with anything?"

"They were just as bad as your family. Or didn't you see all three of their kids recently tried to lead a coup?"

I rolled my eyes. "That's different. What I'm saying is it's off."

"It's not. Our parents never wanted to separate from the purebloods. The second queen forced them to."

"Pulled that from their thoughts, did ya?"

"Yes. And a whole lot of other stuff. All I'm saying is they're not saints."

I stroked the end of my hair. "They're not. But it's different."

"Different, how?"

"I don't know how to be a vampire. Not really. But Ara just willy-nilly names me her heir and hands Elsie over to me. That doesn't sound like the kind of decision a woman who's ruled for thousands of years would make. Then, Jen and Mat just waltz in and give me a new name and several titles. They didn't know what I'd do with the power. What if I was a super villain or the Bellicose leader with the weird magic?"

"When you phrase it that way, it doesn't sound right."

"It's what happened."

"It depends on how you look at it."

I tapped my leg. "Okay, smarty-pants. Tell me what I'm missing."

"What if they were aware of you?"

"Yeah. They said as much. But that still doesn't explain anything."

The look on his face said he thought I was being difficult. "Think about it, Lily. How long between Jed showing up at our door trying to shmooze you and our trip to Allure?"

"Months."

"Right. Follow the logic. Why would he show up?"

"Because Meemaw told him to present me to her."

"Exactly. He thinks you're an abomination and a mistake. Probably because he knew you were the heir. And if he knew, Ara knew. Though I haven't been able to pry it out of her head."

"Ugh."

Alex ignored my discomfort. "Ara can track any vampire. Other than you, they're all connected to her like she's the damn internet or something. So, say she hears about you and shares the information with Jen. Or vice versa. They do a little research, which is plausible considering both Jen and Quin are private detectives."

"At the pissed."

"The PISD, yes. Ara showed up at the bar right before all hell broke loose. How did she find us there?"

"Someone told her about it."

"Right. What if they discovered you live in the valley, and the Firsts adopted you? So she ordered Jed to bring you in, but you won't talk to him. He can't accept rejection, so he plays right into her hands and sends his vampires to spy on you. Through them, she learned you're a somewhat well-adjusted powerhouse who cares about people. So, she wakes Roman up and sends him your way to make sure her assessment is correct. He's fond of you and takes you under his wing, and she learns more."

"Did you read them, or are you guessing?"

"A little of both. My point is that Ara and Quin already knew about you when we showed up at her house. Jen's tone was off when she told Quin they found his granddaughter. As if she had found his lost keys. Even when she learned you were her sister, she shrugged it off. And I didn't have to read minds. I saw Ara's expression. It was bland until she spotted you. Then she lit up like a Christmas tree."

I blinked. "How did I not notice that?"

"Because you convinced yourself they'd torture and kill you. Ara knew you'd run if she didn't make you feel welcome. So they bring you in, tell you who you are, which Ara already knows, of course. Then, she goes all grandma to earn your trust. You respected Elsie's fighting skills, so she dangles that carrot."

"But why make me her heir?"

"A thought ran through Jen's mind about how Lilith took away Ara's ability to produce an heir, so she probably gave up years ago. The idea of one existing gave her hope. So she gives you a vampire who doesn't need much direction and can help train you. And I wouldn't doubt if she can check on you through Elsie."

"No need, with Quin lurking around."

"He likes you and is thrilled to have a grandchild, even if he doesn't show it."

We fell silent. It was a much better perspective than being set up as the butt of a twisted joke, which was my conclusion. "What about Mat and Jen?"

"Drake knew who you were, so maybe he vouched for you. And Jen genuinely likes you."

"Or maybe they talked to Mom and Dad."

"It's a possibility."

Our parents conned us into hiding in Allure to keep us safe. And now we had too many purebloods in our lives. I wouldn't put it past them to manipulate the situation if they thought it was best for us. "What did the Bellicose do to you?" My brother hadn't talked about his kidnapping much, but I knew it affected him far more than he wanted to admit.

A sigh escaped him. "It wasn't so bad at first. They didn't understand my mental abilities, and I attempted to keep it that way. Then Morten showed up." He swept his hair out of his eyes. "He knew all about me, and our plan fell apart."

When he didn't continue, I threw out my hands. "And?"

"And nothing. He wanted me to kill some people in an office building. Drake, I think. When I refused, they beat the hell out of me and locked me in a spelled office. Glac attempted a rescue, and they knocked him out with the remnants of Deva's magic. They had a demon who could store power, but Jen and Deva banished him, and he was too weak to return. So Morten tried to keep Glac until the demon regained his strength. Even with the demons they summoned, he couldn't control us." He stood and stretched. "Those chains didn't work on Glac and barely snared me. In hindsight, I doubt they allowed us to escape. They weren't very organized."

"Drake said something about how their stupidity made them more dangerous."

"Accurate. They failed to use the information their spies gathered to their advantage. It pissed Morten off. They couldn't do what he demanded because they wasted too much energy trying to control people and maintain their spells. It was chaos. I waited until he had them preoccupied with yet another self-inflicted problem and flashed away. They couldn't stop me. But it activated a proximity spell on the chains. Like one of those monitors people put on their dogs. The curse didn't activate until I flashed to Hooves."

Our favorite bartender, Dale, called us for help when Alex and Glac appeared in the middle of a human subdivision near his bar. But I still had a million questions. I didn't ask them because Glacintial appeared in the backyard, two other dragons flanking him. He shifted and flipped his long white hair over his shoulder. "Lily. Alex. My queen requests permission to move a few dragons to your pocket for culinary and security detail."

I started to refuse but hesitated. The dragons made great drinking buddies. If I couldn't find a toxic workplace, then I'd need something else to do. And they made great food. The only issue was how the hybrids would receive them. It would be fun to watch it play out.

"I dunno, Glac. The hybrids might not like dragons hanging around." Alex spoke before I could.

I lifted a hand. "You can stay at our new house." No way I'd move into the thing. The inside was great, but the outside resembled a crayon explosion. I attempted to paint it a different color, but it repelled the paint. So, it had to stay that way until Jen crashed back into my life.

All four heads twisted toward me.

I shrugged. "I like dragon food. How many dragons?"

A chill ran down my spine at Glac's predatory grin. "Three to start. We do not intend to encroach on the hybrids. Our queen wishes to provide them support."

Suuuuuure they didn't. The dragons had their hands in everything within the paranormal community. And they weren't the only ones. I eyed the area where I sensed Gramps. "I take it Flintous and June are two of them?"

He tilted his head. "And I am the third. Queen Jenella wished me to recruit more hybrids into her army and run the division."

I snort-laughed. Even while missing, my new sister trespassed on my life. "Uh-huh."

Alex elbowed me. "You're welcome to stay in our house, but leave our bedrooms and offices alone."

With a dip of his head, Glacintial led the dragons toward the gate.

"Will their presence cause problems?" I asked with too much glee.

The corner of his eyes crinkled. "They're fine."

Chapter Two

Alex needed to focus on boring things like sleep and work, so I was on my own as I pulled into the parking lot of Hooves. Or I had the illusion of being alone. Gramps was never too far away, and Cavil seemed to appear when I needed him. It should have bothered me more, but I couldn't bring myself to care. I was bored, lonely, and restless. It had to change.

The bar's owner, Dale, stood behind the bar with his usual towel slung across his colossal shoulder. His sharp eyes locked onto me the moment I entered. "Your highness."

"Har har." I climbed onto a bar stool and folded my hands, waiting to see what drink he'd serve me.

He lifted an eyebrow.

I grinned.

With a creaky laugh, he turned and poured a vodka and tonic. "I no longer have the time to think about your drinks."

"No shit? Responsibilities weighing you down, are they?"

"Among other things. Where's Alex?"

"Home. What's the word on the street?"

He slid the glass across the bar. "It's been quiet. Too quiet."

"Yeah. I've been out for three nights in a row and haven't heard a peep. It's eerie."

"The privacy spell's still up inside the neighborhood. Some fancy mages are working on rebuilding, but they don't understand city utilities. If they don't fix it soon, humans will notice."

"Not our problem. Where are your regulars?"

"Most moved to the pocket. Some died in the fight. What's it to you?"

I slammed my drink back and pushed the glass forward. "Just curious. Three dragons are moving into the pocket to help with food and whatnot."

Dale's muscles bunched. "Is it wise to mix purebloods in with the hybrid population?"

"There isn't a damn thing about my life I'd call wise at this point."

A deep rumble of laughter echoed through the empty bar.

"Sure. Laugh it up."

He shook a finger at me. "You might need to rethink your life."

"No shit." I hopped off the barstool. "If you hear anything, will you text me?"

"Will do. Oh, and Lily?"

I stopped. "Yeah?"

"Stop telling people to assign me leadership positions."

"You should have thought about that before you decided to call me 'your highness.' Shit rolls downhill."

His laughter cut off as the door closed behind me.

I went fluid and took a lap around one of the two abandoned subdivisions. The one beside the bar wasn't as torn up as the neighborhood across the main street. It didn't take the brunt of the battle.

Movement on the road made me pause. I slipped into the shadows and wrapped them around myself. I was getting better at shadow blending, but still nowhere near the level of Elsie, let alone Gramps.

A mage wandered down the road, marking the torn-up asphalt every few steps. Another one followed behind and added magic. The ragged road smoothed out as it sank into the ground.

I climbed a tree and settled onto a thick branch overlooking the workers. Dale was right about my life. It had become more difficult, yet somehow duller. As we prepared for the battle, all the purebloods hovering around Jen irritated me with their growling, sniping, bickering, and sarcastic comments. I love me some drama. But it was impossible to escape after they put the stupid pocket in my backyard.

After everyone cleared out, I became bored. So, I started applying for jobs and headed to town to poke around in my spare time. The city still felt off. It was almost as if it was too quiet. Unsure what else to do, I often sat in a tree watching the pureblood architectural mages and dwarven engineers. They were competent and wicked-fast learners. Especially since the hybrid construction crew stood to the side, arms crossed, and refused to help, except for a snide comment here and there.

Very few purebloods worked that night. They were still trying to restore power, so they provided a minuscule amount of entertainment. I rested my head against the tree and picked at a piece of bark, wondering how long we had before humans figured out something was wrong. They already posted pictures of gargoyles, and videos of enforcers disappearing into the privacy spell went viral.

The stabbing sensation came a second before Quin appeared on the branch beside mine. The bark slipped out of my hand and bounced on the ground. "Hey, Gramps."

"You are not using shadows properly."

"Nope. I tried Roman's way and blew up an air conditioner."

"Because you do not embrace your vampire side."

"Sure, I do. For example, I went fluid recently."

"You have the power of Lilith, so you should blend seamlessly."

"No shit?"

Gramps understood I wasn't in the mood to discuss my weaknesses because he was silent for a while. Loud voices came from the hybrids down the way, followed by a shout and a laugh. "Perhaps Roman is not the best instructor."

"He tries. He's a little long-winded and monotone, so I can't focus on his lessons. I even tried to trace his magic like Jen showed me, but it's full of these weird mazes and loops I can't follow. And he doesn't understand why I don't understand."

"Interesting."

"It's downright boring." I picked at another piece of bark. "I may have the vampire equivalent of a learning disability. Because even when I follow your lead, I can't replicate it."

"Oh, yes. I'm sure your mind is addled. Tell me, if you are so slow, how did you learn high-level skills without guidance?"

"The vampires at Jed's house taught me the basics. The rest I picked up from books. But I've never understood magic beyond what my biological mother taught me when I was still in diapers. My mom and Jen have come close to helping me. But they're so far out of my league, it doesn't compute."

"Sorceresses do not use much intent, so Ann Marie would not understand it like Jen does. And Jenella has practiced magic her entire life, where you have hobbled yourself. Roman often marches to the beat of his own drummer." He pulled shadow magic around himself. "Study and duplicate this. If you do not, I'll push you out of the tree."

The eerie golden-red glow of my eyes reflected off the branches.

"I will give you to the count of ten." Goosebumps popped up on my arms when Gramps bared his teeth in what might have been a smile.

Not having anything else to do, I pushed my hand into the thick shadows surrounding him, tentatively at first. When I noticed how different they felt, I dove deeper. I attempted to duplicate his shadows during the battle and couldn't. But the new ones were different. "What is this?"

"It is similar to your grandmother's method."

"And Meemaw has magic like mine, right?"

"Correct."

Where Roman's instructions were confusing and chaotic, and Quin's normally too cut-throat, the imitation of Meemaw's shadow magic felt right. Instead of loops and tangles, it felt straightforward and purposeful.

Something clicked in my brain. I focused on the shadows from deep within the tree branches and tried to pull them to me. And failed. Instead of using my crappy method, which was a kind of sinking into the shadows, I layered the ones close to me around myself.

"Better. Each vampire learns the basics and improvises. Release them and try again."

He had me repeat the process several times before I got the combination somewhat right. Sweat ran down my temple, but the shadows stuck well enough to hide me. "Is that good?"

"It is adequate. Let us discuss your fangs."

"My fangs?"

"Bite your tongue should they involuntarily reveal themselves. Do not stop until you have control."

"You expect me to use self-inflicted pain to restrain myself?"

"It is a method used to train baby vampires."

My lips turned down. "I'm not a baby vampire."

A rusty, cartoonish laugh escaped him. "You are very much a baby. A powerful and dangerous one. The pain will teach you control."

"Okay. Want to go spy with me? Or follow from a distance like you usually do?"

Downtown was as dull as West Boise. The deserted streets felt too normal. After the Bellicose clogging the area for the last few months, not running into their putrid magic made me twitchy.

I jammed my hands in my coat pockets and faked being cold as I walked at a brisk human pace. Gramps strolled beside me, wearing jeans and a suede coat. He wasn't a big guy, but his overwhelming presence made up for his lack of height. I shut my eyes to listen when we stopped at a pedestrian crossing.

"Ow." A thump on my head made me hop sideways a little too fast.

"Do not close your eyes."

I massaged my sore noggin. "It helps me concentrate."

"Yes. And it will also help you die."

The light changed, and I watched to make sure he wouldn't smack me again as we started across the road. "How do I listen without concentrating?"

"Stop pretending."

My face scrunched as two guys came out of a bar. "I'm not following."

"You are not now, nor will you ever be, human. Stop pretending and trust your senses."

I relaxed and allowed my body to move naturally. Traffic noises and voices assaulted my ears, and I flinched. "I've adjusted my hearing a million times. Keeping my eyes open while I filter it out is hard."

"As are all unpracticed arts."

My head ached from the assault on my ears. Eyes wide open, I blocked out the traffic noise, the hum of power and lights, the birds and squirrels. A few blocks over, a dog barked. I ignored it, too, focusing on scanning voices. In the downtown area alone, there were thousands of people. I narrowed it down as I fought to hold my eyes open. Bad habits were hard to break. "Got it. Process, discard, move on."

With a wide grin, I practiced again. It had been years since I learned a new vampire skill. Gramps taught me two in a single night. My mouth opened to thank him, but I hesitated when I realized he hung around to train me rather than to make my life miserable. The question was, why? No way I'd agree to be queen of the vampires. Nor would I take Jen's place. Becoming Queen of Umbra or Ahl was less appealing to me than shaving my legs with a cheese grater and taking a bath in alcohol.

A group of men turned the corner and strolled in our direction, interrupting my thoughts. Their eyes were too alert, and their posture too tight for your regular barfly.

Gramps changed his entire demeanor as they approached. "Next time, we'll park closer." He clasped my hand and nudged me toward his other side so he was between me and the guys as they passed. If the men didn't set me on edge, his human behavior right after telling me to stop acting human did the job.

"Yeah. Especially when it's cold." I shivered and hunkered into my coat, playing along.

The men fell silent as we passed. Gramps tugged me around the corner toward a parking garage, not dropping my hand.

"Human," one guy muttered. "We've been here for days and haven't found anything."

"It may take time. Let's check out the area where the anomalies occurred."

Our eyes met, and Gramps pointed toward the exit at the far side of the massive garage and went fluid.

I followed, staying on his heels. When we made it to my van, I flung myself inside and turned to him. "Feds?"

"Perhaps." He scrutinized my shiny new car as if it were a hairy wart. "This is not the ideal way to follow them."

"It'll work. They're going to the battle site."

When I pulled into the concealment spell near Dale's bar, the mages were still working on the utilities. I parked opposite an abandoned house and followed Gramps into the adjacent subdivision. He pulled shadows around himself and crossed his arms.

I practiced layering shadows the way he showed me. Once we started moving, holding them became more difficult. In the past, I'd go fluid and maintain a speed too fast for humans to see. Using shadows conserved energy, I realized as I struggled to pull them with me.

Gramps didn't utter a word when he paused a bazillion times, waiting for my slow ass to catch up. He shot me a contemplative look as we exited the spell around the first neighborhood, and I couldn't find enough shadows. Damn streetlights.

After what seemed like an eternity, we reached the far side near the ruined Bellicose apartments. The houses and yards in the area were pristine. I'd never guess it was where Drake and Deva flattened them when the missile attack knocked them out of the sky. Three massive piles of demon dust still blocked the road, but the blood from the fight was gone. A few hybrids were inside their houses, candles, and fireplaces flickering. It was surreal.

We exited the privacy spell and stopped behind the destroyed Bellicose apartment complex. Police caution tape surrounded the entire area, and two cops guarded it. They were deep into a conversation about football, so I doubted they'd notice us, even if we weren't hidden. I extended my claws, grateful for the spelled shoes I bought in Allure. They allowed my toe-claws out without resistance and fixed themselves when I retracted them. Gramps ducked under the tape and drifted toward the ruins while I scaled a tree for a better view.

A slight movement across the street caught my eye. Several members of my uncle Roman's house monitored the area, so it was most likely them. Three more moved from the corner of a closed business to a hedge. The tingle I recognized as Gramps approached them without disturbing a single shadow. If I didn't recognize family, I'd never realize he was there.

A light glinted from a small slit in the blinds of a ruined apartment, drawing my attention. I focused on it while I attempted to listen for movement. Nothing happened. As I got ready to move on, something flickered in the apartment next door to the original one. Was it flashlights? Or a spell? I was too far away to tell.

Gramps moved away from me as I eased out of the tree. Good. I didn't need a babysitter to guide me when I spied. Keeping the shadows wrapped tight, I moved closer. The cracked or shattered windows where I'd seen the movement were dark. A mixture of stale ozone from spent magic and burned wood clogged my nose as I moved closer to the blackened building. The back apartments where I spotted the light were intact.

I slipped into a singed walkway between buildings and glided over the rubble as I sank into the deepest shadows to listen.

A shuffle came from the floor above, followed by a creak.

I slunk to the opposite wall to examine the stairs. They weren't too bad, but the landing above was barely hanging on. Too risky.

"Found another one," a man said from above me.

"How many is that?" another voice asked.

"Hundreds. They're all over the place."

"Has forensics determined the substance?"

"It'll take a few weeks."

They had to be referring to alchemy vials or some nasty potions the Bellicose created and stashed. Jen mentioned their labs where they held paranormals, but I never asked questions about them.

"Bag the evidence. We'll come back in the daylight."

"Agent Spencer. Back here," a woman's voice called.

My breath hitched. Not just cops, but federal agents. I tiptoed to the edge and craned my neck. Unable to see much, I focused on the stairs. The yearning to see better almost propelled me up them. They were still too risky. The stabbing sensation intensified as Gramps drew closer. Damn it. I needed him to back off so I could do something productive. Like follow federal agents around and eavesdrop.

"Don't move," a male voice said from the walkway.

My heart raced as I swung my head in his direction, ready to confront a cop. It wouldn't be the first time humans tried to arrest me.

But the guy wasn't looking at me. A bush near the building rustled, and a vampire I recognized from my uncle, Roman's house, stepped out and raised his arms.

The agent or cop, I wasn't sure which, lowered his gun. "This is a restricted area."

The vampire's shoulders slumped. "I can read the caution tape. I used to live here until the freaks moved in."

The agent took a half step back. Perceptive of him, considering Roman's people were all high-powered. But his intuition wouldn't save him if the vampire refused to cooperate. The guy raised his gun again. "You came to check it out at night?"

"I'm staying at a friend's house nearby and saw people enter my old apartment."

Plausible. I sauntered closer and leaned against the building.

"Do you have information about what happened here?"

"Not much. The people who moved in next door were odd. I filed a complaint with management, but they didn't care. So I asked my friend to crash at her place for a while."

Oh, he was good. I supposed all of Roman's vampires had a story ready, since they were always creeping around the area.

"Agent Pascal? Everything okay down there?" The woman from upstairs asked.

I turned my head slowly enough not to catch her eye. She was petite, with a short brown bob. Her sharp brown eyes scanned the area and slid over my hiding spot.

The guy who confronted the vampire twitched at her voice. If I were human, I'd never have noticed it. But the slight wrestling of his suit jacket against his side told me she made him nervous.

Roman's vampire must have heard it because his muscles bunched.

The man shook his head without taking his eyes off the vampire. "Just someone poking around. It's fine."

"Do you need backup?"

"I got it. Thanks."

The darkness swallowed her as she disappeared back inside the apartment.

The scuffle of a shoe was the only sound as the vampire struck.

"Don't kill him," I said in a low enough tone the agents upstairs wouldn't hear. I'd spent hours testing the limits of human hearing while working in toxic workplaces. One of my favorite games was to insult a power-hungry boss just outside their hearing range and watch their faces scrunch. It gave me a pretty good idea of how loud to be based on distance and acoustics.

The vampire hesitated.

A flash of steel and the crack of a gun sent me into action. I burst out of the shadows, extended my fangs, and struck. As they sank into the man's throat, I cast the intention of sleep, pushing aside the slight worry that always ran through my mind when I used venom. Or any type of magic, for that matter. I sealed the wound and lowered him before he collapsed.

Roman's vampire slammed into me. I dragged him with me as I hit the ground, reversed our positions, and crouched on his chest. "It's me, you idiot."

"What are you doing here?" he asked in a hushed tone.

Gramps appeared near the stairs. His head ticked as he scanned the scene with glowing red eyes.

My brow furrowed, and I mouthed 'what?'

He motioned toward the shadows.

I shoved the vampire one more time and followed him.

The other agents' voices rumbled above as I wrapped shadows around myself.

Gramps zipped up the steps without making a sound.

The vampire dusted off his clothes and followed. It was still tricky to drag shadows as I moved, so I couldn't keep up with them.

Chapter Three

Gramps wasn't visible when I reached the apartment. His familiar stabbing pattern guided me as I tiptoed around a pile of alchemy vials wrapped in individual evidence bags. The ozone scent was so pungent it nearly covered the faint smell of death. I moved inside a scorched bathroom, careful to stay hidden, and peered out. Gramps stood inside the bedroom across the hall with three humans on their knees, as if they were praying to him.

Movement registered a second before an arm clamped around my waist, and a crisp, masculine scent enveloped me. I went limp and fell sideways toward the weakest point. One hand extended to catch myself as I moved my legs in a sweeping motion so fast my assailant didn't have time to react before his feet left the ground. He swung a leg around and caught himself with one foot.

Sharp pain racked my body as my back took out a chunk of the wall when he jammed his shoulder into my stomach. We crashed through the doorway and careened across the hall. I struck at his neck with my fangs and plunged my claws into his back. Shooting pain radiated across my hip and down my leg.

I tried to reverse our positions, but he tweaked my arm so hard I lost my grip. My toe-claws dug into his shins, and I used my forearm to throat-punch him. When his grip loosened, I rolled to take control. He tried to take it back, and I countered. We resorted to punching and kicking each other until my shredded back slammed into a charred dresser, and we hopped away from each other.

Folomi, Roman's second, stood across the room, bleeding from several wounds. My muscles relaxed, and I retracted my fangs and claws.

"Reacting to the slightest confrontation with drastic actions will not teach you control." Gramps couldn't have sounded more bored.

I tore my attention away from Folomi. Gramps leaned against a closet, his arms and ankles crossed. The three human agents still kneeling at his feet. Their glassy eyes and relaxed posture made it clear they were in his thrall. Roman's other vampire stood in the corner, his eyes wide. "No shit? Who'd have thunk." I pointed at his captives. "When will I learn that?"

"Perhaps once you learn control." He refocused on the agents.

Excitement bubbled inside me as I staggered toward him. Folomi followed, as silent and deadly as always. I liked all of Roman's vampires, but I had a soft spot for him because he had my back at that terrible, bloody dinner Jed and Ara forced me to attend.

Gramps pulled an agent toward him. "Why are you here?"

The man blinked, though his eyes remained glassy. "To do my job."

"What job?"

"Sort through this mess and look for paranormal activity."

"Why?"

"It's a punishment. My superiors picked the troublemakers."

"What have you found?"

"A shitload of liquid drugs and a pile of bodies."

"What agency are you from?"

"Homeland Security."

"Have you found paranormal activity?"

"Undetermined."

"Explain."

"We found video evidence of several people vanishing and the DNA of creatures we can't identify."

My heart thudded, and my mind raced as Gramps questioned the three agents one at a time. They were grunts with little information, yet they knew about us. And there were still a few thousand hybrids living in the city. I needed to figure out how to convince them to leave before the agents found them.

Gramps slumped against the wall. "Many years have passed since I dealt with humans."

"You nailed it." I tapped my filthy fingers on my ruined pants. It felt great to be useful again. "Ask them how many agents are in town and where they're staying. Can you mess with their memories?"

The look he gave me would have cut me to the bone if I didn't understand him.

"I take it that's a dumb question."

"Even if we wipe their memories, the other agents will notice the discharged firearm and the disturbance in the ash," Folomi said. "Roman is looking for new vampires if you wish to turn them."

"We are also taking applications." Gramps examined the three agents. "However, my love is the one who determines whether the candidates are adequate."

I followed their conversation with an enthusiasm I normally saved for bosses with enormous egos. I didn't expect to find out how to make a vampire that night, and I found the fact they were even considering it fascinating.

Gramps cocked his head. "Jen does not wish to harm humans."

"Because she's worried about hiding the internal war. I doubt she gives a shit if we make new vampires," I said.

They stared at me with unreadable expressions.

I shrugged and pulled my phone out, relieved to see the screen intact. "These agents will be missed, so it's best you leave them alone. Should I call Glacintial for the mind wipe?"

Gramps shot me another look of disgust, then one-by-one, talked them through replacement memories, starting with the gun going off, then filling in everything that followed with mundane tasks. He also planted a memory of the biggest one falling into the bathroom door. Roman's vampires tried to make the soot look undisturbed. When the agents stirred, we high-tailed away from the apartment.

"What now?" I spoke in a quiet tone.

Gramps stopped beside the agent I put to sleep. "Why did you bite this one?"

"She wouldn't let me kill him," Roman's vampire answered for me.

An unreadable expression crossed Gramps's face. "Leave."

"Yes, Consort." Folomi bowed and dragged the other vampire with him as he went fluid.

"What venom did you use?"

"Sleep. Is something wrong?" I used sleep venom several times during fights, so I didn't see the problem.

"He is turning. We cannot leave him here."

Dizziness washed over me, and I had to latch onto Gramps to keep from falling. "No way. Nope. I didn't inject the vampire virus. I'm sure of it."

"Yes. Because humans often spontaneously combust into vampires." He hefted the guy on his shoulder and motioned toward the gun and the bullet casing.

I stashed them in my pocket, and we went fluid all the way to Hooves. Dale grumbled, but let us use the gate. I worried the magic wouldn't let the human through, but Jen screwed up when she made the gates. Anyone with permission could enter, human or not. I only hoped it wouldn't bite us in the ass later.

We spilled onto a snake-like road that wound around nothing for no reason. They were a pain to walk but would be fun to drive. My van wasn't ideal for racing, so I'd have to buy a new car. I considered the best vehicle for the task as we dragged the guy towards my house.

Gramps placed the man on the garage floor and stepped back.

I bounced around faster than I intended. "I only meant to disable him."

"When training, one often makes mistakes."

My heart thudded. "Not helping."

He scanned the empty garage. "Do you not have furniture?"

"There's some inside."

He disappeared and returned seconds later with two chairs I'd never seen. "Sit, Lily." His tone left no room for argument.

I folded my arms. "Why?"

His serious blue eyes radiated power as they bore into me. "Sit, Lily."

I complied with a huff.

He spun his chair around so it faced me. "Can you monitor his heart?"

Unsure where he was going with it, I closed my eyes. "Yeah."

"Eyes."

"Right. Bad habit." The guy's heartbeat was sluggish, and his breathing shallow. "What? Why?" My mind spun, trying to remember what I'd done. I intended to put him to sleep. We had several venoms that were activated by intention with our bite. Lust, sleep, mind-fog, and some I'd never tried. The vampire virus was the most powerful. But I didn't activate it when I bit him. The intrusive thought fluttered through my mind. "Shit." Cavil insisted my fear of my darker side was the problem with my mage magic, but I never had an issue with my vampire skills.

Alex burst into the garage. "What did you do?"

"Unknown."

"Holy shit." He moved closer and gave the guy a deeper sniff. "You created your own vampire?"

The sharp pain kept me focused as I bit my tongue to control my fangs. I had conflicting emotions about the matter. On one hand, the thought horrified me. On the other, it soothed something deep inside I was reluctant to confront. "We aren't sure yet."

"Really? Because he sure as hell smells like a vampire."

My eyes landed on Gramps. Though his face stayed bland, pride reflected in his eyes. "Holy hell." I clutched my stomach and leaned over. "This is not how I wanted my life to go."

"The fates rarely give us what we expect."

"Yeah. No shit." I sat up. "What in the hell will I do with him?"

"My love will guide you should he live through the change." He glanced around the garage. "Perhaps retrieve a spell to keep the mess to a minimum."

The only spell casters I trusted enough not to blab were my mom and Jen's friend, Tracy. My parents were at their house in Allure, and Tracy would go straight to Jen. And she would bulldoze her way into the situation and take over. A thought struck, and I stood. "Cavil might help."

The twisted maze Jen created in the fake DMZ looked nothing like the one Alex, Flemming, and I built. But it had a certain artistic quality to it I admired. I raced through it and stopped at the wards surrounding Cavil's new monstrosity of a house. The front still reflected a farmhouse, but the rest resembled a lavish mansion.

A bear shifter appeared and strode toward me. "Hello, Princess Lily."

"Not funny. Is Cavil around?"

A laugh escaped her. "Yes. He'll be out in a minute."

It occurred to me I'd never asked Cavil how he met the bear family. My guess was that my new sister planted them since she knew the family's leader, Colonel Ballard. Jen came across all cooperative and nice, but inside, the woman was solid steel and had a manipulative streak a mile wide. She probably planted them to keep tabs on Cavil. I adored her more than I'd admit.

Cavil appeared behind the bear, and his smile lit up the area. "Hello, Lily."

My stomach fluttered. "Hello, your holiness. You're looking awfully edible today."

Humor danced in his eyes. "Yes. What can I do for you?"

"I need your expertise. Do you have some spare time?

"Of course. I swear I will help any time you ask."

I scratched my head when tingling from the contract swept over it. "Not the time." I was sure he'd regret it when he learned what I'd done.

Cavil crossed the wards, took my hand, and kissed it. "I am not the only one looking good today. The torn, bloody look suits you."

My entire body throbbed with lust. Shaking it off, I pulled him toward the fake DMZ. "I messed up, and Gramps said we need a spell."

"I am a god. Spells are beyond my abilities."

"Will you at least try?"

"Of course. Anything for you."

When we reached the garage, I yanked him through the side door and slammed it behind me. Gramps sat upright and still as he monitored the agent. Alex lounged in a recliner as if he didn't have a care in the world.

The vampire Meemaw forced me to keep crouched next to the guy. She ran a hand through her purple-tipped hair and raised her eyes. "I leave you alone for one minute, and you go and make a baby."

"Hey, Elsie. Aren't you supposed to answer to me?"

"Sure. But sometimes I wonder why."

"That makes two of us." I focused on Cavil, who stood beside the door with a blank expression. "I may or may not have accidentally turned a federal agent. Gramps says it'll be messy. Can you protect the garage, and maybe Alex?"

He crossed his arms. "Is that all?"

"Yeah. I'd rather not call my mom."

"Brock, brock," Alex teased.

I raised my middle finger.

Cavil's lips twitched. "Only if you allow me to stay and watch."

I wrung my hands, realized how weak it looked, and dropped them. "Will all these people watching screw it up or humiliate him?"

"No," Elsie answered. "A turning is cause for celebration. The entire house normally attends, and when the change is complete, we throw a birthing party. Since I'm the only one in your house, the others can help make it more festive."

"Oh, hell no. I am not interested in a house. He'll need to go somewhere else."

She glided toward the door. "I'll invite the dragons."

"Effective learning requires accepting the consequences for your actions," Gramps drawled.

I tugged Cavil toward the unconscious man. "I liked you better when you were sarcastic all the time."

"Your likes and dislikes do not change the circumstances."

I banged my forehead against Cavil's shoulder. "What can we expect?"

Elsie returned with two more chairs. She pushed one toward Cavil. "The dragons are unsure they should attend."

I rubbed the back of my neck. "We don't need them involved in this."

"I can place a thin barrier over the garage, but your chairs may not survive," Cavil said, as if the conversation with Elsie hadn't happened.

"Fine with me." Maybe the dragons would leave when they saw the mess. I doubted even an explosion would pry Gramps or Elsie away.

Cavil's bright magic lit the room, causing the entire garage to glow until it settled in and faded. "Done." He pulled a chair next to the one I'd abandoned. "I shall try to eliminate the blood as it spills."

Glacintial stuck his head through the door. "We respectfully decline your invitation to join in the turning. Dragons are forbidden to interfere in the matters of other factions."

My shoulders sagged in relief. "Perfect. Thank you, Glac." I turned to Gramps. "So, how's this going to go?"

Three hours later, I questioned my life choices even more than before the turning. After Roman rejected me as a young teen, I became obsessed with learning about vampires. Scarred from my stay at good ole Jed's house of horrors, I was determined to learn enough so no one would trap me again. So, I spent hours reading books about their abilities and my heritage. If I'd known my abilities came from Lilith, I'd have studied different material.

The guy bled so much my heart ached, even though he stayed unconscious as he turned. Cavil worked at a steady pace but struggled to clean the constant mess. Gramps and Elsie sat completely still the entire time, monitoring vital signs. My nerves were fried, and I couldn't concentrate on his heartbeat. It seemed like a turning point in both our lives. I'd had enough change in the previous few months to last me several hundred years. And the guy didn't deserve to be ripped from his life in such a violent way.

Alex fell asleep halfway through but startled awake when the agent groaned. "His brain is online."

Gramps disappeared, then reappeared with the blood bags from our fridge. "This will not be enough."

"What happens if we run out?" I was the only vampire in the house until Elsie arrived, so we didn't stock much blood. And distribution wasn't available in the hybrid pocket. Driving to Allure was an option, but it would take hours. "Should I text Roman and see if we can borrow some?"

Cavil stood. "I will go to Allure."

When I met his eyes, my heart sank. Cool calculation had replaced his flirty, fun demeanor. I dragged my eyes away and focused on my latest mistake. "Sure."

His warm hand burned when he squeezed my shoulder. "It will be okay, Lily."

"Only vampires may purchase blood in Allure," Gramps said.

"I'll go. It's my mistake."

Elsie stood. "No. Baby vampires need their master to control them. Stay here." She flinched at Gramps's icy glare. "Please."

I watched the exchange with interest. Elsie was expected to be subservient to me, but always ordered me around. If her casual attitude irritated Quin too much, he'd say something. Or kill her. He was more than capable of fast and efficient violence. For some reason, his protective instincts centered on me. I didn't know how much crap he'd take from those he deemed my subordinates.

"How much blood does he need to survive, Tarquin?" Cavil asked.

Gramps pulled his attention away from Elsie. "One crate at a minimum. Two is ideal."

Cavil and Elsie vanished.

I grabbed a bag and crouched beside the groaning man. "What was that about?"

"It is unfortunate your grandmother's genetics did not override the hesitation to lead common to Lissa's descendants."

A laugh escaped as I bit into the blood bag and squeezed some into the man's mouth. His reference to the First Queen of Ahl, or my biological grandmother, was hilarious. Especially since no one dared say anything like that to my biological mother, who had once been the Second Queen.

Alex adjusted his recliner to a sitting position. "If Elsie becomes too disrespectful, Lily will slap her down."

"Then perhaps there is hope." Gramps watched me with a singular focus.

My entire blood stash was gone when Cavil returned. The new guy was a little rowdy, so I held him in a headlock while Gramps dug a knee into his back. My weight shifted as he once again tried to fight. "Relax."

His body turned to jelly.

Gramps tapped his temple. "Perhaps a little less persuasion is in order."

"I didn't use persuasion."

"You did." Alex still sat in his recliner, though he gave up lounging to watch us fight the new guy. "You've used it several times since you started drinking blood. Lucky for me, I'm used to your bossiness."

Chapter Four

When the two crates Cavil and Elsie retrieved were low, Gramps tugged at the guy's eyelid and examined his pupils. "I have not seen this in thousands of years."

My stomach clinched. "What haven't you seen?"

"I cannot recall more than a feeling of doom." He tapped a thumb on his knee. "We must take him to my love."

His words increased the sickening feeling. "Please tell me I didn't create a freak vampire."

"What part of I cannot recall was not clear?" He zipped into the house.

Alex stood. "He's right, Lily. This guy doesn't register as a regular vampire any more than you do. Ara can help."

My shoulders slumped. "Great." As an ancient, Gramps had seen some shit, so if he thought we needed help, we did.

Which was why, moments later, I found myself sick to my stomach and standing at the gates of Allure with a baby vampire in tow. I struggled to keep him under control without physical force.

Meemaw stood beyond the checkpoint, her hands clasped. She bounced on her toes when she spotted us.

I dragged the agent to the checkpoint and braced myself for the usual harassment.

The mage's eyes swept over me. "Have you registered this vampire, Your Highness?"

Meemaw appeared beside her and pulled the guy through. "It's fine, dear. He needs my guidance under the public protection act. I will take full responsibility."

The mage nodded and motioned toward the magic scanner. "Register him within thirty days."

The tension drained from the new vampire's body when Ara touched his arm.

Gramps came through last and kissed her on the cheek. "Hello, my love."

Her face flushed. "It is wonderful to have you home." She turned her attention to me. "Let's settle your first turn in so we can bask in this joyous occasion."

I wouldn't call it joyous, I thought as we appeared inside a flashing circle near the palace. "Thanks, Cavil." I half-heartedly waved at the griffins on the palace wall as I spotted the snarky mage who always manned the checkpoint. "Bet you won't give me any shit today, eh?"

Her lips flattened to hide a smile. "Hello, Mistress Ara. You have quite the procession with you today."

"Didn't think so." When I noticed everyone's attention on me, I shrugged. "We go way back."

The guard lost the laughter battle. "I wouldn't recommend angering *Princess* Lily."

Meemaw arched an eyebrow. "Oh?"

"Long story. This guy is new." I pulled the glassy-eyed agent along behind me like he was a puppy or a balloon. "Is it a problem?"

The castle guard started to make a snarky reply, but changed her mind when Gramps stepped up to scan himself in. "No, Your Highness. You have thirty days to register him."

"We heard." I gazed toward the palace. It didn't look any different, but the lack of stabbing from Jen and Mat's presence felt like a giant hole in my heart. "Who's running things while Jen's gone?"

"She's in regular contact with her assistant. Should Jenella take time off, then you will fill in," Meemaw said in a conversational tone.

I skidded to a stop. "What?"

"Jenella named you her heir, since Mathias is no longer with us."

A sense of dread washed over me. "Nope. Not going to happen."

She patted my hand. "Don't worry, dear. I'm sure it will be fine."

It had to be fine because I couldn't even run my life, let alone an entire coalition.

Cavil flashed us from inside the gates to the circle near my grandparent's house deep inside the neighborhood. He motioned toward the street where he owned a kickass Victorian-style house. "If you no longer need my help, I'll take my leave."

I stared longingly in that direction. "Sure. Thanks for your help, Cavil."

"Text if you need me." He disappeared.

Alex shoulder-bumped me. "Jen will not like him flashing without using the circles."

"You going to tattle on him?" I asked in a lame attempt to lighten the mood.

"No. But she notices every little detail."

"She likes Cavil so much she gave him a position of power."

"True."

I caught the new vampire watching the conversation and stared him down until he dropped his eyes.

Meemaw led us into the light and airy vampire mansion and continued to the back. She opened a door with stairs leading down and heaved open a reinforced door at the bottom. I found myself inside a spacious sitting area with a TV mounted above a fireplace. A pool table took up the opposite side. Dark wood floors stretched through the whole place. A massive magichef sat behind a short counter on one end, and two hallways flanked it.

She pointed at a room just inside the hall on the left. "Your new vampire can stay here and mingle with my elites for a few days. I've instructed them to treat him well. When he learns a bit of control, we will move him to your home in the hybrid pocket. Have you thought about giving it a name?"

My head spun at how casual she sounded about the situation. "I'm pretty sure he has a name."

Her tinkering laugh rang through the room. "Yes. He is a grown man, after all. Have you named your new pocket?"

"It's not mine. And no one told us we were supposed to name it." I looked at Alex. "Did you name it?"

"No." He peered into a room. "Is this where you keep all the new vampires?"

"Yes. However, I rarely practice turning since I bring in vampires who need help. Lily can use it for hers until she learns to fully control them."

"What if I don't want to keep one?" I tried to sound casual, as if my stomach wasn't spinning with the force of a hurricane.

She took the guy's chin in her hands and examined his eyes. "Your venom runs through his veins. Venom creates a much stronger bond than blood. No other master will be able to fully control him, and he will always be linked to you and your house."

"I have no desire to become a housemaster." I also didn't want to sink further into the pureblood world. Being around them still made me uneasy.

"Excellent excuse to shrug your responsibilities," Gramps murmured.

My sigh was so exaggerated it sounded like a hiss. "Fine."

The new vampire stumbled toward the sofa, lost his balance, and fell on his ass. "What's happening to me?"

Meemaw lifted him off the floor with one arm. "We'll explain everything soon."

I wanted to be her when I grew up. I crouched beside the guy. "Open your mouth."

He complied. Instead of the two fangs normal vampires had, every tooth in his mouth was pointed. My eyes grew wide. "Is this normal?"

Gramps leaned toward the guy, then threw a speculative look my way. "No."

Meemaw's eyes glowed when the guy tried to snap at her, and he settled back down. "Oh my. It is not normal for modern vampires, no." She patted him on the head. "Taming him will give you much-needed training."

My chest tightened. "Yeah. The teeth?"

"It is nothing to worry about for now. Your power is quite unique." Pride laced her voice.

Alex sensed my temper rising and elbowed me. "He's alert and determined to fight his way out of here. It's like he's cataloging everything to report back to his superiors."

"Great." We didn't need the feds breathing down our necks. I shuffled toward the living area. "So, what now?"

Meemaw's head ticked, and vampires flooded the room. "I'll have some of my elites stay with him tonight. His training will begin in the morning."

I wasn't thrilled about staying in the vampire mansion, but I didn't want to insult my new grandparents. So, I stayed for the small turning celebration and accepted the massive two-bedroom suite they gave Alex and me. The minute we could slip out, we went to visit our parents. I was too mentally exhausted to argue when Elsie insisted on going with us.

Every house surrounding the palace was upscale, including our parents' place. The Mediterranean-style mansion was light tan and had a decorative pool in front with a center fountain. The lush shifter woods butted up against their back yard and extended to the extensive palace grounds. A dusting of snow covered the trees, and I couldn't help but admire the beautiful scenery.

Alex rubbed his chin. "Is it weird that I never imagined our parents living like this?"

I eyed the arched doorways of the three-story mansion. The second and third stories reminded me of a human wedding cake with flat roofs and multiple tiers. "No. I thought they'd have a mountain chalet."

A man stepped out of an arch and looked down his nose at us for a full thirty seconds. "May I help you?"

I copied his stance. "Yeah. You can let us in."

"I think not. What business do vampires have with the shifters?"

Alex's muscles tensed. "I'm a shifter."

The guy assessed my brother with a look of disdain that made my fangs ache. "Not entirely."

Right before I snapped, Mom appeared. "Lily! Alex! We didn't expect you. Come on in." She pulled us through the wards. "What on earth are you doing in Allure?"

"I made a mistake. My grandparents are helping me with it."

"Is that so?" Her eyes sharpened as they landed on the shifter, who stood beside the wards, his arms crossed. "These are our kids, Lily and Alex. They can visit whenever they want."

"And the vampire?"

"Mine," I said without thinking.

Mom gave me a curious look. "She's welcome if Lily is with her. Come. Your dad will be thrilled you came to visit."

As we followed her through an arched front door, I was so shocked at the miles of cream-colored marble floors that I veered into Alex. "Sorry." The potent scent of cleaning spells hit me, and I sneezed. "Sorry, again."

Two staircases with ornate iron banisters flanked the room. A round table sat in the center, with a vase of pink flowers spilling out of it. An arched doorway led toward the back, revealing an equally posh living area. Floor-to-ceiling arched windows with dark wood trim overlooked the woods. It was so different from the farm where we grew up that it baffled me that the same people owned both. My heart ached with the realization that I never really knew my parents. Especially if the pristine mansion was their true idea of a home.

Shifters were everywhere. Some even stopped what they were doing and glared as Mom led us through the room, down a hallway, and out a sliding glass door onto a spotless porch.

A toe-curling roar thundered through the forest. Several shifters, in a variety of forms, poured out of the woods and scattered. A second set trotted behind them and paused. The ground shook. A flash of orange caught my eye seconds before a gigantic greenish-brown dinosaur with orange plates down its back stomped into the yard.

My eyes drifted to the gouges Dad's feet left in the grass. "Flemming would cuss up a storm if this were his yard."

Mom chuckled. "Our gnomes are used to it. There's always gouges in the yard from all the shifters."

Dad spotted us and morphed into his usual unassuming self. A woman sprinted across the yard and handed him some sweats. He put them on and strode toward us, ignoring the shifters attempting to steal his attention. "Well, I'll be damned. My kids decided to grace us with their presence." He enveloped me in a warm hug before moving to Alex to shake his hand. "What brings you here?"

"Long story." I flicked my head towards the yard where shifters gathered in groups.

"I see. Well, come on then." He guided us back through the house and into an office, thew on a T-shirt, and tapped on a tablet secured to a massive, ornate desk with gold accents. Visions of him working in the garage or barn crossed my mind. The dad I knew didn't belong in such a fancy office.

I moved to the large windows framing the woods and plopped into a cream-colored chair. "I screwed up."

Dad settled beside me. "How so?"

I glanced in Elsie's direction and spilled the story. When I finished, I scanned my parents with both my eyes and hearing to gauge their reactions. Mom had taken the chair beside Dad. Alex rested against the window, staring longingly out at the forest. Elsie stayed near the door, fighting to keep her expression blank.

"I wondered when your grandparents would force you to become more involved," Mom said after a pause.

"They didn't force me, but they *are* holding me accountable."

Dad rubbed his chin. "Want me to sugar-coat what I say, or do you prefer brutal honesty?"

One thing I loved most about my dad was his straight-forward manner. "Brutal honesty."

"You are not human, nor are you two normal hybrids. The quicker you recognize it, the faster you can adjust."

I couldn't help but laugh. "No kidding? I wouldn't have guessed."

"My point is we raised you amongst humans, so you learned how to fit in with them. After you bought your house, your lives became idle, and it stunted your magical growth. It was one reason we sent you here, even knowing you'd collide with your biological family."

"Okay." I shifted in my chair, my stomach tight with nerves. When dad started a conversation with such a reasonable tone, it meant the other shoe was about to drop. "Is that why you came back to Allure? Because you'd become too comfortable?"

"No. We returned because the shifters needed me, and Jenella made a valid point about where my responsibility lies."

I scanned the room. "And you wanted to live in this museum. It's like I don't even know you."

Mom laughed. "I went through a Mediterranean phase a couple hundred years ago. If I had it to do over, it wouldn't be so...."

"Posh? Snooty?"

"Pristine. But it will have to stay this way until the architectural mages finish rebuilding those subdivisions in the valley."

"To answer your question," Dad continued, "Yes. Our lives had become far too lax and idle."

Alex cocked his head. "And the other part?"

"Because I love the shifters as much as I love you. It tore my heart out to see what they'd become since I abandoned them. As I said, Jenella was right about me. If she ever gets her ass back here, I'll apologize."

"Where is she?" I tried to keep my tone neutral.

Dad shrugged. "Drake took her somewhere, but her assistant won't tell anyone her location."

Jen's assistant, Verity, had a backbone of steel. I swallowed the lump in my throat. "What should I do about my problem? The vampires think it's a joyous occasion." I shot Elsie a look. "But it feels so...final."

"It's not a problem, firefly. It's the natural progression of your calling." Mom tapped her leg. "You are the heir to not only the vampire throne but to the throne of Ahl until Jen has kids. You can't live your life skating by and absorbing drama inside human businesses anymore. It's time to take responsibility."

Dad nodded. "What you see as a mistake is an opportunity. Use it. Learn from it. And don't screw it up."

"Thanks, Dad. That's soooooo helpful."

He shrugged. "The faster you accept your true nature and learn your full potential, the easier your life will become."

My parents were always right, but not as helpful as I hoped. And all the shifters hanging around made me uneasy. Alex stayed with them in their pompous house to shift and run through the woods. And honestly? It would be good for him. He wasn't one of us and needed to spend more time around shifters. It still stung how my little brother didn't need me anymore.

"Do you think this is wise?" Elsie asked as we strolled towards the downtown area.

"You don't have to go with me."

"Are you out of your mind? There's no way I'm leaving you alone in dragon territory."

I examined the top of Dragon Headquarters. The new dragon glass shone brightly in the evening sun. It looked like they'd finished construction, and for a second, I wondered if they'd give me a tour. "They won't hurt me. Besides, you hate hanging out in bars."

Elsie scanned the street as we approached the hotel where Alex and I had stayed. "Not true. I hate hanging out in *dragon* bars."

"Then don't." I approached the doorman, whose name I never learned. "Hey. Did you miss me?"

His yellow eyes sparkled with humor. "Hello, Lily. I see you've brought your curmudgeon vampire with you."

I jerked a thumb toward Elsie. "She's already grumbling about my drinking habits."

A laugh rumbled from him as he opened the door. "Perhaps some delicious dragon nachos will ease her discomfort."

"I guess we'll see." My shoulders slumped when I saw the deserted bar. It was still early, so I hoped the dragons would show up later. Elsie and I took a booth, and I tapped the table. "Well, this blows." The three dragons I considered friends were the ones who moved to the new pocket, but there were others I hoped to see.

Elsie tapped a blue menu spell, and a hologram of food and drink choices hovered above the table. "This place is always terrible. It just took you a long time to figure it out."

I selected nachos and a vodka tonic from the menu. A dragon with long silver hair and sparkling eyes the same color sauntered over and waved his hand. Our food and drinks appeared. "Lily. It's good to see you. Where's Flintous and June?"

I often drank with the two dragons when we stayed at the hotel. They were loads of fun. "They're living in the weird new pocket. How have you been?"

"Hangin' in there. You're early tonight."

"Yeah." I didn't elaborate. "What's the word on the street?" A pang of longing for my old life reverberated through my chest. It was something I'd often asked Dale.

"Hell if I know. No one warns me about the constant impending doom. How's life in the valley?"

I didn't believe him for a second because everyone talked to bartenders. It was in the job description. "Quiet."

He slid into the booth next to me, and I scrambled to move over before I got squished. "And that's the problem, isn't it?"

"Yeah." I wanted to blurt how federal agents were snooping around. But I was at the bar to forget my new responsibilities, not to talk about them. "Hopefully, they forget about us soon."

A massive man with lime green hair swept through the door. His face lit up when he spotted me. "Lily! I heard a rumor you were back in town." He motioned for Elsie to scoot over.

She gave him a nasty look before complying. "Do you think being trapped in this booth by dragons is wise?"

The green dragon threw his head back and laughed. "I forgot what a spoil sport you are, Elsie."

"What are your names again?" I asked.

He clutched his heart. "I am hurt."

"Sorry about that. There were too many fresh faces to remember when we stayed here."

"I am Lyran. My friend is called Kalth." The silver dragon conjured a drink for the newcomer.

"Those names are doozies. No wonder I didn't remember them." I downed my drink. "So, what's on the agenda for tonight, Kalth?"

"You got this, Lily!" a woman with orange hair shouted from the small crowd gathered around us.

"Bet your ass I do." I eyed a drunken Kalth, who'd transformed into a massive green wyrm dragon. "Whenever you're ready."

Waiting for you. Even his mind voice was a little slurred.

Which meant I totally had it. I was buzzed, sure. But not nearly as drunk as him.

"Go!" Lyran's voice boomed over the crowd gathered beside the hotel.

I hooked my claws into the mortar and went fluid, climbing up the building. A bright green flash made me increase my pace, racing toward the top.

Ten feet to go. Five.

As I hooked my right claw on the top of the building, I realized the crowd had gone quiet. At first, I thought I was too high to hear them or automatically tuned them out to concentrate on the race. No such luck. As I swung my legs over the ledge, something massive locked around me. In a moment I'd never live down, I screamed. The grip on me tightened, and my claws dug into my sides. I had to retract them.

My drunken brain hadn't come up with an alternate strategy before I tumbled through the air and landed on a soft surface. I bounced to my feet and re-extended my claws.

A hand grabbed my shirt and yanked me to my toes before I fully focused. A pair of fiery black eyes stared back at me. "What do you think you're doing?"

I retracted my claws and fangs. "Damn it, Bastien! I had him. I would have won!"

He released me and ignored my stumble. "You came into *my* territory and riled *my* dragons up on purpose. Again." The Dragon Prince leaned forward, so we were nose to nose. "Do you want to start a war?"

I threw my arms out and stepped back. "Oh, please. We were just blowing off steam. Besides, it's not *your* territory. It's your mother's."

Smoke rolled out of his nose.

It probably wasn't smart to piss him off. Bastien didn't suffer fools and had quite a temper. But I couldn't help myself. "And, since when did you become the fun police?"

A sultry laugh from behind me sent chills down my spine. I did one of those freeze-and-slow-mo turn moves and flinched. My style points were seriously suffering that night. "Hey, Deva."

She stood near the doorway, an amused expression on her face. Jen's BFF, Tracy, leaned against the wall nearby, her arms crossed and her face unreadable.

"Well, that was certainly exciting." The Dragon Queen moved toward the window. "But please avoid doing it again."

We were in a sitting room with brand new overstuffed furniture, so I stumbled toward a chair. "We were just having some fun."

Gramps came through the door with Elsie on his heels. Her eyes burned with anger. "I told you it was a bad idea."

"That you did." I crossed my arms. "So, what stick-up-the-butt rule did I break this time?"

Tracy's shoulders shook with laughter. "None. I mean, it *was* fun to watch, but probably not the smartest move, considering your title."

I opened my mouth to say what I thought about the title but snapped it closed when Gramps bopped me on the back of the head. "Fine. No more drinking with dragons." I sighed. "It was fun while it lasted."

Deva's dark, seductive laugh made me wince. "Oh, to be young and invincible again. Hold on to that as long as you can, love. But perhaps find other amusements to fill your time."

I whipped out a thumbs up. "Sure. What about my friendship with Lyran and Kalth?"

"I believe such friendships are healthy, but perhaps consider causing less of a spectacle."

Chapter Five

As I entered my grandparents' basement the next day, I once again found myself grateful for my vampire metabolism. After Deva gave me a not-so-stern lecture about the decorum of royalty, she sent me home with Gramps and a disgruntled Elsie. Her intervention gave me plenty of time to sober up. Good thing, because if I had a hangover, my new vampire would have died.

Furniture sat in tatters against the ripped and scratched pool table. The magichef had dents in it. I almost tripped over a large gouge carved on the floor. I swung my head around and noticed the wall leading to the bedrooms had a line of holes. Five of Ara's vampires milled around, trying to clean up. The new vampire wasn't in the room. "What the actual fuck?"

A hand landed on my arm. "It's okay, dear. These things happen from time to time. A spell will repair this area once the furniture is in place."

"I don't care how spelled it is. This is not okay."

Elsie slipped past me. "No, it's not. But it happens sometimes. Would you like me to retrieve the new guy to answer for it, Mistress Lily?"

I blinked at her formal tone, then realized Ara's vampires were watching the exchange with unwavering stares. "No." My scowl deepened as I turned toward Meemaw. "What should I do about this?"

She linked our arms and tugged me toward the ruined hallway. "Let's begin with control. A new vampire engages in one of three types of destruction. The first is bloodlust." She motioned toward the kitchenette. "The second stems from anger from the abrupt change in their circumstances. It is why I changed the recruitment policies to only accept vetted volunteers."

After so much change in my own life, I understood the anger. "And the third?"

"To escape. The gouge near the door shows very acute reasoning skills." She dragged me toward the five vampires who hadn't moved a muscle since we arrived. We stopped in front of a man with black hair who I recognized from the fight Alex and I had when I first met my grandparents. "What caused your intervention, Robert?"

"The new guy mumbled something about how important it was to report to his supervisor. We allowed him to think about it for a while before intervening. He likes to organize and plan. You chose well, Mistress Lily."

When the group continued to stare, I cleared my throat. "Thanks."

Memaw released my arm and clasped her hands. "Elsie, please retrieve him."

She disappeared down the hall. When she reappeared with the guy, he no longer looked the same. His eyes were glowing the same gold-red color as mine. His hair stood on end, and his clothes were in tatters.

"Use your blood bond, dear. Monitor his bloodlust and teach him his skills. Always remember you are much more powerful, so don't expect him to perform on your level."

"Is that all?"

"It is quite simple once you practice," Meemaw continued, missing my sarcasm. Or maybe she ignored it because Gramps was always sarcastic. "It will require you to pay close attention and intervene until he acclimates. I suggest you set rigid rules at first, then revoke or relax them as necessary." With a tick of her head, Meemaw's vampires exited the room and closed the door. "You may take control when you're ready."

When I first bonded Elsie, I processed it fast and rarely touched it. It never occurred to me to check on her to make sure she was okay. Likewise, I did the same with the agent's bond when he changed. Their feelings flooded me the second I tapped into them. Elsie had a sense of pride mixed with a little hope. The new guy's gnawing hunger slammed into me. It would have made me double over had I not experienced extreme hunger as a kid. "Elsie, will you bring him some blood?"

She went fluid and stopped at the magichef, not even trying to hide her vampire nature.

The wide-eyed man crossed his arms, his loyalty to his former job and utter defiance clear through the blood bond. "I'm not like you. I don't need that shit."

Elsie returned and held out two blood bags. "Mistress."

I took them and pointed toward the ruined furniture. "Have a seat."

He shuffled over and lowered himself to the sofa.

I scooted a chair across from him. After saving hybrids for years, dealing with angry, reluctant people was a skill I'd picked up. "My name's Lily. This is my grandmother, Ara, and my friend, Elsie. What's your name?"

The man ran a hand through his dark brown hair. "I don't have to tell you shit."

Meemaw rested a hip against my chair, and her aura expanded. She didn't comment. She didn't need to because her power spoke for her. It told any vampire within a five-mile radius who was in charge. Neat.

I soaked in the warm feeling of her magic and expanded my own as I stared the man down. "Your name?" I tried to add a touch of persuasion.

His chocolate brown eyes narrowed. "Agent Pascal Lopez. Just Pascal is fine."

With rescues, it was always best to be honest. "Here's the deal. You were in the wrong place at the wrong time. My intention was to knock you out, but I accidentally turned you into a vampire." I paused to let it sink in. "Some myths humans believe are true, but not all. For example, you're going to crave blood for a while." I jiggled a blood bag. "If you don't drink it, you'll go insane, and we'll have to kill you. You still need to eat and drink regular food."

I scanned his face. He was young. Maybe in his mid-to-late twenties, so I hoped he didn't have a partner or kids. "As much as you want to, you can't return to your life. And you won't be able to tolerate the sun for a few years. Right now, you need to concentrate on drinking blood and assimilating. You can't report to your superiors, so don't even try." I explained a few basic things about his new situation and turned to Meemaw. "Did I miss anything?"

"You will not receive many privileges until you assimilate," she said in an even tone. "The faster you accept your new situation, the better quality of life you may live."

His eyes narrowed. "You're not my boss, bitch. And I don't have to do shit."

A hiss came from behind me. Apparently, Elsie didn't like his tone any more than I did. I leaned forward and pressed the blood bond. "This is the Queen of Umbra. Umbra is another term for vampires. She's also my grandmother." Images of what she did to good old Jed flashed through my mind. "If you use that kind of language in her presence again, I'll beat your ass."

Meemaw patted my shoulder. "You may call me Mistress. My granddaughter is less formal and does not like to flash her title, but she is my heir. Treat her as such."

I shivered at her icy tone. "Right. You can call me Lily. I'm in charge of you. As a federal agent, you understand the importance of following the rules. We'll start simple. Act like a child and get punished like one. And not the ones from this century. You tear this place up again, and it'll get bloody. Understood?" Both Alex and I liked a clean house. If he messed ours up, one of us would lose our temper, and the baby vamp was no match for my brother.

He launched himself at me.

I reacted fast, but not fast enough. His shark-like teeth sunk into my shoulder. I detached him with a palm to his temple, flipped him to the floor, smashed his face in it a couple of times, and pushed into the blood bonds. "Try that again, and I will kill you. Understood?"

His eyes reflected sheer defiance as he tried to shake off my orders. I ramped up my essence. His muscles bunched as he nodded.

I drew in a deep breath. "Do not attack anyone again unless I tell you to." My words came out in a guttural growl.

He bucked underneath me.

I pushed the command.

A deep scowl formed on Pascal's face. "Fine."

Before I released him, I glanced at Meemaw. "Is this normal?"

"For the feral ones, yes. You must always push your commands until he gains control."

I didn't have the patience for his bullshit, so I pushed harder. "You'll drink blood without argument and be respectful to my grandmother's vampires. If Elsie gives you a command, comply as if it's me. There will be no more schemes to report to your boss. You will spend every waking minute learning your skills and about your new world until I say otherwise. Acknowledge."

It took a couple of hours to go through the rules. Whenever I thought I'd finished, something else popped into my head. I perched on his chest and used persuasion to make a point. Afterward, I gave him a blood bag and stood. That's when I noticed the room had repaired itself. One of the many advantages of living in a pocket.

Meemaw seemed pleased as she set him up with a series of tutors, and we left him in their capable hands.

As we left the room, I glanced back and saw a flash of defiance in his eyes. "This is going to suck." I didn't mean to say it out loud.

"Perhaps," Meemaw said. "It will take days for him to learn control. I believe he will be a great asset once he learns his place."

"Yeah." As soon as we got him under control, I planned to find out what he knew about the agents sniffing around the valley.

She led me to her human-style kitchen and offered me a glass of tea. "What would you like for dinner, dear?"

I eyed the glass. "Everything you cook is delicious, so whatever you want to make is fine with me." I took a sip of tea and rolled it around in my mouth. When she first served it to me, I couldn't decide whether it was tea or punch. It wasn't until that moment that I realized why it tasted so good. "Do you add blood to your tea?"

She clasped her hands, and a smile lit her face. "Yes. I have a special recipe reserved for drinks we serve vampires. The tea served to non-vampires is similar but lacks blood."

"It's good." So good I couldn't bring myself to gag at the idea of being fed blood. "Can I get the recipe?"

"Of course! I will text it to you." Her pure joy at sharing a recipe made me feel bad that no one ever took the time to see how she was doing or take an interest in her hobby. I couldn't imagine good ole Jed or his vile sister caring enough. And although Gramps took every opportunity to praise her food, I couldn't imagine him cooking.

I made a mental note to ask her for recipes when she made a special meal. "Hey, Meemaw? I hate to change the subject, but what happened to Jed?"

The smile melted off her face. "He is around. You need not worry about him until he relearns his place."

"And his vampires?"

"They assimilated into other houses. It is much better to control your house if your people respect you. It is also important to allow your vampires to think for themselves and make their own choices. A lesson my children forgot."

I tapped my glass. "I spent the last several years seeking toxic workplaces for their drama. So, I have a good idea of what I don't want to become."

She dug in the fridge and emerged with an armload of vegetables. "Your ego is not an issue now. Ensure you remember those lessons as you age."

"Sure. Do you want me to help chop those?"

The smile my question wiped off her face returned. "It would be lovely to cook with you."

After dinner, I sat back, rubbed my stomach, and reveled in my connection with Ara. Her food knowledge was extensive, and I learned a lot as we made dinner together. More than that, I enjoyed her company. We shared a kinship I'd never felt with anyone else, and I wondered if it was because our power was similar. Not that I cared. I was too busy basking in the feeling of belonging. It felt like breathing in fresh air on the first day of spring.

A blonde vampire strolling into the dining room to collect our dishes interrupted my euphoric thoughts. His brown eyes scanned us, and he froze when they landed on me. I'd met him before but couldn't place him.

"Scott. You remember our granddaughter, Lily?"

He bowed. "Yes, mistress. She has grown into quite the young lady."

Memories of him laughing as he went fluid around the trees and challenging me to catch him crashed through my mind. "Holy hell. I remember you." I turned my attention back to my grandparents. "Scott was one of the vampires who helped me during my stay with Jed."

"We are aware," Gramps murmured. "Jenella, Tracy, and I found him in a Bellicose lab. He explained the conditions Jedediah kept you in."

I shuddered. "Yeah. Let's not revisit it. How are you doing, Scott?"

"Very well. Mistress Ara and Consort Tarquin are most generous."

I blinked. "Yeah."

He bowed, then continued with his duties.

After he left the room, I stared at a crumb on the table, trying to shake those memories. "Is he the only one left?"

"I'm afraid so, dear." When I met Meemaw's eyes, she continued. "Scott is a quality vampire and is thriving in our house. He will remain here indefinitely."

My throat was too tight to talk, so I nodded. Scott was a young vampire who got turned not long before my mother dumped me at Jed's house. Because he wasn't as fast and strong as the others who helped me, he often trained me on basic things like going fluid. He didn't have darting eyes filled with mistrust back then, and I wondered what Jed and the Bellicose did to him. We'd all seen some shit since then, so I didn't ask.

Alex leaned against the wall and watched my new vampire with eyes much too knowledgeable for his twenty-five years. A product of his mental abilities. He'd learned way too much at a young age by catching people's thoughts. When he was a kid, he always knew when the abuse from his biological family was coming. Which was an extra kind of torture for a small child to endure. When Mom and Dad tried to teach him about sex, he kept correcting them. Since then, he'd learned to hide his extra knowledge, but it still showed sometimes. He folded his arms. "I dunno. He's still determined to report everything he's learned to his true master."

"We don't have masters," Pascal said through gritted teeth.

It had been three weeks since I accidentally turned him, and Meemaw thought he was ready to transfer to my house. So, I brought Alex to gauge him mentally. I stared Pascal down until he lowered his head. Point made, I tapped my chin. "We can't have him at our house with all the attitude. The dragons will eat him."

Alex chuckled. "Literally."

The guy's eyes widened, but he didn't comment.

"He must follow your orders, even if he appears resistant. You have a good heart, but new vampires need structure." Meemaw pushed Pascal's head back and examined his teeth. "He still manifests sharp teeth instead of fangs."

Apparently, any vampires I created would be as weird as me. "Is it a problem?"

"Only time will tell." She released him. "He will not act on his treasonous thoughts because you've ordered him not to. You must monitor him closely until you have complete compliance. Ensure someone else supervises him when you cannot. Perhaps Elsie, or one of your dragon friends."

"Are you sure he shouldn't stay here for a while longer?"

She patted Pascal's head like he was a little kid. "It is time. However, if he remains feral, we will readjust our plans."

Chapter Six

The sun sank over the horizon as we strolled the transport station downtown. Pascal stumbled as he stared at the flying, shifted, naked, and other odd-shaped paranormals in Allure. I supposed it was more than a little overwhelming for a guy who was human a few weeks before. Elsie and Alex pointed out the different factions as we walked and explained what they were.

Two dragons swooped low and wiggled their tails at us. A sharp pang of longing ran through my chest at the thought of how I'd never again drink with them.

Cavil stood inside the station, watching the massive discs loading and unloading paranormals. His face lit up when he spotted us. "Hello, Lily." He inclined his head in Alex and Elsie's direction. "How is your new vampire?"

Butterflies took a lap around my stomach. "He's planning to report us to his human masters and still hates drinking blood. How are you?"

"I am well. Mistress Ara requested I escort you home."

We didn't need his help. But I appreciated it so I could concentrate on keeping control over my baby vamp. I hoped I didn't have to monitor him for long. The last thing I needed was a mindless servant rattling around the house. If he were going to live with me, he'd need to contribute and learn to think for himself. "Great."

The transport was fun. Especially when the other passengers recognized Cavil and fawned over him. He didn't seem to mind, and Alex and I had a great time making fun of the situation. The entire time, the former agent stared at the scene like he was cataloging it. A familiar pang of guilt pinged through my chest. He wasn't married and had no family, so I got lucky there. But he still thought he'd return to his life. It made me feel terrible, but I didn't let it show. No need to give the guy ammunition to use against me.

We stepped out of the small transport station in our new pocket, and my head pounded from the color explosion. Even dark, the skies were emerald green. Puffy white clouds with bright yellow accents floated across it. The blue grass didn't die in the late fall temperatures. Instead, they curled up and resembled close-cropped curly hair. I hoped it would straighten out in the spring.

Ahead of us, the round and triangular houses had been replicated as the hybrid population grew. I wasn't sure if it was the pocket creating the ugly buildings or the architectural mages. Thick turquoise raindrops fell from the sky and splatted on the tan streets. "How in the hell did Jen come up with these colors?"

"The First, Drake, said she pulled them from our heads as she created the pocket," Cavil said, a wry grin on his face.

"Not mine," I grumbled. "They're odd."

Alex glanced toward the center trapezoid square thing with the strange fountain. "They're unique and fun. You don't like them because you're no fun."

"Har, har."

Pascal shook his head. "Is this real?"

"Yup. My big sister made it."

He rubbed his eyes. "A vampire made all of this?"

"Queen Jenella is a god," Cavil explained. "Though she denies her heritage because her blood is not pure. Likewise, Lily and Mistress Ara are not vampires. Mistress Ara hails from the realm of night, and Lily is a goddess of both dark and light."

I blinked. "Nope. I'm a mage-vampire hybrid. Period. End of story. My half-sister is our queen. I'm just a reject who got swept up in the whole royalty thing."

Alex kicked a stray orange vine that snaked across the road. "Keep telling yourself that, and someday you'll believe it."

After we settled Pascal into the room next to Elsie's, I sat him at the new, much bigger table in the breakfast nook and ordered food from the magichef. "So, you worked for homeland security?"

Pascal's lips flattened.

I plucked his blood bond like a guitar string.

"Yes."

Making the guy talk was like pulling teeth. "What did you do for them?"

"I'm studying to be a field agent."

When he didn't continue, I leaned forward. "Tell me everything about your mission here." I pushed the command.

The defiance in his eyes sharpened. "I wasn't told the details. Only how we were supposed to assess the area. The senior agents said the apartment building explosions were an ongoing terrorist threat. As a field agent in training, I was assigned to patrol and look for potential evidence of terrorism outside. They didn't include me in most of their meetings, but I heard rumors of paranormal activity." He ran his hand through his hair. "I thought it was far-fetched until...."

"Until Lily came along and ruined your life," Alex finished for him. "This guy hadn't received the proper security clearance yet, so they kept a lot of information from him."

I sat back and sipped my water. It was just my luck that the one agent I accidentally turned was a low-level nobody with very little information. "Where were you and the other agents staying?"

"In the long-term suites by the mall. Others stayed downtown or by the airport."

After Pascal settled in, I returned to our human house for a sleep period. I'd just reached the dreaming stage when panic flooded my senses. Heart pounding, I went fluid. I slammed through the door of the fake house and screeched to a stop.

Our three dragon roommates surrounded my new vampire. Glacintial leaned over and sniffed him. "This one smells deceitful."

I let out a breath as relief flooded me. Pascal's fear tasted bitter as the dragons loomed over him. Smart guy. "He's a former federal agent."

"Ah. That explains the stench." Glacintial manifested a row of sharp teeth that made ours look like thumbtacks. "Is he available to join my division in the queen's army?"

"No." I squeezed past him and froze. The place was a mess. Empty glasses and discarded food sat abandoned on the counter. The spell on the magichef blinked, showing it needed a refill. Something sticky made me lift my foot. "If you three are going to live here, make yourselves useful and clean this mess up."

Flintous swiped his bright red hair out of his face. "Sorry, Lily. We've been busy working and didn't notice how messy it became."

I hadn't noticed it either. My attention had been on my new vampire when we settled him in.

"I thought you were dragons, not pigs. How did you not notice it?" Alex asked as he came through the back door.

I pointed at him. "Exactly. Either clean it up or find your own places."

Elsie poked at a mystery bag someone had left on the counter. "If we're going to establish a house, everyone needs a role."

I started to argue, then decided against it and headed toward the door. "Right. Figure that shit out, and don't put all the responsibility on the new guy." No way I'd turn my forced house into a toxic workplace. "Don't tell Alex what to do."

It was difficult to monitor my new vampire and keep my senses open as I strolled through the park where Mat wanted to have the last battle. My chest tightened at the thought of my older brother. He was an excellent strategist and fun to mess with because he didn't put up with my shit. The guy even gave it right back to me. I missed him, even though I'd only known him for a short time.

Dismissing the thought, I scanned the area. There wasn't much going on other than a couple of homeless people camping on the riverbank. I checked on Pascal, who was sound asleep, so there wasn't much to monitor.

Gramps was absent. He was handy to have around, but it was a relief to be on my own. There were so many powerful people with big personalities hanging around since I found my biological family. They were on my last nerve, and I needed a break before I gave into the urge to put them inside one of my violent magical boxes. I didn't want to kill them, per se. But I wished they'd shut the hell up and leave me alone.

A vibration shot up my calf and settled into my knee as soon as my foot hit the bridge spanning the river running through the city. I frowned and turned in a slow circle to scan the area before continuing to the center. The buzzing increased. Back when the Bellicose was everywhere, I probably wouldn't have noticed it. But with the town so quiet, the sensation stood out. A hand landed on the railing, and I took an automatic step back, keeping my hands loose at my sides in case I needed to fight.

A massive block of a woman climbed over the railing. "We got a live one!"

A male troll came from the other side and landed behind me.

I whipped around to keep them both in sight.

His eyes lit with excitement, and he rubbed his hands together. "Finally."

The female scurried to his side and hip-checked him. "You!" She extended a chunky finger toward me.

Adrenaline flooded my body, and I felt more alive than I had in weeks. "Yes, me. You guys looking for a fight?"

They shared a wary look before the male troll schooled his face. "You will pay for passage."

My shoulders slumped. Damn it. My life sucked if I couldn't even pick a fight with trolls. "What are you doing out here? Aren't all you purebloods supposed to live inside the pockets?"

His chest puffed out. "Our king has ordered us to guard the human bridges."

"No shit? Against what?"

"He did not offer an explanation," the woman answered.

I glanced at the nearby greenbelt. "How are you hiding yourselves from humans?"

"They don't see us. It is the advantage of being a troll."

"Huh." It wasn't the first time I wondered what Jen was thinking, but that one was a doozy. A thought struck me. "Does Jen know you're here?"

"Who?"

"The Queen. Jenella."

The male leaned down until his eyes were level with mine. "Why do you call her Jen?"

"Because she told me to." I bounced on my toes, hoping they'd fight me over me calling my sister by her first name. "You gonna answer me, or do I need to extract the answer?"

His eyebrows drew together. "You are not like other vampires who spy here."

"Tell me something I don't know. Like, did my sister order you to monitor this bridge?"

The woman yanked the man away from me. "You're her! The new princess! Why are you wandering around in the dark?"

"Well, I am a vampire, so...." I shook my head. "Never mind. Your answer?"

"The queen approved our pilgrimage."

Weird. I wondered if she knew something I didn't. "Have you heard about the human government snooping around?"

"Yes," the male troll answered. "We have not received your payment, so the information will remain ours."

I pulled out a twenty and waved it in front of his face. "Information first." The only thing I knew about trolls was they were greedy. They'd probably extort me for more if I paid them before they answered my questions.

"Your payment is meager," the woman protested.

I shrugged. "Fine. I'll just be on my way, then." I turned and sauntered toward the end of the bridge.

"Wait! We have information!"

I paused and cocked my head. "Oh?"

"They had gadgets and spoke of magic as if it weren't real."

When I turned and met her eyes, she cowered. Yet another bite on my tongue helped control my temper as I reeled in my aura. "Did you register?"

"What?"

"Did their gadgets register your presence?"

"No. But we are trolls. We're difficult to spot."

My shoulders relaxed. I pulled out another twenty. "Go back to Allure and tell your king to remove his spies from my city. If he has a problem with it, send him my way." My confidence made me sound almost like actual royalty. Or at least, like I wasn't fighting with my damn fangs again as I held out the money. "And don't come back. The humans are looking for us."

The idiots bowed. Until then, I always found Jen's bowing dilemma amusing.

If federal agents were still snooping around, they were probably investigating all the areas where apartment complexes exploded. Which meant I needed to spy on them all. Impossible for one person. So I pulled my van onto the main road and turned toward the only vampire house in town.

My uncle Roman lived in a house he'd registered as 'sober living' with the human government. Nestled near downtown in the north end, the parking was a nightmare. I didn't want to deal with it, so I left my van a couple of blocks away and walked. The chest stabbing started before the dark blue western colonial-style house came into view. I did a courtesy pause at the end of the sidewalk. The place looked majestic at night, with its manicured lawn and pristine landscaping, accented with strategically placed outdoor lights. When I spotted an out-of-place shadow, I waved. "Hey. It's Lily." I continued to the door, ignoring the other vampires who hid near the porch.

The door swung open, revealing a middle-aged woman. Her face lit up when she saw me. "Lily!"

"Hey, Susan." My former co-worker beckoned me inside, looking more relaxed and happier than I'd ever seen her. We worked in adjacent cubicles in my last toxic workplace, and I paid off her house after I quit. She had a touch of death magic and used it as her side gig. "What are you doing here?"

She waved a hand. "Roman told me all about magic and convinced that big hunk of a dragon to give me a job." She closed the door behind me and touched my arm. "Thank you for all your help. I always suspected it was you."

My eyes narrowed. "Who told you?"

"No one. Once I learned about vampires, I knew. Your aura was always off, and you never had the hunger in your eyes when Kevin threatened to fire you."

"And you're working here now?"

"Yes. I'm doing Roman's administrative work."

I scanned her one more time. "They're treating you well?"

"Absolutely." She leaned in. "I got to meet the queen."

"Which one?"

Her forehead creased. "The one who's married to the dragon. Is there more than one?"

"Yeah. There are several. You met Jenella, who's the queen of everyone."

A vampire appeared behind Susan, her face hard and her eyes assessing.

"Hey, Senga. How's it going?" She used to belong to my biological father. Roman took her as payment for a territory breach when good ole Jed and his crew showed up at my house unannounced.

"Very well, thank you. What brings you here this fine night?"

"Is Roman around?" I already knew the answer, but wanted to give him a chance to throw me out. Again.

"Of course." She turned to Susan. "I'll escort Lily to her uncle."

"Sure. It's good to see you again, Lily."

"Yeah. You, too. Text me if you need anything."

Senga motioned for me to follow her. "Master Roman is this way. He'll be thrilled to see you."

"Doubtful," I murmured as I took in the décor. From what I'd heard, the older vampires usually had expensive homes. Not Roman. His house was an eclectic mix of what I'd consider a thrift store hodgepodge. The sitting room on the right had two mismatched sofas and three different styles of cheap lamps. The rugs were threadbare, and the wooden floors needed a refinish. His place was as strange and twisted as the man himself.

My uncle emerged from the kitchen. His dark hair was damp from a recent shower, and he wore a long-sleeved black T-shirt and sweats. "Lily. It is so kind of you to visit."

"Hey, Uncle Roman."

He dismissed Senga and led me down a wide hallway that spilled into a kitchen with dark orange countertops and chipped linoleum flooring with an orange flower pattern. He opened the almond-colored fridge. "Would you like something to drink?"

"No, thanks." I moved to a glass kitchen table and lowered myself into a vinyl chair. "Sorry to disturb you. I wondered what you know about the feds hanging around the apartment buildings."

"Oh, yes, of course. They are looking for us. I hear your attempt to rescue Felix didn't go so well the other day."

"Long story, that. The agent I turned was a low-level grunt and didn't have details about the investigation."

His eyes lit with interest. "You turned your first vampire?"

"Yeah. It was an accident."

"Accident or not, it is a cause for celebration." He rummaged around in the pantry. When he returned, he held a bottle of champagne and two expensive crystal glasses. "There is so little to celebrate since my awakening. We must take the opportunities presented to us." He popped it open, poured two glasses, and slid one to me before raising the other. "To your first turn."

It was hard not to sigh as I picked up the second glass. I didn't understand why everyone thought ripping a man away from his life and turning him into a blood-thirsty monster was so exciting and fun. "Thanks."

After a ceremonial sip, Roman pushed the champagne away and got down to business. "The agents are most active during the day. But some recently started snooping around at night." He leaned forward. "Tell me, have you spoken to the hybrid leader, Sheila?"

"No. I've been in Allure for the last few weeks. Why?"

Shrewd brown eyes assessed me. "It has come to my attention she is not working in the best interest of the hybrids these days. I suspect she may even be feeding the humans information."

I pulled out my phone to text Mom. "No shit? What makes you suspect her?"

"She had a run-in with Queen Jenella before we took back the city. Then there are rumors about replacing her with a bartender. According to my vampires, she is awful jumpy these days." A predatory smile darted across his face.

I sent the text to Mom, then returned my attention to Roman. The guy pretended to be the kindly uncle who cared about others. But he was as old as dirt, and his aura had an underlying feeling of terror. The only other vampire who put me on edge like him was Gramps. Only in a much different way. "Is there anything else I need to know?"

"The queen is missing. My sister has informed me she works remotely, but I am unsure I believe her. Jenella has a very distinct leadership style, and the orders being handed down are much more direct."

I snorted. "She's in touch with her assistant, from what I hear."

"I see." He drummed his fingers on the table. "There have been many times throughout history where humans have discovered us. The time has come to start worrying about protecting ourselves because it never goes well for either party."

I imagined not. And now, with their advanced weapons systems, they'd slaughter us before we organized. "And you think that's what's happening here?" When I met his eyes, they were so serious, I gasped.

Roman leaned forward, his congenial mask slipping, and the ancient being behind them peered out at me. "I am never wrong about these things, Lily. We must do everything within our power to protect our own."

After wiping my sweaty hands on my jeans, I held one up. "I'm not implying you're wrong." When his eyes melted to his regular kind gaze, I continued. "What can I do to help?"

"Do not turn more federal agents. If Shiela is after revenge, you will be the first on her list."

"Okay. Will you keep me updated?"

"Of course." He stood. "Senga, please escort my lovely niece to her vehicle."

We'd taken two steps when something popped into my head. "Did you tell Sheila about your house?"

"Of course. But do not worry about us. We can survive turbulent times."

I nodded. "Thanks, Uncle Roman. Please be careful."

He gave me a slight bow.

Chapter Seven

The conversation stuck with me all the way home. Roman and his house provided a good chunk of the intelligence about the Bellicose before the hybrid battle. They broke into apartments and offices to steal documents and eavesdrop. They also followed members of the Bellicose around and reported their activities. Through all of it, I'd never seen him lose control of his persona. If Roman was gearing up to protect his house and talking about turbulent times, we were in trouble.

Dismissing the thought, I raced to my room in our silent human house to shower. Alex must have stayed in the pocket with the dragons, where I sensed Elsie and Pascal. Pascal was still sleeping, but Elsie was angry about something. With a sigh, I threw on some clothes and headed through the gate.

The scent of cleaning potions stung my nose as I stepped inside. Elsie looked up from the spotless dining room table. "Where the hell have you been?"

"None of your business."

Her brow furrowed. "I didn't sign up to run a house full of dragons."

"You're right." I slid into the chair across from her. "I was at Roman's house. He's worried about the humans."

"No kidding? Huh." She slid a laminated paper toward me. "This is everyone's assigned role. I let the dragons pick their chores. Your new vampire is worthless around the house, so we'll need to teach him."

I looked over the list. Alex chose kitchen cleaning and laundry duty. Glacintial was listed as head of security. June chose food duty, while Flintous assigned himself to general maintenance. Flemming and his gnome family were on yard duty. Elsie gave herself and Pascal the house cleaning. "Why is my name missing?"

"You're the housemaster."

I slid the list back to her. "Nope. I won't let everyone trip over themselves for me. If everyone else has chores, I will, too. It's how leaders are supposed to operate."

Her forehead crinkled. "Housemasters don't do menial tasks."

"Then what do they do?"

"Run the house."

"What does running a house mean?"

"Take care of the house's businesses and finances, discipline vampires, create schemes to be noticed by the queen, and stay in her good graces."

"You think I need to scheme to be closer to Meemaw? Or were you talking about Jen?"

"Well, no." Elsie tapped the table. "But what about finances?"

"Dude. The dragons have hordes. I'm loaded, and my brother is a financial genius. The money's covered. We don't need someone who toils all day trying to out-asshole the other housemasters." I stabbed a finger at the assignment list. "If everyone else is going to pitch in, I will too. Assign me chores."

She tapped her chin. "You can help us with cleaning."

"Perfect. I'll vacuum, but only when Alex is home so I can watch him do the zoomies." I smirked at my brother, who'd slunk into the kitchen while we were talking.

"You're so funny, I forgot to laugh." He moved to the magichef and tapped at it. "June stocked us up on food and will help Glac with security."

"Nice." I filled him in on what I'd learned from Roman. "He's got thousands of years of experience. If he's worried, I'm worried."

He picked up a bowl of cereal and shook his spoon at me. "Which is why you should stay in the pocket."

I eyed a drop of milk as it landed on the floor. "Yuck. Clean that up."

"It's not my job, it's yours. I have laundry to do."

Elsie went fluid and cleaned the spot. "Do you two argue like children all the time?"

"No," I said. "Sometimes we argue like adults. Did you not have siblings?"

She tilted her head. "Times were different. If we argued, our parents beat our butts with a belt and forced us to kneel in a cold corner to pray for an hour. Back then, children were seen and not heard. Especially girls."

"Yikes. Sounds like my biological mother's parenting style. Only she liked to punch instead of spank and insisted I worship her instead of a god."

Elsie blinked. "Yet here you are, arguing with your *adult* brother like a child."

"Yep. Alex and I are lucky we found our lenient parents. Besides, it's harmless."

Alex's eyes bounced between us, but he didn't comment.

I moved to the kitchen and poked around. "What did you do with the blood?"

"We need more. I've ordered some, and it should arrive on a transport at around noon."

That would work. I wasn't quite at the critical point. Hell, I'd gone my whole life without it, so a few hours shouldn't make a difference. I headed to my new, much larger home office, closing the door behind me.

By noon, I had the jitters. I lurched out of my chair to see if the blood came in. When I swung the door open, knuckles greeted me. I resisted the urge to jump back. "Hey, Cavil."

His hand fell to his side as a brilliant smile stretched across his face, then melted. "I was about to knock. What is wrong with you?"

I motioned him inside. "Have a seat. I need to check on something."

Elsie stood at the back door, bouncing from foot to foot. "The blood delivery didn't come in, and the new guy is getting antsy."

"When will it be here?"

"Tomorrow at the earliest. I'm going to go to Allure for more. The transport leaves in thirty minutes."

Except I'd already waited too long and was jumping out of my skin. "Thanks, Elsie."

I returned to my office and shut the door. "Remember when you swore to help me when I got in trouble?"

Cavil's lips turned down. "I take my oaths very seriously."

"Right. I need help."

"Are you in danger?"

"Actually, *I'm* the danger." I dipped my head. "IthinkIneedblood."

It came out so fast it took him a minute to process. "You said you didn't need blood to survive."

"Yeah. Apparently, that was a bunch of hogwash."

"Hogwash?"

"Crap. I lied to myself and everyone else. According to Gramps, not having blood hobbled my abilities. And since I found out, I drink the minimum. But my new vamp drank our entire supply, and I waited too long. Now, I'm a mess. My head is pounding, and I'm ready to jump out of my skin. I have a house to run, and...."

He stood and massaged my shoulders. "You may have some of mine."

I choked. "Um. I hoped you'd flash me to Allure."

He ignored my suggestion, dragging me to one of the two chairs in my office. "Sit."

I sat.

He scooted the other chair close. "You are almost feral, and I am a god. My blood is not like the supply from Allure. You won't need to drink it as often, and it suits your physiology better."

My heart pounded as he extended his arm. The scent of sunshine washed over me. I swallowed. "I don't think this is a good idea."

"You won't hurt me, and I don't mind." He shoved his arm in my face.

My instincts took over, and I struck. Sweet liquid spilled into my mouth. My muscles turned to jelly as my anxiety melted away. Heat spread through my body. Not erotic heat, but like a beach on a warm summer's day. Fruity drinks and carefree fun danced through my head. When I started trembling, I pulled back. "Thanks."

"You're welcome."

"What did you need?" My mind whirled, and spots danced in front of my eyes. I shook my head to clear it. "When you..." I tried to stand, but the room spun, and I stretched out a hand to catch myself but missed and smashed into the floor.

"Lily!" The voice sounded muffled.

My mouth was glued shut. After trying to pry my eyes open and failing, I tried again. They wouldn't budge, even when bright white light flashed in front of them. I focused on my breathing so I didn't die. It pissed me off how no one warned me how vulnerable drinking blood from the source made me. At least it was Cavil and not some stranger who got in my way and became a vampire. Poor guy.

A tickle started in my belly. I patted my stomach with a half-limp hand to stop it. It didn't work. The tickling expanded up my chest. I fought to open my mouth to warn Cavil to leave, but it came out as 'hmpf.' The sensation climbed down my legs and into my arms, then started up my neck.

My senses snapped back online. A loud belly laugh escaped me as my eyes sprung open. A mid-century modern room greeted me. The tickling increased, and I clutched my stomach and laughed. The laughter turned into guffaws when the tickling spread through my whole body. I launched from the couch. Wrong move. Every inch of my skin tingled, and the tickle spread. Tears streaked down my face as I laughed so hard I had to brace myself to keep from falling.

Cavil tried to grip my shoulders, but his hands made the sensation worse, so I pushed him away. He grabbed my arms. "Lily, are you okay?"

My watery gaze landed on him. "Damn, you're sexy."

I didn't see his reaction because another fit of uncontrollable laughter rolled through me. When I spotted the neon green couch, I doubled over. A lightning bolt of energy jolted through my muscles. My laugh died, and my body stiffened. Unsure what to do with the enormous energy coursing through my veins, I went fluid around the room. When the tickling ramped back up, I shouted 'woo hoo' and spilled out into the hallway, doing flips all the way down it. Cavil managed to snake an arm around my waist and drag me back into the room.

I broke into a dance. First, I did the twist, but that wasn't fun enough, so I did the hokey pokey, seamlessly transferring to the Y.M.C.A., then doing an ultra-fast moonwalk. I found my groove with the macarena and started singing. The energy surged again, and another belly laugh exploded as I did the monster mash. Unsatisfied, I did a handstand and tried to walk on my hands. When Cavil opened the door, and Gramps strolled in, I lost my balance and landed on my face. "Ow."

His eyes swept over me.

I burst out laughing as the energy surged. They'd left the door open, so I went fluid and bolted. I flew through a house I'd never been in, bouncing down a hall. A woman screamed as I blew through the kitchen and out the back door. My bright blue house sat in the distance, so I booked it through the DMZ, leaping over bushes and adding some spins and flips.

I caught movement out of the corner of my eye and veered around the house and out the gate. I landed on my ass in the back of my real house, climbed to my feet, and raced around it. Something smashed into me with enough force to knock the air out of my lungs. Dirt and grass filled my nose as I skidded across the lawn. My laughter sounded ragged as I tried to clear dirt from my mouth.

Someone yanked me up and shook me like a rag doll. "Expel the extra magic."

I thrashed, trying to free myself, but the hands around my arms felt like steel bands.

A surge of vampire persuasion washed over me. "Expel magic that is not your own. You must do it fast."

My thoughts swam. My belly tickled. I trembled. But the words, mixed with the persuasion, broke through the fog. I turned my senses inside myself and wrapped them around my magic. Bright, shiny magic in my body clashed with my dark power. I used the sanity I had left to expand my darkness and release the bright stuff into the air. My body deflated like a balloon, and I sank to my knees. A series of coughs made me double over. When they stopped, I took two long breaths. Just to be sure, I checked for the shiny stuff again and raised my head.

Flemming stood twenty feet away, his tiny gnome hat clutched in his hands against his chest, his eyes brimming with concern. "Are you okay, Lily?"

"I'm good." I searched the area. Gramps loomed over me in the front yard of my human house. Cavil stood near the corner, his face an unreadable mask. Across the street, a woman stood, her mouth open and her phone up, recording. "Shit." I stumbled to my feet. "Sorry about the lawn."

Flemming took two steps forward, then ducked behind a rock to hide from the woman. "Fuck the lawn. If you lose your damn mind, people will lose their homes. We're counting on you, so keep your shit together."

I glanced toward the pocket. Thankfully, no one followed us. "Gotcha."

Flemming bowed toward Gramps and Cavil, then scurried into the DMZ.

A beam of sunlight shot from Cavil, and the woman lowered her phone. She blinked and shook her head. Gramps appeared in front of her, said some words, and she returned to her car and drove off.

When he reappeared near me, I ran my hands over my face. "What the hell just happened?"

Gramps dragged me toward the back porch and deposited me in a chair. "You drank the blood from a powerful magical being without expelling the magic."

"How in the hell is that a thing?"

Cavil scanned the field. "It has always been a thing. If I knew you lacked the knowledge, I wouldn't have offered. I retrieved your grandfather because I couldn't break through the magic poisoning."

"Right. Can you explain what happened like I'm five?"

"Your ignorance almost got you killed. Another trait inherited from Lissa." Gramps rubbed his chin and stared at me with unblinking eyes.

He had some strange ideas about my heritage. "Right. How do I handle it in the future?"

His eyes flicked between me and Cavil. "You must expel the magic as you feed." Gramps leaned in, his dark blue eyes so close I saw tiny red flecks in them. "And never feed from a god unless the situation is dire."

My face flushed. "Why?"

Cavil crossed his arms. "Lily was on the verge of bloodlust."

"The blood of a god will strengthen you, increase your speed, and has some restorative properties. It is okay to drink occasionally. But it may cause you to begin idolizing him. It has been known to cause addiction."

It made sense, I supposed. "Right. So why don't the blood bags do the same?"

"They extract magic prior to packaging."

"Okay." I didn't need another reason to be addicted to Cavil. My heart already did the pitter-patter routine every time I spotted him. No way was I taking a chance on feeling so out of control again. I scanned the road. "What happened to the woman recording me?"

"I erased her video. However, she was talking to someone," Cavil said.

Great, just what we needed.

CHAPTER EIGHT

THE BRIGHT BLUE HOUSE and the pocket creeped me out. It was possible there was nothing wrong with either of them, and I disliked them because of how the purebloods always treated me when I went to Allure. Or maybe it was my time locked in the shack at Jed's house. Either way, my new vampire needed to stay inside the pocket, so I did, too. The guy was still defiant. The government's brainwashing tactics were as effective as they were admirable. I'd need to propose Jen use them for her army to see the look of horror on her face.

I stood in a game room and watched June and Flintous shoot pool. Nearby, Alex reclined on a heated massage chair, working on his laptop. Elsie was downstairs dusting because I suggested I'd do it later. The woman hated the idea of me doing manual labor, so she asked me to babysit the new vampire and ran to do it herself. Though, I didn't consider it babysitting since he was mine. It was more my responsibility to watch him than hers. When I brought it up, she took offense and accused me of implying she was incompetent.

My gaze landed on Pascal, who lounged on a black beanbag like the one I tried to make when I practiced magic with Jen. It had to have been a joke for her to create it inside my house, though I doubt she realized she'd done it. Too bad, because it was funny.

I launched into the blue one beside him and landed with a 'poof.' The thing didn't feel like a beanbag chair. It was more like an enormous ball of memory foam. "Hey, Pascal. How are you settling in?"

His eyes darted to me before refocusing on the TV. "Fine."

I snorted. "Bullshit. Look, I apologize for all of this. It wasn't my plan to turn you. But there is no way you can go back to your old life now."

He muted the TV and focused on me. "Yes, I can. Several gifted people work for the government."

I already knew about the paranormals in the government because we planted most of them there to spy. "Sure. But not a single vampire, which is what you are."

His brow furrowed. "You've heard of them?"

"Yep."

"That's not what I was told."

I tried to shrug, but the chair was too bulky. "Governments only tell people what they want them to know."

His eyes trailed across June and Flintous. "They aren't vampires."

"Nope. They're dragons. Fun to drink with, but I wouldn't recommend pissing them off."

The wheels in his head turned for a few seconds before he refocused on me. "Why do I feel so normal?"

"What do you mean?"

"I'm still me. If I died and came back, why am I not better looking or more vampire-like?"

"I don't know. I'm a natural-born vampire, so I've never turned. Elsie did, though. Have you talked to her?"

His eyes widened. "I can still have kids? Even though I'm dead?"

Elsie appeared at the door, a large potion bottle in her hand. "You're not dead, nor can you have kids. We call it the vampire virus, though it's a venom that spreads through your system and turns you. The magic involved sterilizes us."

Pascal tapped his chin. "Then how are you a natural-born vampire?"

Alex closed his laptop. "Lily's not like other girls."

I threw an arm over my face and groaned.

Pascal shifted. "Why do you guys seem so human?"

"We've lived in the human world most of our lives, so Lily and I have adapted," my brother said. "The three dragons have been around for a long time, so they can fake it. And Elsie *was* a human, same as you."

"Not like me," he mumbled.

A bell interrupted our conversation. When I tried to jump up, I flopped back down and had to roll off the damn chair. "What the hell is that noise?"

Elsie waved a hand. "Someone's at the front door of your human house."

I didn't even realize we had a doorbell. No one came to our house except other paranormals, and they tapped the wards. We were too far out in the country for religious groups or door-to-door salespeople.

"I'll get it," Alex said as the entire group, except for Pascal, raced down the stairs. "I'll see who it is. You stay back."

"Someone stay with Pascal." I raced after my brother.

My stomach soured when I stepped out of the gate. The flap of a wing sounded behind me, and I glanced back but didn't see anything, so I assumed a cloaked dragon followed us.

When I sauntered inside, Alex stood at the front door and glanced back with a tight expression. "Hey Lily, some guys are here to see you."

"I'm not buying anything," I said a little too loud as I sauntered toward him.

Four men stood on the front porch. They wore black suits with white shirts and black ties. Two also wore mirrored sunglasses.

I stepped out and tilted my head toward the overcast sky. "We haven't spotted aliens, UFOs, or UAPs. Nor have we been abducted." I wiggled my eyebrows.

They remained expressionless. The one with silver running through his dark hair shifted. "Are you Liliana First?"

"Last time I checked. What can I help you with?"

"I'm Agent Harper. This is my partner, Agent Davis." He motioned toward the other guy with sunglasses. "We'd like to ask you a few questions."

Alex crossed his arms. "Not without ID."

All four men whipped out badges. They tried to be quick, but I caught their agency. The CIA. "What do you want to know?"

Agent Davis glanced toward the spare guys. "May we come in?"

Alex's expression was tight as he waved them through the door. The two agents with sunglasses came inside, but the other two stayed on the porch. They'd shit their pants if they knew there were two dragons close enough to bite them. Or I assumed they were near. Jen's ability to sense them would come in handy for times like those.

The agents scanned the house as if cataloging everything as I led them to the breakfast nook. I wasn't worried. Until recently, Alex and I were careful to live like humans. And their senses wouldn't pick up the spells and wards blanketing the place. But their eyes lingered a little longer on the cameras.

Their presence made me both grateful and nervous about having a human and magical security system. "Can we get you a drink?" My voice sounded flat.

"Coffee, if you have it." Agent Harper answered.

Agent Davis examined every inch of the house without taking off his sunglasses. "Just water for me. Thanks."

Alex moved toward the kitchen. "I've got it."

I perched in a chair across from them and laced my hands together while I fought to suppress a smile at their arrogance. They had no idea how fast I could kill them. Or worse, how fast Alex would drop them if they stepped out of line. "So, what brings you to our door?"

"We received a report of unusual activity on this property."

My face scrunched. "Like what?"

"What do you do for a living, Miss First?"

They already knew the answer. I was sure of it, so I went into professional mode. "Our parents set us up with a trust fund. I work occasionally but am currently unemployed."

Agent Harper nodded a thank you to Alex when his coffee and condiments landed in front of him. "And you, Mr. First?"

"I'm a financial advisor." He set a bottle of water near Agent Davis and took the chair beside me.

The guy opened the bottle in slow motion and sipped like he had all the time in the world. "Been to the mountains lately?"

I bit my lip to keep from making a snide comment. His lame attempt to intimidate or make us uncomfortable was funny. "Sure. We like the outdoors."

Agent Harper stirred his coffee in a slow, deliberate manner. "You said you're both financially secure?"

My eyes narrowed. "Yes."

"No offense, Ms. First. I'm just trying to understand why you share a house." He glanced around. "It's large, but not something I'd imagine a rich person living in. Let alone siblings."

"It's none of your business."

Alex sent a stab of pain through my head. "I take it you haven't looked into our backgrounds," he said with certainty. "Lily and I were adopted out of the foster system."

Agent Davis's eyes bounced between us. "Your point?"

I leaned forward. "What my brother means is that we don't trust easily, but we also understand the concept of safety in numbers. We don't flash our wealth because it's an invitation for some asshole to rob us. Or did you not notice the expensive security system?"

"We did."

"Great. Then forget the fishing trip and tell us why you're here."

Agent Harper sighed. "We had a report of some unusual activity at this location."

"Really? The police got a report of something weird going on way out here in the boonies and sent the feds? I find that hard to believe."

My foot throbbed when a boot landed on it. "What my sister means is nothing weird has happened since the homicidal old man sold the farmhouse next door."

"Yes. To another wealthy person. How well do you know this new neighbor?"

"Well," I blurted as my heart rate increased. If they suspected Cavil of being paranormal, I needed to warn him.

He raised an eyebrow. "And when did you meet him?"

"A couple of months ago."

"When he bought the house?"

"No. I met him at a bar and suggested he buy the house."

The agents shared a look. Though, it was hard to read their expressions since they didn't remove their sunglasses.

I almost said as much until Alex's hand twitched left, then right. A signal for me to shut my trap.

He waited for me to understand, then leaned his elbows on the table. "Did our neighbor do something wrong?"

"No," Agent Harper pulled out his phone. "We found this live stream." He flipped it around.

The video started as Gramps tackled me the day before. Cavil approached at a human pace. "I swear they just appeared there. I didn't see them come around the house. You guys probably won't believe me," a woman's voice rambled. A bright flash cut off the livestream.

"What happened before and after this video started, Ms. First?"

"What you should ask is why that woman invaded my privacy." I pointed at his phone. "As you can see, we didn't just appear. We ran from the back of the house. My friend and I were just messing around. My neighbor spotted us and came to see what was going on." I glanced at Alex. "What's so strange about it?"

Agent Davis leaned forward. "What happened to her phone as your neighbor approached?"

"How in the hell am I supposed to know?"

The two were quiet for a full minute by design. They were trying to make us fill in the uncomfortable silence. It would have been hilarious if I wasn't terrified. They suspected I had supernatural abilities. Worse, they were watching Cavil, who wasn't as careful about using his magic as we were. I couldn't wait to discover what Alex fished from their heads.

When we didn't take the bait, Agent Davis continued. "Have you crossed paths with a man named Pascal Lopez?"

I tapped my chin. "No."

"You were seen with him and this man in West Boise the other day." He showed another picture of Gramps.

My heart pounded as I shrugged. "It wasn't me. That guy has a wife, and I'm not a home wrecker."

"And who is *that guy*?"

Gramps never mentioned what name he used in the human world. And if I made something up, the agents would check.

"Jacob Smith," Alex answered. "He's a friend."

"So, you haven't witnessed strange activity. You haven't seen Agent Pascal Lopez. And you weren't with Jacob Smith in West Boise." He leaned back and tapped the table. "You're lying, Miss First."

I cocked an eyebrow. "Or you're wrong."

"We wouldn't be here if we were wrong."

I wondered if I should use persuasion on the guy.

Alex leaned forward. "Would you like more coffee or water?"

"No." Agent Harper blinked several times.

Agent Davis shook his head as if to clear it. "We don't, no." Their faces relaxed.

An amber glow reflected in their sunglasses from Alex's eyes. "The woman you are looking for is not Lily First. You have confirmed Lily was home and not involved in any paranormal activity. Are you sure you don't want another drink?"

Agent Davis stood. "No. I think we got what we needed." He pulled a card out and offered it to me. "Call me if you notice anything odd at your neighbor's house or spot Agent Lopez." They strode out the door.

Alex moved to the front window. "What do you suppose that was about?"

Since he still used his human persona, I played along. "No idea. Who would have thought playing around in the yard would bring the feds down on us?"

"Yeah. Do you think Cavil was involved with that Lopez guy?" He moved toward the table and dipped his head under it to check for listening devices. "Or a drug dealer or something?"

I snorted. "No. He's too squeaky clean. But it wouldn't surprise me if he escaped a fashion show or went AWOL from a movie set."

"Yeah." He slunk toward the sink with the cup, turned on the water, and pointed down the hall to where we kept our security equipment. "But why ask you about Jacob? And what was that lady livestreaming?"

"Be careful around Jacob until you find out what he's up to. Are you going back to work? Because I need to use the office to job hunt."

Alex paused. We had separate offices, so sharing wasn't necessary and would probably be a disaster if we tried it. "Use the little desk. Just be quiet."

"Sure." We raced toward the security room.

"They circled the house and snooped around, but it doesn't look like they planted anything." I leaned forward as Alex's intense eyes focused on the agents' movement in the monitoring spell.

He jammed his finger into the controls. "There. See that? Mom's wards will neutralize any signal not approved by her, so they're SOL."

I gasped when I saw they'd planted a mini camera pointing in the general direction of the gate. "Cavil's wards will, too. But we need to warn everyone." The hybrids usually used either the gate at the bar or the one across the street from our parents' farm, but we used ours all the time. "Is bugging our house even legal?"

"Not without a warrant. But if we destroy their equipment, they can charge us with the destruction of government property. And if we take it down without destroying it and give it back, they'll figure out another way to spy on us. It's best to leave them there and act human when not in the pocket. Those agents' minds were humming with information about the coalition, so we need to be careful."

"I'll call Cavil and give him a heads-up." I pulled out my phone. "Gramps is always zipping around the property, so I'll warn him, too. Tell the dragons to stay cloaked."

"What about Flemming and his family?"

Good point. The gnomes wouldn't be able to help themselves from maintaining the lawn. "I'll warn him, but he won't listen. How can we redirect their attention?"

"I'm not sure we can."

After I texted Gramps and left a voicemail for Cavil, I headed toward my actual office. The humans had someone feeding them information. Both Dale and Roman suggested it was one of the area leaders, Sheila. Even though she hated me for some unknown reason, she loved the hybrids. She tried to sell us out to the Bellicose, so it was a good place to start.

Alex slunk into my office and closed the door. "I texted Mom and Dad."

"Good. After Pascal's settled, I'll head to the bar to talk to Dale and stop by Sheila's place. Dale knows they're snooping around, but if they're willing to knock on our door, they're probably watching other hybrids, too. Do you find it odd how Pascal got sent across the country without knowing why?"

"Sure. I'll do some research on those agents."

Chapter Nine

Elsie stood next to the dining room table, digging through bags when we returned to the pocket. She raised her head and flicked a vial with her fingers. "We got a delivery from Allure."

"Great. We also got a visit from the feds. They put cameras on the property."

"Huh." She moved to the next bag. "Who sent all this?"

"You didn't order it?"

"No. I thought you did."

I moved around the table, peering into the bags. An old-fashioned-looking card rested on the top of one, so I pulled it out and traced my finger over the waxed seal. Loopy writing showed the delivery was for me, so I broke the seal. I couldn't help but smile as I read it. "It's from Jen's griffin, Helen. Apparently, she thinks she needs to take care of us now." A laugh bubbled out of me as I held up a spelled shirt in my exact size and style. "Jen wouldn't, in a million years, think to send this stuff. It wouldn't even cross her mind."

She dug in the last bag and opened a box. "Cookies. They have Alex's name on them."

"Yeah? Why would she do this?"

"Griffins nest. When they decide you're worthy of joining their nest, they take care of you. It's entirely possible she's adopted you and Alex."

I wondered where all these well-intentioned people were when I was a kid. Not a single pureblood cared about me when I needed them most. Now that I was independent and strong, they all wanted to spoil me rotten. It was too much, too fast, and part of the reason I felt off my game. "I'll send her a thank-you card. But if they decide to establish a nest here, it's a big 'no' for me."

Elsie moved to the next bag. "If she sends some of her family, there's not a damn thing either of us can do about it. Same with Mistress Ara. They'll spoil you even if you don't like it."

I closed my eyes and drew in a breath. There was a time when I would have jumped at the chance to be showered with attention. But not anymore. And as much as I appreciated and liked them, I was too independent to be coddled. "I'm going to town to talk to Sheila and warn Dale about the feds. You want to go?"

"Sure. Who's going to watch Pascal?"

My eyes trailed in the direction where I sensed him. "Good question. Is that why vampires have such large houses?"

"No. The larger the house, the more powerful the vampire. It's a status thing. It's also safer and has more money-making potential."

"How does that work? Like everyone hands their money over to the housemaster? Or is it a taxation system?"

"Neither. Most houses own several businesses where the members work. Their positions within the business and their pay are based on rank within the house."

I'd never thought about vampire houses as cults before, but her description sounded like the ones I'd seen on the internet. "I don't want to open a business any more than I want to start a house."

"You're the heir. You can do what you want."

My stomach soured at the suggestion of being an heir to anything. My fangs ached. Gramps was right about how biting my tongue taught me control. It took less time for the sensation to go away each time. "I'll see if a dragon can stay with Pascal for a couple of hours."

"I'll do it." Flintous sauntered into the kitchen. Fire lit in his red eyes when he spotted our Helen haul. "Are those homemade cookies?"

"They're for Alex," I said. "But if you stay with Pascal, I'll pay you with cookies made by my meemaw. She cooks using human methods."

His predatory grin made me like the guy even more. "Is she good at it?"

"She makes the best food I've ever tasted."

He ran a hand through his bright red hair. "I pride myself on finding the best food. How did I not hear about her cooking?"

"I don't know. Did Alex tell you about the government agents?"

"Yes. Glacintial witnessed the exchange and is not concerned, so I'm not."

"You should be. It was their missiles that took down Deva and Drake."

Dragon eyes were expressive if you knew what to look for. Most people only saw the glow and looked away in fear. But after spending time around them, I learned there were different layers to the light in their eyes. Flickering fire meant excitement. A slight glow meant they were communicating using telepathy. And if you ever notice a raging inferno, someone was about to die.

My statement ignited a raging inferno in Flintous's eyes. It was gone so fast that I would have missed it if I wasn't watching for the reaction.

Elsie froze and lowered her hands to her sides.

"Calm that shit down, Flint. I didn't mean to cause offense. Drake's family." Sort of. I didn't think of him as family. Not really. But he was a good guy. And he kept Jen occupied, so she didn't inject herself into my life more often.

"It's best we do not mention the incident."

"Right." Elsie returned her attention to the bags.

"Back to the task at hand. I'm going to town for a while. Do you know how to take care of a new vampire?"

"Of course. Feed him and feed him some more while monitoring his treasonous thoughts."

"I'll text my meemaw to see if she'll send cookies."

He licked his lips. "Fair trade. But if he attempts to contact his human superiors again, I may eat him as a snack before the cookies arrive."

"I'll reinforce my orders before I go." I'd given him the order not to contact them several times, and he kept trying to find a way around it. Almost as if his brain was pre-programmed to report to them. "Have you gotten anything from his mind?"

"No more than Alex."

"It takes time, especially when the turning isn't voluntary. We might have to deal with this for a few months." Elsie's voice held a tinge of bitterness.

"Not looking forward to that, eh?"

"Not even a little."

"You didn't need to come with us." When June didn't answer, I put the car in park and glanced in the mirror. Our house was under surveillance, so I needed to leave it occasionally to keep up appearances. If not, I would have used the gate. It would have been much faster. But we needed to look like normal humans who weren't living in a pocket dimension in the yard. As soon as the federal agents tailing us drove by, I opened the door. "Go."

The sliding door opened, and the tingling between my shoulder blades disappeared. June kept herself and Elsie cloaked as they spilled out. I sauntered toward the bar's entrance to give the government agents a good look. When they turned in the other direction, I slid into the shadows.

June remained cloaked. I caught up with Elsie, and we went fluid, heading deeper into the subdivision. The privacy spell had shrunk by a few blocks, and hybrids had moved back into several houses. We slowed once we passed the barrier and scanned the street. There were more mages than before working on the utilities and cleaning up the demon dust. The hybrids, who always stood by and taunted the mages, helped. With everyone helping, the cleanup wouldn't take much longer.

We came to a stop outside Sheila's house, and I tapped her wards. They were good. Not as good as my mom's, but better than most. The front door swung open, and she stepped out. Mom often speculated about how the mage-witch hybrids had magic comparable to sorceresses. Sheila's magic was unique and powerful, sure. But not even close to a sorceress.

Her face pinched in disgust. She strolled down the sidewalk and her defiant brown eyes landed on me. "Lily. What do you want?"

"Hey, Sheila. I wondered if you knew anything about the federal agents sniffing around."

A deep frown formed on her face. "Yes. They've been swarming the area. The crews we sent to help repair the damage were dragging their feet, so I lit a fire under them."

"Ha! I wondered why they suddenly started working. Nice." I twisted my head toward the still intact privacy bubble. "Roman thinks you're feeding the humans information."

She bared her teeth. "That old dust bag doesn't know what he's talking about. He didn't even know Jonas's kids were traitors. Yet he has the balls to imply *I'm* leaking information to the vile humans?"

My lips twitched. "Well, you almost sold out your people to the Bellicose."

She crossed her arms. "The Bellicose were not human and fighting for a cause. And I learned my lesson."

"Right. For the record, I didn't think it was you." I waved a hand toward the restored houses. "I see people are moving back in."

"Many moved to the pocket. I've been trying to convince them to come back."

I shifted my weight. "Why?"

"Because we have no place in the coalition, so it's best to avoid it. The queen doesn't know what she's doing and even admitted she could force us to her will. It's too dangerous."

The urge to strangle her was real. "So, you're trying to convince hybrids to move back out here where they have to check their every move because Jen pissed you off?"

She dropped her arms. "That's not what I said."

"Right."

"You wouldn't understand, since you favor purebloods." She motioned toward Elsie.

"I understand." I leaned in. "Be careful, Sheila. The federal government is looking for people with magic. They even came to my house. And you might want to check your ego and think about how it will play out when they figure out you're one of us."

She crossed her arms. "I suppose you want me to move in that ghastly pocket."

"I don't give a shit what you do. Just don't risk other hybrids over your personal grievance. And if I find out you're feeding the humans information, I'll kill you." I went fluid, heading back toward Hooves.

My entire body stiffened as we stepped inside. Humans lined the far wall and took up most of the bar stools. Dale worked behind it, slinging drinks without moving too fast. His match, Darla, carried a large tray stacked with food. She glanced at me as she passed.

A human occupied my barstool, but I spotted June sitting at a table. I gave her a half-wave. "Busy in here tonight." I took a seat across from her while Elsie chose the chair next to June.

When she raised her head, I bit my lip to keep from laughing. Although her hair was still purple, her face looked daintier. She raised a dark brown eyebrow. "Yeah. We might need to find another bar." One of her dark brown eyes disappeared when she winked.

The laugh escaped. I'd heard some dragons used glamour but never witnessed it first-hand. "Have you ordered?"

Elsie twisted a ring on her finger. "They're busy, so it might take a while."

I tapped the table as I wondered if glamour would work on me. Probably not, considering most magic didn't. A tingle in my chest ignited, and I scanned the bar, trying to spot Gramps.

Darla's eyes swept the room as she approached our table. "What can I get you ladies?"

We put in our drink orders. When she leaned over the bar and relayed them to Dale, he raised his head, and his left eye twitched. Anger flared in them and vanished.

Elsie shifted in her seat. "That's not good."

"No, it's not," I agreed.

When Darla returned with our drinks, she set a napkin with writing under the beer I didn't order. I picked up the drink and read the napkin, then slid it toward Elsie, who spun it toward June and tucked it in her pocket.

I tuned my hearing to the individual conversations and confirmed Dale's suspicions. The humans were all federal agents. And they weren't there to blow off steam. Someone tipped them off about the gate Jen installed in the back office.

The beer tasted bitter, and my instincts screamed at me to run. "Let's finish our drinks and head to the other bar."

As June opened her mouth to answer, the door burst open, and several men dressed in black and carrying rifles poured in. "Everyone down on the ground, now!"

"It's a floor, you idiot," an owl shifter-elf hybrid corrected.

My ears blew out at the sound of gunfire, and the hybrid slumped in his seat.

We hit the floor.

June scooted to position herself between us and the bullets, a purple sheen coating her skin.

"No. Don't...." Another round of roaring gunshots cut off my words.

The guys in black shot without aiming as they made their way towards the bar. Bullets pinged off the walls and tables. Biting pain in my calf caused me to flinch as I swung my head toward a cussing Elsie. Darla lay on the ground beside June, her eyes tight with pain. Holy hell. If June's scales didn't give us away, our fast healing from bullet wounds would. I needed to do something fast. Heart pounding, I coiled, getting ready to strike.

"This is a test." Gramps's voice was close, but I still couldn't spot him.

June's eyes ignited with purple fire. "Hell of a test."

Elsie wiggled closer to me. "Shut up and act scared."

I threw my arms over my head. It had been a long time since I showed fear. There were predators within the paranormal world who sensed fear and would attack when they did. My dad and Alex were two of them. Even some vampires liked the taste of blood laced with adrenaline. But my biological mother beat the fear out of me before I could walk, so my adopted family never needed to fight their instincts around me.

Elsie slung an arm over her dry eyes and sobbed. Darla cried out in pain as June shoved her against my other side and shot me a look. Fear. Right. It was hard pretending to shake when red-hot anger burned in my chest.

Someone yelled, and thundering footsteps followed as the shooters raced out the front door.

Boom!

A fireball burst through the swinging doors leading into the kitchen. Dale swore, then slithered to Darla's side, leaving a trail of blood from his gunshot wounds.

Engines fired up outside, and I hopped to my feet and caught myself on the table when my left leg gave out.

Boom! Boom! Boom!

I ignored the ache in my calf as I hit the floor again.

"Those are coming from outside." Elsie climbed to her feet. "I'll find some healers." She disappeared into the back.

Dale pulled Darla onto his lap. "If the healers aren't here in the next few minutes, she won't make it."

Gramps appeared in front of him, bit his wrist, and held it out. "This will speed her healing."

My face pinched when Dale nodded, and Gramps dripped his blood into Darla's mouth.

Sirens sounded in the distance, and I tore my eyes away from them and scanned the room. Several people lay in a pool of blood. Bullet casings littered the floor, and the scent of gunpowder filled the smoky air. No fire, though.

June checked a couple of hybrids for pulses. "You would be dead if not for my scales."

"Yeah. Thanks. I owe you one." My head tingled when the magical contract settled into place.

She scanned the bar, pausing when Gramps offered his blood to Dale. "You have allowed me into your home and given me one of the most treasured things amongst dragons, a purpose. I consider your contract fulfilled."

With a zing, the contract disappeared. "Okay." A human woman tried to sit up, then fell back and groaned. My hearing tuned to vital signs. Seven humans had sluggish heartbeats, indicating their wounds were bad. Three were already gone. Two hybrids were also beyond saving.

Elsie spilled out the doors, followed by three hybrid healers. She pulled out the potions Helen sent and handed one to Darla and another to Dale.

I went fluid to Gramps, who leaned over one of the dying humans. "What are you doing?"

"Saving them. These two will die within minutes if we do not act." He motioned toward three others near the center of the bar. "Those three are still alive but will not make it to a medical care facility. The ones on the other end of the bar are already on death's door."

"You're turning them?"

"Yes." He leaned over a man who danced on the edge of death. "If I gave you a chance to live, but you had to give up everyone and everything in your present life, would you take it?"

The man blinked. "Yes."

Gramps turned his attention to the woman beside him and raised an eyebrow. She eyed the man, her breathing taking on a death rattle. She nodded.

"You must say it."

"Yes. I want to live."

Gramps struck one, then the other so fast, I wouldn't have seen him move if I weren't also a vampire. His eyes met mine. "You may offer the two dying in the corner the same option. I can only control five."

My head shook in an automatic response. "I don't want more vampires. Especially not federal agents."

"A fair decision. Then you must allow them a dignified death."

My eyes drifted toward the dying people. Out of the corner of my eye, I saw Elsie helping June with a hybrid. "We have potions."

"Potions do not work on humans. I am unsure if healing magic works on them."

"Well, shit." Talk about a rock and a hard place. I could let them die and save myself the hassle. Living with the decision was another matter. Because saving people was something I took pride in despite my dark nature. Letting them die felt like letting it win. With a sigh, I moved toward the woman who fought to put pressure on a leg wound. Smart. But she would still bleed out from the other two holes in her. I crouched beside her. "Hey."

"I heard that conversation. You're not human."

I shrugged. "So, what's your choice?"

"I'll make it."

"You won't." I tapped my ear. "Your heartbeat's fading."

Her sharp brown eyes met mine. "I'll make it."

"I choose life," the man beside her said.

It took me a few seconds to concentrate. When venom flooded my fangs, I picked up his arm and bit.

He closed his eyes, and his muscles relaxed. "Thank you."

The woman coughed, and blood spilled down her chin. "What are you offering, exactly?"

"You'd become a vampire."

She drew in a ragged breath. "So, I'm going to die either way."

"Vampires aren't dead, just altered. The death thing is some bullshit the humans made up."

"But I'll need to sleep during the day and be awake at night. I hate the night shift."

I liked her. She was a fighter and a much better choice than sniveling Pascal. "We don't sleep more than once or twice per week. And it will be decades before you can go outside during the day."

Her eyes scanned my face. "You're serious."

"As serious as your wounds."

A laugh escaped her, and she broke out in more bloody coughs. "Then I want to live."

I injected venom and stepped back.

Dale was on his feet behind the bar, staring at the swinging doors with glassy eyes. Darla stood by his side, rubbing her bloody clothes. They disappeared into the kitchen. After a few seconds, Dale returned. "Notice anything odd, Lily?"

I swung my head around. Elsie and June lined up the uninjured humans, but nothing else seemed off. Then it hit me. Not a single bullet had penetrated the walls or the furniture. Blood was everywhere, and shattered glass was strewn across the floor, but not so much as a single dent in the bar's walls or furniture. "My sister's doing?"

"She added protection to the wards."

"Yeah. She's a badass when she wants to be." The sassy woman passed out, so I moved her into a more comfortable position.

Dale's face grew hard as he scanned the scene. "Evacuate these people before the cops arrive, and I'll clean up." He pointed toward the front door. "Those shooters weren't all humans. Some were hybrids."

"I noticed. We'll need to take our new vampires and the other hybrids through the gate and come back for my van."

"Do what you gotta do. Just leave so we can bury this mess."

Darla swung through the doors with an armload of potions and set them on the bar. "Send a few people back to pose as patrons. They blew up the cars in the parking lot, so we'll need to alter IDs to match the vehicles."

"Shit." I peered out the door. My new van was a blackened husk. The one time I parked in the lot, and it got destroyed. My insurance premiums were going to suck if they didn't throw me off the policy. Those companies were bigger predators than me. And they didn't like it when cars got totaled every couple of months, no matter who was at fault. "I'll call my mom." I slung the woman over my shoulders.

Elsie lifted the man. "You ready, June?"

"I'll stay. I'm Lily's roommate, so I'll claim I borrowed her van."

"Except they followed me here and saw me driving." I sighed. "I need to stay with these two."

Dale pointed toward the back. "Get a move on. I'll hide your van. Send some people back who can act distraught. The dragon can stay and help alter memories."

Gramps somehow moved all five of his vampires to my garage in the time it took Elsie and me to trek through the pocket carrying my latest victims. Thankfully, I learned from my past mistake and had a massive supply of blood on hand. Plus, Gramps brought in several magical storage units and filled them with bagged blood. It was a relief, but I'd need to talk to him about boundaries. Because I didn't know he'd done it until we reached the house and Elsie mentioned them. When I asked him why, he scoffed and said, 'So the god's charisma does not override your reasoning skills again.' Like it was possible to stop being tempted by the sexy god.

Chapter Ten

The new vampires transitioned much smoother than Pascal. I theorized it was the amount of venom I used. The venom I injected him with was only supposed to knock him out, not turn him. He only turned because doubt crept into my mind. I thought back to all the people I'd used my sleep venom on over the years. My breath caught when I realized none were human. Pascal's turning was my biggest mistake thus far and one I planned to learn from. Even worse than encroaching on my grandparents' territory twice, believing I'd get away with it. It wasn't lost on me how I always learned the most important life lessons the hard way.

Mom agreed to take some trusted people back to the bar to alter IDs and pose as patrons for the cops to question. She wasn't happy when I told her about the incident.

Gramps took the people he turned to Allure, and I settled mine into their rooms. The woman wanted a downstairs bedroom, so we gave her the one next to June's. The man opted to take the last bedroom on my side of the upstairs. Glacintial and Flintous stayed on Alex's side, and Elsie, Pascal, and the new guy took up all three spare rooms on mine. It left one bedroom without an occupant.

A house full of people wasn't something I looked forward to. Alex and I liked our solitude. Especially him. I wondered if the dragons could help him block thoughts or if we'd need to change our living arrangements.

After I showered, I fell face-first on my new, too-comfortable bed. I read somewhere how it was vital for new moms to sleep when their babies slept and applied the philosophy to new vampires. They'd need my guidance when they woke up, and I'd make too many stupid mistakes if I were tired.

Pounding on my door dragged me from a deep sleep. I lay in bed, trying to bring myself to consciousness. More pounding. I slid out of bed, lurched toward the door, and swung it open.

"You look terrible, Lily."

"Huh?" My head pounded, and I wasn't entirely conscious, so I must have been hallucinating. My fangs extended, and I blinked. "Is this a nightmare?"

"Clean up and put on some clothes. And don't even think about using those fangs on me." The woman turned and stomped down the stairs.

I peered down the hall, noting how quiet the house was. "What?" I swung the door shut and headed to the bathroom. It had to be a nightmare. Or I woke up in an alternate reality. I bit my tongue for the fang slip.

When I shuffled into the kitchen, the tension was so thick I could cut it with a knife. The new male vampire sat across from Pascal, his eyes filled with fury. The three dragons lounged around the table with amused expressions on their faces. Elsie leaned against the bar next to the new woman, watching the scene with tight eyes. Alex drummed his fingers on the magichef.

Jen's assistant, Verity, perched at the head of the table, sipping a cup of coffee. Her match, Titus, stood behind her, his arms crossed.

June conjured another cup of coffee and shoved it into my hands as I lowered myself into the chair between Pascal and Verity. "Thanks." I took a sip.

Glacintial cleared his throat as he tore his dancing white eyes away from the new vampires. "Perhaps a little intervention is in order."

"Perhaps," I agreed and took another gulp of coffee. The anger radiating off my two male vampires made it taste bitter. Frowning, I set the mug down and turned my attention to them. "Your bullshit is making my coffee even more bitter than usual. So drop the attitude, or I'll drop it for you."

Alex snorted. "You're channeling Mom?"

"What did I tell you, Pascal? Act like a kid, and I'll treat you like one." I motioned to Verity. "We have guests."

"Rule fifteen," Elsie murmured.

June's purple eyebrows drew together. "We have numbered rules? Why didn't anyone tell me?"

I shrugged. "They only somewhat apply to you."

The new guy leaned back and folded his arms. "My apologies."

My head swung toward Elsie. "You already explained the rules?"

"It's my job as your second."

"Huh." I took another gulp of coffee and savored the lack of bitterness. I made those rules up and spouted them on impulse when I turned Pascal. They were basic and included things like leave Alex alone when he's working and don't piss the dragons off. If Elsie made them permanent, we'd need to tweak them. "Will you give them to the dragons?" I met Glacintial's eyes. "We'll have a house meeting about it later."

He stood. "Of course. No need for us to interfere with the Crown's business." He motioned the other two toward the back door. If anyone noticed my flinch at his words, they didn't show it.

The blood bonds gave me a lot of information about the well-being of my vampires. Pascal was a lot more conflicted than the two new people. They also weren't as hungry as him. Interesting. "I need your names."

"I'm Agent Spencer. This is Agent Monroe." The guy motioned toward the woman.

"I'm Elizabeth. Not Liz, Beth, or any other shortened version."

"No shit?" I met her eyes. "Touchy about it, are you?"

She swiped her dark hair out of her face. "Very."

"Yeah, me too. My given name's Liliana, but I'll rip out your throat if you use it. I go by Lily. That's my brother Alex, and you've met Elsie. Our guests work with my sister. This is Verity and her match, or what you'd call husband, Titus." I pointed toward the back door. "Did you meet the dragons?"

The woman's eyes lit with excitement. "We did. Are they really dragons?"

"Yep." I stood and headed toward the magichef for more coffee. "Anyone offer our guests refreshments?"

Verity stood. "We declined, but the dragon insisted I have a cup of coffee. Where did all these people come from?"

"The government. They're here to help." I laughed at my own joke. "And June takes great pride in her coffee."

Alex cleared his throat. "Did you hear about the shooting at the bar?"

Titus stirred. "What shooting?"

I ordered coffee. "You don't want something to eat?"

Verity scanned my vampires. "No, thank you. Do you have a place where we can talk in private?"

I motioned toward the hallway. "You know I do." They'd been inside my house several times. Verity even took over my office for a couple of days. I padded toward it without checking to see if she followed. The coffee wasn't helping with my sluggishness, which only meant one thing. I needed blood. Damn it. I rubbed the ache in my chest that always came with the yearning for my old life.

As soon as we settled, Verity struck. "I need you to come to Allure and fill in for Jen."

I choked. Coffee spit out my nose, and I swung around, looking for a tissue. Except we were in my new office, so there weren't any. I mopped up the mess with the tail of my shirt. "Have you lost your damn mind?"

"I ask myself the same question every day. But so far, so good. Jen named you her heir, so it's your responsibility to fill in while she's absent. She's finalizing my decisions, but the Leadership Council has refused to take my orders because I don't have a title. I need you to push your weight around."

I motioned toward my sides. "Weightless here. Besides, they don't even listen to Jen. What makes you think they'll follow a filthy hybrid?" The words stung to say. It was what they called me when I dared sit with my dad during a meeting. Mat thought their disgust over such a silly thing was hilarious. A pang of loss swept over me, and I brushed it away. "Besides, as you witnessed, I have my own shit to deal with."

Verity's spine straightened. "Adults always need to juggle multiple responsibilities. And you, young lady, are royalty even if you don't like it. You can either help now or spend years cleaning up the fallout later. Your choice."

A smile lit my face. Jen's assistant was great. "Well, when you put it like that..."

"This is not funny."

"Sure, it is. It'll be even funnier when I screw everything up, and Jen has to clean up the mess."

She crossed her arms. "I won't let that happen."

"Uh-huh." My biological mother trained me for Jen's job for the first twelve years of my life. Stepping into the role, even temporarily, felt like letting her win. And that's before I factored in how it would give my sister another foothold in my life. "Look. I'm not emotionally or mentally prepared for this. But if you need me to swoop in and bust some heads, I'm game. Just don't expect much."

She nodded. "You need to come to the palace and meet with Jen's advisors first."

As I rubbed my eyes, an idea struck. "Okay. But I'm bringing people to help me."

Her eyes narrowed. "Who?"

"Cavil."

"He's already an advisor."

"A few of the hybrid leaders."

She leaned back in her chair. "Why?"

I explained the events of the last couple of weeks. After I finished, I stood. "You purebloods think this war is over and done, but it's not. If anything, we kicked a hornet's nest. You want me to fill in for Jen? Fine. But I'm doing it my way."

Luxury made me twitchy. Or maybe the plethora of griffins and palace guards who watched us with varying degrees of interest as Verity and Titus led me toward Jen's office had something to do with my shaking hands. Alex and Elsie stayed behind with my vampires, so I was alone. Fine with me, considering the circumstances. I didn't need to lose more style points by letting them see me play queen.

The office was on the fourth floor in the front corner of one of the many wings and looked over the public entrance. Jen's scent washed over me as we passed a half-moon desk that blocked the door. I glanced at the colossal desk and snooty furniture as I stepped inside, then made myself comfortable at a conference table. Verity settled at Jen's desk. "Most of this can wait until Jen returns, but there are a few things we need to take care of today."

"Great. Let's do it so I can go home."

Her eyes narrowed. "These decisions may affect millions of lives."

I leaned my elbows on the table to hide the shaking. "Fine. Do you have any blood?"

The look of disgust that rolled across her face would have made me laugh if I weren't both drained and terrified. "You didn't take care of that before we left?"

"Are you parenting me?"

She reared back. "You're a vampire, so blood is a priority. Why on earth would I parent you?"

I shrugged. "Because you sounded a lot like my mom when we took road trips, and Alex had to pee five minutes in."

She ran her hands over her gaunt face, then tapped something on her tablet. "I'll see if Helen can help you."

Great. The griffins fussing over me did not sound like a good time. But I needed to be alert if I was going to screw up Jen's job, so I supposed I had to dial back my attitude. Being difficult was my go-to when forced to deal with the shit my mother dumped on me. But Verity didn't deserve it.

After two bags of blood and a long briefing about the fallout from the awful things the Bellicose did while living near humans, a fresh fear unlocked. One that settled into my bones and would be hard to shake when my temp job was over. With the information, I realized my life and the lives of everyone else in the coalition would never be the same. And trying to sweep the mess under the rug and hope the humans would forget about us wasn't an option.

After playing it cool with Verity, I tried to calm my nerves by going fluid in circles after she stepped out. When it didn't work, I resorted to what I always did when I got myself into trouble I couldn't handle. I called my dad.

He strode through the door and scanned the room before his unassuming brown eyes landed on me. The second they did, I burst into tears. Dad strode across the room and swept me into his arms. "You got yourself into deep shit this time, firefly."

I stepped back and swiped a sleeve across my eyes. "Yeah. And then Verity showed up and made it worse."

A crooked grin formed on his face. "I highly doubt any of this is her fault."

"It's not. Most of it is my fault or Jen's. And she's not here." I motioned toward her desk. "This is what Anitta tried to make me. She wanted me here. In this position." I'd wrestled with the wave of hopelessness the entire time I'd been there. Although I kept telling myself to think rationally, my emotions wouldn't let me. Dad anchored me in a way no one else could.

He rubbed his chin. "If it were up to her, you'd have killed Jen on sight, somehow stolen her ruling magic, and made Anitta a shadow queen. This is not even close to what she wanted."

My throat was too raw to speak, so I nodded.

"Jenella has lost the one person who kept her coloring within the lines. She needed this time away. If Verity needs help, it makes sense for you to step up." He ran a finger over the conference table. "And you needed to face your fears to move your life forward."

It wasn't exactly the support I was looking for. A watery smile formed. "So, I need to suck it up and deal with it."

"In a way. Look at it like you're helping to save her."

"It's what we do. We save people." I repeated the words my family said a million times while helping hybrids settle in the city. But they sounded right. When I first met Jen, I vowed to save her. She seemed so conflicted and needed someone to point out her lack of confidence. In hindsight, it was a selfish move. I planned to use her to save my adopted family and the hybrids. Either way, helping her with confidence was fine, but becoming her sole heir wasn't. "I turned two more federal agents."

"Your brother told me."

"That little tattletale."

"He's just wired differently from you."

"That's an understatement." My brother was even more honest than my dad. Alex idolized him, so he talked to him whenever he became uncomfortable or uncertain. And I was almost always the cause of his anxiety. I didn't give a shit about the consequences of my actions most of the time, and it caused him and his analytical mind a lot of stress. "So, what should I do?"

"The best you can. Rely on those of us with experience. But don't let anyone push you around. Your mom and I raised you to take charge. Use those lessons."

I crossed my arms. "Shouldn't we consider Jen's wishes?"

"She has a simple vision of unity and peace. Same as the rest of us." He tapped his chin. "Why don't you text her and ask?"

"Because I'm pissed at her and can't figure out why."

"She intruded on your territory, and you're a vampire. It's fundamental."

I blinked. The explanation seemed too simple, but also right. "Well, hell. How did I not see that?"

"Willful ignorance. Where should I sit?"

"I don't care. I've invited a few hybrid leaders to join us. We need to deal with the feds."

When Jen's advisors poured through the door, I realized they were people I'd met before the battle. Some had even fought by my side. Before the fight, they sat around on their asses gathering information about the Bellicose while I ran between them and Roman, relaying information. The guy refused to text. Some of his vampires had cell phones and texted, but he didn't tell them everything, and Jen needed as much information as possible. Being the Lily Express kept me busy.

I scanned the group as they settled. "We have a problem. Federal agents are snooping around the valley, looking for paranormals. They've gathered a ton of information about us and are analyzing spent potions from the Bellicose apartments." I sat back and folded my arms. "Let's start there before we move on to your council drama."

The elven-fairy-looking lady leaned forward, a mischievous gleam in her eyes. "Is Jenella dead?"

"No. But you come at me, and you will be."

She threw her head back and laughed. "Oh, Jonas. Your daughter is a gem."

"I agree. I also have things to do. So cut the crap, Razazia."

Meemaw cocked her head and peered at the office door. A few seconds later, it swung open, and my sister strutted through it. Her skin glowed with health, and her eyes were sharper than I'd ever seen. Drake loomed behind her like an unshakable, terrifying, hard-ass guardian.

The tension drained from my muscles. When her eyes landed on me, I amped up my bravado.

She scanned the rest of the room. "So, what are we meeting about?"

Verity shifted in her seat at Jen's desk. "Nope. You don't get to disappear and then just waltz in and take over our meeting."

"You knew where we were." Chills ran down my spine when Drake peered over my shoulder. I shoved the tablet toward him, and he moved on.

Jen sauntered toward a chair and lowered herself into it, power rolling off her in waves. "And it's my office."

Drake moved to stand behind Jen. "Yes. And it's Jenella's office."

"One would think you would spend more time in it." Gramps took a sip of the fancy blood Helen had served us. It was rare for him to drink blood, and it made me wonder if turning five vampires at one time drained his energy.

After an awkward silence, Tracy broke the tension by shooting out of her seat and hugging Jen. When they broke apart, my sister stepped back and squared her shoulders. "It's time to get back to work. Where's Emine?"

"Gone," Verity said. "She packed up her stuff and disappeared."

I hadn't thought to check on Emine, and it made me feel like shit. Luckily, Meemaw didn't make the same mistake. "Nonsense, dear. She is at the manor reserved for the mage leadership. She's hurting and needs some time."

"You've talked to Emine?" Jen asked.

"Yes. Daily."

"So, what's going on?" A devious glint lit her eyes when they met mine.

I needed to hurry home to deal with my own problems, so I decided it was best to cough up the information. "We hid most of our activities from the humans, but not all. The neighborhood we fought in is still a mess. Humans being unable to enter is a problem. I caught a cop studying the spell the other day."

A look of pure dread ghosted across her face. "How bad is it?"

Mom answered the question. "Bad. We hid the battle but not the dragons, enforcers, and gargoyles who came to back us up. Hundreds of people witnessed them disappearing into our privacy spell and recorded them."

After a few more questions, she asked about my favorite subject. Action. My parents were busy people, but they always got the job done. The rest of the hybrid leaders? Not so much. When Jen asked about their plans, Chuck opened his mouth to argue with her. She'd slap him down for too much attitude, so I kicked him.

Jen was the most perceptive person I'd ever met and caught on. She fought to suppress a smile.

Dad noticed, too, so he moved the meeting along, and I zoned out. Since she was back, it wasn't my business. When Jen asked about the various crowns, something in her tone made me examine her. Before, she wouldn't have been so direct. And her demeanor was what you'd expect from a confident queen. The change was so drastic a laugh escaped me. "Damn! You've changed." I craned my neck toward Drake. "What did you do while you were gone, harvest backbones?"

"He helped me work through some stuff," Jen answered in a less queenly tone.

I tuned them out again as they updated her on the coalition's stability. All I wanted was for the meeting to end.

"I am taking over the shifters."

My thoughts screeched to a halt when Dad's words registered. If he took over the shifters, the hybrids would fall apart with their half-assed leadership. On top of that, we'd need to trek to Allure to see them in their fancy house. I slammed a hand down on the table. "How the hell are you going to do that?"

"We're moving back to Allure and appointing a new leader to take over the hybrids," Mom answered, a slight warning in her voice. One I understood as 'We'll talk about it later.'

Dad raised his hand to placate my anger. "Jenella rightly pointed out a power imbalance within the hybrids, so I've asked Dale O'Donnell and Darla Smith to take over."

When they continued with the political conversation, I thought about what it would mean to not have my parents right down the street. It would suck. I'd had them close to me for most of my life. To lose the comfort and safety of their presence caused dread to wash over me.

Before I processed it, Jen got up and left. I blinked when everyone's attention refocused on me.

"Meeting adjourned, I guess." When I stood, Verity shot me a look. There was no reason for me to hang around, and I had my own problems to deal with, so I ignored her as I zipped out of the room.

Chapter Eleven

The four vampires stood in a cluster as Elsie flashed her sparkling white fangs. She had two sharp, elongated canines, and the rest were human. I moved to Spencer next and whirled my wrist. He flashed his fangs, revealing hyena teeth, only straighter. His two fangs were longer than the rest of his pointed teeth, but they were all razor sharp.

Cavil rested his hand on the small of my back and leaned forward, causing my whole body to light up. "Interesting."

I clenched my hands, so I didn't run them across his perfect abs. "What do you make of this?"

He stepped back with a thoughtful expression on his face. "In the realm of Nought, where the dark goddesses rule, the staff they hire undergo a similar change. It makes keeping track of their servants easier and ensures loyalty."

"Huh." I refocused on my vampires. "Do any of you feel an overwhelming loyalty to me?"

"Not exactly," Elizabeth answered. "It's more a feeling of kinship. As if I can trust you to have my back. And when you order me to do something, I can't resist."

"No kidding? Is it the same for you two?"

Spencer nodded. Pascal stared at his feet, so I took it as a yes.

"What about you, Elsie?"

"I only feel compelled when you use persuasion. You feel a lot like Mistress Ara, but with a twist."

"What kind of twist?"

"It's hard to explain. I never knew when Mistress Ara monitored me. But when your anger surfaces, I want to cower. When you're happy or high on Cavil's blood, I have the urge to burst with joy myself. It's...odd."

The last thing I wanted was for anyone to feel my emotions with me. The dragons got too drunk one night and explained their bonds. I wanted no part of the intimacy those types of bonds created. After all, I already had a brother who could read my thoughts. People tuned into my emotions was too much. "Thanks. You guys can go."

Cavil rubbed his chin as they zipped toward the too-bright house. "Have you noticed any other differences?"

"I don't have a lot of experience with other vampires, but they don't look or act like any I've met."

"How so?"

"Elizabeth walked straight to the kitchen window at sunrise and peered out this morning. When I threw a fit, she explained how she had a premonition the sunlight wouldn't hurt her. And it didn't." I stabbed a finger toward the fake sky. "They're all fine in the daylight. And Pascal keeps drinking blood like he's new. The only one even remotely sane is Spencer. But only because of his lack of stupid actions." More reserved than the other two, he thought things through before he acted. I bet he made a great federal agent with his calm and measured personality.

Cavil dropped his hand. "I don't know what you want me to do."

"How do I stop it?"

He stayed silent for a long minute. "I still don't understand the question."

I threw my hands in the air. "They can feel my emotions. What happens if I'm all hot and intimate with someone? It'll throw the entire house into chaos."

His shoulders shook with laughter. "I suggest you block the bonds so such an incident doesn't occur." The heat in his eyes lit me on fire. "Should you wish to experiment, I am available."

Tingles broke out over my entire body at the thought. "I'm serious here."

"As am I," he mumbled, turning toward the maze where one of his bear shifter guards waited. "You live inside a pocket now. I suggest you use the opportunity to practice control of both your magic and your new bonds."

"Will you help?"

His eyes landed on me and darkened. "The queen has given me many responsibilities, and I have accumulated a strong following. It's good for my power level but limits my time. As a result, I'll need to adjust my schedule to assist you with your magic. Ara can help with the bonds."

Cavil was getting everything he wanted and more from our realm. It stung to think he'd soon leave me behind for a more popular life. But it was inevitable, so I needed to brace myself. Because it wouldn't be long before he saw me as nothing more than the woman who helped him adjust to a new realm. I kept my eyes focused on a bright purple rock with silver streaks to hide the pain those thoughts caused. "Sure."

He pulled me against him before I realized he'd moved. His warmth sank into my bones and lit my whole body on fire. "Don't worry, Lily. I swear I will always make time for you."

My face flushed. Damn it. I usually had better control of my emotions. "We both know that's not true, so don't lie to me."

He stepped back and lifted my chin. "You still don't see it?"

I swallowed the sudden lump in my throat. "See what?"

Several emotions swirled in his electric blue eyes. "Perhaps I have gone about this all wrong. You're a very direct person."

"Sure. And a complete smartass when I'm nervous." The look in his eyes made me want to melt. Or run away like a coward. It was one thing to flirt with someone way out of my league. But the promise in those eyes was something entirely different. My body trembled.

He leaned down until our faces were even. I fought not to step back. Or dive into that warmth and never leave. I wasn't sure which. "I did not stay in this realm to become their god. Followers are important for me to maintain a strong power level, so I must do what I can to gain and keep them. But make no mistake, the one and only reason I am still here is because it's where you are. And I will tear this realm apart if you need me."

Butterflies erupted in my stomach, and my knees almost gave out. "That's extreme." I tried to keep the snark to a minimum. "Sorry. I'm a little overwhelmed."

He rewarded me with one of his sunny smiles. "Of course you are." His lips met mine.

My head almost exploded. Heat like I'd never known lit in my core and swirled through my entire body. I gripped his biceps and deepened the kiss. His lips were soft, and he tasted like sin and salvation. I wasn't sure how matches formed, but I knew then and there that if I had a choice, I would pick him.

He ran his hands up my back and clutched my shirt before breaking the kiss and stepping back, his breathing uneven.

My hand came up and touched my mouth like some flabbergasted actress in an old movie. I'd been kissed before, but no one had ever done it so thoroughly. Or sparked so much turmoil inside me. When I realized what I was doing, I met his eyes. Big mistake. They looked back at me with the same molten heat coursing through my body.

He reached up and caressed my cheek with a featherlight touch. "You're so damn beautiful, Lily."

My mouth watered at his husky tone, and my fangs ached. A sloppy smile formed when his words registered. "That's my line."

Another bright smile. "I must go. Text should you need me." A desperate tone laced his words.

My stomach quivered, and my mind spun, so I nodded.

He turned and strode toward the bear shifter.

"Holy hell." I rubbed my eyes and headed toward the house. Never in my life had I been in so much trouble in so many ways. The entire house gathered in the spacious kitchen when I stepped through the door. Knowing or amused looks in their eyes. "Nope. I'm not talking about it."

"Please don't," Alex mumbled.

Elizabeth shifted in her seat. "We're totally going to talk about the toe-curling lust. How do I find it for myself?"

A deep rumble rolled through the kitchen, and it took me a second to realize it was Glacintial laughing. "Because humans are incapable of such a deep connection. Now that you are one of us, you may find your match. Only then will you experience the joys of pure and overwhelming lust."

Alex's face puckered. "Let's not talk about Lily's lust."

"No?" June flipped her purple hair over her shoulder. "Tell me every detail."

"Yes. Spill it, girl." Flintous agreed.

Pascal slammed his glass onto the table. "This is not a normal conversation. You people are a bunch of freaks, and I don't belong here."

Everyone's eyes landed on him. Before I could think of a response, Spencer spoke for me. "They're not your problem. You are. We all feel for you and the circumstances which brought you here. It wasn't fair, and I'm sure Lily would take it back if she could. But it's your reality now. You won't be happy until you accept it."

Pascal rubbed his face. "And if I don't?"

"Then I'll send you to my grandmother's house for reconditioning. She uses pain and mental coercion." I motioned around the room. "We have a lot of problems to deal with and don't have the resources or energy to babysit a grown-ass man twenty-four-seven. So, either suck it up, or off you go. Either way, this is your new life, so it's best to accept it."

He slammed his chair back so hard it hit the wall. Thudding echoed through the house as he stomped up the stairs.

"That guy is a problem," Alex said. "He stole my phone and thinks he can use it to tattle on us."

Fire lit in Flintous's eyes. "Can I retrieve it?"

With a sigh, I stood and headed toward the stairs. "I got it." Tech mages infused our phones with magic, so once we added a drop of our power, they became keyed to us and were useless to anyone else without our magical permission. Pascal couldn't use the phone, but his theft still needed to be addressed.

First turn, first fail, I admitted two days later as I drove toward Dale's bar in yet another new van. Pascal wouldn't adjust, no matter how much reasoning, cajoling, or begging I used. When I had enough of his attitude, I sent him to his room and called Meemaw. She gave me a few pointers I'd try later. I sent Elsie to buy a new van and enjoyed a few hours of peace. She came back with a black one. My least favorite color. But it would work until some new idiot crashed it or blew it up. It needed to be broken in, so I grabbed Alex and drove toward the bar.

Mom said the police suspected gang activity in the area. They were partially right. There were several hybrids unhappy about joining the coalition. Even more were uneasy about the federal agents snooping around. So we still didn't know who shot up the bar.

The privacy bubble had shrunk again since my last visit to the battle site. I wondered if the mages would move faster now that Jen was back. I parked on the street and gave one a friendly wave. "Mind if I leave this here for an hour?" The mage shrugged, so I locked it up.

Alex loped beside me, scanning the area. "They're moving too slow."

"Yeah. Pureblood mages aren't used to working around humans, and it scares them. The hybrids assigned to help stand on the sidelines and laugh at them. They were working together when I went to Sheila's place."

"You'd think the taunting would make them work faster, not slower."

We exited the privacy bubble in the fenced backyard of someone's home and squared our shoulders as we moved through the gate and headed toward the bar. The parking lot still had scorch marks and police tape blocking it off. There were three cars parked on the street around it belonging to regulars.

When I opened the door, heat smashed into me, along with the familiar scent of fried food and stale booze. I shuffled inside and swung my head around in wonder. If I hadn't been there, I'd never guess a mass shooting happened.

Dale was deep in conversation with a phoenix and glanced in our direction as we settled into our usual spots.

Alex pulled out his phone. "Another shooting took place in Florida near the pocket of Arcadia."

"Not Texas this time?"

"Stop bashing Texas."

"You're right. I should bash Florida."

"Or don't bash either of them."

"You're no fun anymore."

"Bashing entire states isn't fun."

A dark beer landed in front of me, and Dale rested his elbows on the bar. "It's beneath you, your highness."

I pointed at the beer. "I take it you're still pissed at me."

"Understatement. When I first heard rumors about being considered for a leadership position, I wondered who in the ever-loving hell thought I'd be a good choice. It certainly wasn't Jonas or Ann Marie, so it had to be you."

"Yeah. We already established it was me. But our parents would never have considered you if you hadn't got all bossy with Jen. You sealed your own fate, buddy."

"I'm not your buddy."

"Sure you are."

Alex cleared his throat. "Have you heard anything about the shootings in Texas and Florida?"

"I've heard rumors the government is leaking information about us. A hybrid Jonas planted said they plan to release information in small doses before revealing our existence." Dale straightened to his full height. "The more militant humans aren't taking the news well. And it's going to get worse before it gets better, I'm afraid."

My face puckered as I sipped the beer. "Hybrids and humans shot up your bar."

Dale's eyes bore into me. "Yes. I told your stubborn sister some hybrids wouldn't join the coalition no matter what she did, but the bitch didn't listen and instead plowed forward with her plans."

My aura ramped up, and my fangs almost dropped. "Don't call my sister a bitch."

Alex's shoulders shook with laughter. "Yeah. I dare you to call her that to her face."

"Jenella's tolerant for a queen. It's the big-ass dragon she runs with I need to worry about. He would most likely kill me before the words left my mouth."

"Drake's a good guy. But yeah. He's not a fan of people disrespecting Jen."

Alex shook with laughter. "Like it ever stopped you from running your mouth." He jerked a thumb toward me. "She made him feed an entire crew of people who showed up at our house unannounced."

"Everyone was hungry, and he thought it was fun. I'd have made Jen help if I knew she made me her heir."

"I guess we're all moving up in the world." Dale's head tilted. "Incoming humans."

Alex and I slumped over our beers and tried to look bored as the door swung open.

Two men in cheap suits scanned the place, their heartbeats too fast as they moved toward Dale and raised their badges. He motioned them around the bar and led them to the back, outside my hearing range.

Alex returned his attention to his phone. "This is getting bad. There are entire online forums dedicated to locating and hunting paranormals."

"It'll calm down." I hoped. "If they give us enough time, I'm sure the purebloods will take care of it. They always do."

"You think Jen is as good about covering things up as Mat?"

Not even close. Mat was a master at maneuvering the entire world to fit his narrative. Jen would be even better one day, but it would take time. She still had a lot to learn. "What did you learn from those guys?"

"Coworkers of your new friends. They're fishing for clues about their disappearance."

I polished off the nasty beer and eyed the door. My heart told me I did the right thing by taking the federal agents in, but my brain disagreed. And I wouldn't be in such a mess if I left the guy from Roman's house alone when Pascal confronted him. If I could go back, I'd mind my own business. I threw the thoughts out of my head. "Are you about ready to go?"

We circled the area but didn't see or sense anything suspicious. If rogue hybrids were shooting up Dale's bar, the group knew about his leadership position and, most likely, the gate. Which meant they had access to the pocket. Lucky for us, the population of the new pocket was still sparse, and we had three dragons and an Alex who could read minds. I was about to suggest we snoop around the pocket when some idiot cut me off and slammed on the brakes.

"Human," Alex said, without looking up from his phone.

"Why is everyone determined to total my vans?"

"Maybe your winning personality soaks into your vehicles."

"Funny." I changed lanes to take another route. We didn't need to be involved in a road rage incident.

Halfway home, Alex lowered his phone and rubbed his head. "The guys following us are bored and frustrated because we're so normal."

"Are you scanning minds as we drive?"

"Just theirs. It's fascinating how little information these guys have on paranormals, considering we exist under their noses."

"We should go to their hotels and learn what they've found."

"No. It's not our problem. Besides, the ones running the operation rented houses."

My head snapped toward my brother. "Where?"

"I'm not telling you because you'll find them, and it won't go well. Besides, we don't need more roommates."

No argument there. "At least tell Roman. His people are out spying all the time." Unless the government was on to them, too. If so, they'd act like humans until the agents moved on. Roman had a lot more experience than me, so he was smarter about how he spied. "Let's check out the hybrids moving to the pocket. Maybe they've heard something."

Chapter Twelve

We drove home, went straight through the gate, and peered out the one near our parent's house. Federal agents sat in a car parked down the street from their farm but didn't look our way. Mom's dusty magic coated the area, hiding us from their view. Hybrid farmhands moved around their property, caring for the land and animals. Every so often, one would glance toward the agents, but it was subtle.

Fat turquoise snowflakes fell as we dipped back inside, near a replica of our parents' farm. It also buzzed with activity. We headed down the winding road leading to our house.

Alex opened his hand to catch a snowflake, and a smile stretched from ear to ear. "You should take your newbies and teach them how to spy."

"Yeah. What are you going to do?"

"I'll explore the shifter areas."

"Be careful. If anyone attacks you, kill them."

"Yes, Mother." He changed into his lion form and trotted off.

A mass of new houses popped up in the last few days. A new town was forming near a lop-sided peach-colored hill. I made a mental note to train my vampires there to see why they formed a separate town. Familial stabbing punched into my chest as soon as I stepped through our wards.

I rested my hand on the doorknob, squared my shoulders, and stepped inside.

There was no way I could have braced myself for what I walked into. Elsie stood on one side of the family room, her fangs and claws out. Flintous's red hair flowed over his shoulders as he struggled to hold her back. To the left, Elizabeth and Spencer huddled together behind what used to be the sofa. Stuffing coated every surface, a few pieces still floating around. In the center of the room, Pascal was on his stomach, blood flowing from several wounds. The left side of his face was purple. Gramps perched on top of him while Meemaw sat cross-legged on the floor.

I folded my arms. "Did you start the party without me?"

Meemaw raised her head, and her ancient eyes sparkled. "Hello, dear. It seems you are correct about this one. He is not developing."

I dropped my arms. "What happened this time?" I directed the question toward Elsie.

She retracted her fangs. "That little fuck tried to jump me."

Elsie was one hell of a fighter and super hard to sneak up on. I'd only managed it twice, and I had a lot of practice from trying to jump-attack a cat shifter. "Dumb."

Flintous let Elsie go and stepped back, but the red fire in his eyes remained. "He is unaware of many dangers."

I pinched the bridge of my nose. "Let me guess, he challenged you?"

"Not me, no." His eyes flicked toward the kitchen.

Drake appeared in the doorway, a tray of food in his hand. "Hello, Lily."

"Oh, holy hell." If there were a dumb way-to-die award handy, I would have handed it to my new vampire. "Please tell me he didn't attack you."

"He did try." Drake motioned for Elizabeth to take the tray. "I doubt he will make that mistake again."

"Yeah, no shit." I jabbed a finger in his direction. "This guy can transform into the biggest dragon you've ever seen, so don't fuck with him. Because if he doesn't kill you, I'll do it myself."

"I am a very patient dragon, but will act should the need arise." Drake slid his hands in his pockets in such a casual way you'd think he was human. A very large, beat-up human with an aura so powerful it was unsettling. "I see you've been busy."

"Yeah." I refused to explain the situation while everyone stood around wide-eyed and full of adrenaline. "Can we save him, Meemaw?"

"Perhaps. His blood tastes similar to the other two. You may have a point about the venom. I suggest you inject him again."

"Meemaw?" Elizabeth whispered.

I ignored her. "Sure. Who tore up my house?"

Spencer leaned against the wall next to me. "Pascal tried to sneak up on the big guy. Elsie lost her shit. When she turned to apologize to your guest, he jumped her. She reacted fast, but not before the big guy turned into a giant furry thing."

My fists clenched and unclenched. Good thing we had tall ceilings. "And?"

"The two powerful vampires stashed Elizabeth and me behind the couch and talked the big guy into changing back. Meanwhile, Elsie tore Pascal up. Flintous came in and tried to break it up. Your *meemaw* ended the fight using that weird energy you share, and the sarcastic male pinned him." He motioned toward Drake. "That guy turned normal and stayed naked until it was under control. When you came down the drive, he headed toward the kitchen."

I made a mental note about how observant Spencer was as I sucked in some air to calm myself. "Thanks. The sarcastic male is my Gramps. And it's normal to see naked paranormals running around because many of them shift. The big guy's name is Drake, and he's my sister's match."

"Oh, my. You are such a good housemaster." Meemaw went from the floor to standing so fast my eyes couldn't track the movement. "This one will continue to cause issues until he learns his place." She tapped her chin. "You have your hands full with the two lovely additions to your house, so if you inject him with more venom, I will take him home to monitor him. If he does not improve, you must use force to ensure compliance."

My muscles relaxed a little. "Thanks, Meemaw." I glanced around the wrecked room. "Can any of you clean this mess up with magic? No?" I motioned toward Elsie. "You made the mess, so you clean it up. You too, Pascal." I used a little persuasion as our guests allowed me to herd them toward the dining room. "Spencer, grab the food, please."

Drake waved a hand, and more snacks and drinks appeared on the table.

My mouth watered. "Can June do that?"

Drake's lips twitched. "Perhaps. She prefers using her observation skills more than her culinary talents."

"What brings you here?"

"I hoped you would fill me in on the issues within the city."

"How should I know? I live in this hideous blue house inside a pocket now."

He raised an eyebrow.

"Fine." It took me a minute to gather my thoughts. "Should I explain what my instincts tell me or stick to the facts?"

"Both."

"There haven't been any Bellicose sightings. The mages Jen hired to rebuild the neighborhoods are taking too long because the hybrid contractors won't help them learn how human utilities work. Though they were working together the other day."

"Yes. I paid them a visit."

"Sheila said she handled it."

His eyes sparkled with humor. "Interesting how she waited until I returned to lead."

A laugh escaped me. "Yeah. I wondered if Jen's return would speed things up. Federal agents have many of us under surveillance, and a few rogue hybrids worked with humans to shoot up Dale's bar. Jen's protection magic saved it. Unfortunately, it didn't save the cars outside, including my new van."

Drake's eyes sharpened. "You were there?"

"Yeah. June used her scales to protect Elsie and me from most of the bullets. Then Gramps and I turned the dying humans, which is where I got Spencer and Elizabeth." I raised a hand. "Those are the facts. My instincts are screaming at me that something's off. It was too quiet for a while. A few days earlier, we found the feds digging through some ruins outside the privacy bubble. It's where I screwed up and turned Pascal. He cornered one of Roman's vampires and I tried to knock him out to save his life."

"You said the bar was undamaged?" A note of pride rang through Drake's voice.

"Yes. The bullets didn't so much as chip a wall. But we lost a couple more hybrids and three humans. All the humans in the bar were federal agents. Mom and Dale covered it up. Before the shooting, the CIA showed up here, or rather at my real house, and questioned Alex and me."

"And what else are your instincts telling you?" Gramps asked.

"That something big is coming, and we need to prepare. That those hybrids were working with humans is worrying. I planned to take my house spying inside the pocket to see if we could learn more. It's almost as if the agents at the bar were expendable and placed there on purpose. If so, we screwed ourselves by changing them. By covering it up, we may have raised the humans' suspicions." I popped a fancy mini-sandwich into my mouth. "Some hybrids responsible for it might already live here."

"If so, I'm sure you will find them." Drake leaned back. "Perhaps everyone should stay inside the pocket for a while."

I raised an eyebrow. "By everyone, you mean me, right?"

"Yes. I'll deploy my team of dragons to see what intel we can pick up." He tapped his temple.

"Alex learned some things he won't share with me. He even knows where the guys in charge are staying."

"So do we," Spencer said. "It's not classified information. Pascal and I were new, and our supervisor assigned us to this case to gain experience. Elizabeth was well-liked and trusted within her team."

Drake considered him for a minute. "Has Alex assessed their motives?"

"Yes. Why?"

"We don't have a motive. Lily asked if we wanted to live. I do, so here I am."

Gramps came out of his listening stupor. "Do not remove him from Lily's care, First. He is well-behaved, but will not do well without her guidance."

"I have no use for a new vampire on my team." Drake tore his eyes away from Spencer. "He wasn't happy in his human life but is honorable and looks forward to the new opportunity. The woman is happiest surrounded by people, no matter the circumstances."

Spencer lowered himself into the chair beside me. "How did you learn about us?"

"Dragons can read minds." I jerked a thumb in Drake's direction. "This guy is as good as Alex."

"No kidding? What superpowers do we have?"

"Oh, I'm sure you will have many gifts." Pure delight radiated from Meemaw.

I didn't ask what she meant. The weirdness of my vampires wasn't Drake's business. "We'll go over some skills later. I think you'll like what you learn."

Alex strode through the back door, wearing sweatpants and nothing else. He scanned our gathering and pulled out a chair. "Drake. What brings you here?"

Drake pushed a plate of food toward him. "We were discussing the current situation in the valley."

"Did Lily tell you about our visit from the Men in Black?"

Everyone's heads swung toward me.

"I told them they questioned us."

"What about the militias?"

"It was two incidents clear across the country. No one's hunting us."

"So you say."

A rumble of laughter came from Drake. "It seems I have missed quite a lot." He stood. "I will contact Roman."

A thought struck me. "Be careful going to his house. The feds might watch him, too."

He inclined his head. "Please contact Jenella soon."

My face sobered. "Sure."

As soon as he left, I focused on Spencer. "Vampires develop skills with age. Right now, you're faster, stronger, and your senses are better than when you were human. You'll also heal much faster. As far as other abilities, they'll reveal themselves later."

Meemaw tapped the table. "It is possible you will develop skills sooner. Lily has the power of our creator, Lilith. Some of her creations were quite unique until she settled on a specific formula."

My left eye twitched. "So I can change people with a stray thought and choose what they become?"

"Of course not, dear. Even though Mother altered her venom to suit her needs, you may only have the skills to create one type of vampire."

"Mother?" Spencer asked in a strangled voice. "The person who invented vampires is your mother?"

A tinkling laugh burst out of her. "I adore the innocence of youth. My mother was what we called a First, yes. As is Drake. They are our creators."

"Except for those of us who are natural born."

Meemaw nodded. "Correct. Lily is an anomaly because she is the direct descendent of three Firsts. Only time will tell what you become."

He paled, but didn't ask more questions.

Fine by me. "So, you examined their teeth?"

"Yes. They are works of art. Monitor them closely as they develop, but it is not something to worry about today."

Relief flooded me. "When should I worry?"

Another tinkling laugh. "It depends. If one of them gives in to bloodlust, starts hunting for sport, or becomes deformed, then put them down. I shall help you work through other issues, including rehabilitating the feral one.

In the future, I advise you to use caution when deploying your fangs as a weapon."

Yeah, no shit. "Cavil said my doubts cause my magic to do strange things. I'm pretty sure that's what happened when I turned Pascal. I'll work on it."

She stood. "Of course you will, dear." Meemaw was around the table and had me in a hug before I could dodge. "Take care of your new house members. They are truly special."

"Sure." Her delight made me uneasy.

After I injected Pascal with more venom, she latched onto his collar and vanished. Gramps gave me a long, considering look and followed.

Spencer watched them go. "Can I do that?"

"Not for a few thousand years. Trust me, I've tried."

"A few thousand?" His voice sounded strained.

Alex refilled his plate. "You didn't tell him?"

My forehead crinkled. "Tell him what?"

He focused on Spencer. "Lily is the heir to both the vampire throne and the throne of Ahl. Her sister oversees the entire paranormal community. We call it the Coalition. Her assistant was the one who came and dragged Lily away the other day."

"Oh, come on! Do you have to blab all my business?"

My lovely little brother ignored my protest. "The woman who just left is not only Lily's grandmother, but the queen of vampires. The man is her consort. Drake is a dragon and the consort to Lily's sister, the Queen of Ahl."

"I am *not* taking a throne. They're my biological family, and I just met them. Alex and I were adopted. I have no desire to rule, but I like my sister, her quirky friends, and my grandparents." I pointed at the door. "A word of warning. My Gramps is usually hanging around, and he is great at hiding."

Spencer's eyes grew as big as saucers. "So, I hit the vampire jackpot?"

"Pretty much," Alex continued, ignoring me. "Lily's nicer than other vampire masters. She's also half god, which means no one knows what you'll become."

"He's a vampire. Period. End of story." I stood and stomped out of the room.

Chapter Thirteen

Adjusting my body temperature against the bone-chilling cold, I exited the gate into my normal backyard. Cavil walked beside me, a grim expression on his face. Christmas lights covered the entire house and twinkled in unique patterns. Excitement bubbled in my chest at the sight. We used to celebrate Christmas every year, and I had a lot of fond memories of opening presents and laughing together as a family. Though we hadn't in a while. The decorations were probably Elizabeth's idea. The woman had so much energy she was hard to keep up with. A couple of snowmen stood guard in the backyard, their tattered scarves flapping in the wind.

Fat white snowflakes floated down from the sky so fast they coated us in seconds. I stomped up the deck and flung the sliding glass door open. The scent of home wrapped around me, and my muscles relaxed. I turned to Cavil's bear shifters. "Make yourselves at home."

They stayed by the back door as I peered out the front window. Someone plowed the driveway and shoveled the walkway. Since Elsie appointed herself my second, she insisted I didn't do what she called menial chores. She tried to think of everything and have it done so I couldn't do housework. It frustrated me, but she was relentless about it. I sighed as I focused on the property across the street.

The humans visibly shivered as they huddled in the loft of an abandoned barn. I bet they thought they were clever with their hiding spot. But my parents owned the property and had monitoring spells on them. We let them watch as we did our regular human home maintenance. Alex probably cleared the drive and decorated the house since they didn't know about our roommates.

I dropped the blinds. "They're not giving up."

"No, they're not. It's wise for them to stay persistent. Someone will eventually slip up, and they'll catch it on camera."

"Yeah." I thought back to everyone who appeared at our gate over the last few months. "Or they already have proof."

Cavil ran a perfect hand through his immaculate hair. "I have been to many realms. Some are at war, while others enjoy peace. But never have I seen one as divided." His eyes scanned my face. "A reckoning between paranormals and humans is inevitable."

I supposed he was right. Anyone with half a brain could have seen it coming the moment the first hybrid got tossed out of a pocket. My parents worked hard to hide us, but their efforts only bought time.

My gaze settled on Cavil, and I drank in his appearance. His muscular body balanced with his perfect face. Those magnificent eyes weren't a standard shade of blue any more than mine were a regular brown. And contrary to popular pureblood opinion, humans weren't stupid.

One look at a dragon with matching hair and eyes, and they'd realize something was off. It wasn't a problem when they were in denial. But now they knew about us, so they'd watch for it. "We need better information. I need to find out what they know and plan to do about us."

Cavil's eyes flashed, proving my point. "And how will you accomplish this goal?"

"Good question."

He took my hand and rubbed the back of it with his thumb. "Let the dragons handle it. The men across the street already believe you and Alex are magical. Should you try to spy, you will prove them right."

"Yeah." It was a chance I'd take to protect the hybrids. I tapped my chin. "I've been hanging around the neighborhood where the battle took place. It wouldn't be hard to shadow one of their agents when they leave."

"What if we tapped into their electronic devices?" Spencer asked from the direction of the security office. When our attention turned to him, he gave me a half-wave. "I'm not doing anything wrong. Elsie suggested I take a more active role in security, so Alex is showing me the ropes."

"Alex is here?"

"Yes. And you're stupid if you think you can follow those guys," Alex's muffled voice came from down the hall.

"Don't call me stupid, stupid." Not my best comeback. "What are you two up to?"

Alex slunk to the doorway and paused beside Spencer. "We have resources now, so you don't need to risk yourself. June and Glac have spent days perched on that barn, reading their minds."

I crossed my arms. "What have they found, and why did they keep it from me?"

"Because the dragons do what they want, and you aren't their boss."

I raised an eyebrow.

He threw his hands up. "You're not! Besides, you've been busy establishing a house."

"It's not a house."

"Keep telling yourself that."

"What have the humans learned about us?" Cavil interjected.

Spencer shrugged. "More than you want them to. They've employed paranormals in the military for decades. They expanded the program after a dragon incident went viral a couple of years ago."

I rested a hand on Cavil's arm. If they knew about us, they might have been watching for unusual activity for a while. "Have you told Dale?"

"Sure." Alex wiggled his phone. "He met with Jen about it."

I should have felt relief. Instead, an old scar created by watching vampires from afar during my time with my biological parents ripped open, and the pain of rejection stabbed me in the heart. I folded my arms, so I didn't grab my chest as I scanned the three faces. Alex and Spencer had knowing looks while Cavil's eyes shimmered with concern. "Stop looking at me like that." I went fluid and fled back to the pocket.

I barely made it through the gate before Cavil appeared in front of me. "Why are you running?"

"I'm not." The pain in my chest throbbed. "Okay, maybe I am. But it wasn't intentional. Can I hang at your place for a bit? I want to figure out my blood bonds, and I can't without a quiet place to think."

"Of course." He motioned toward a fresh path Flemming created, connecting our house to his. "Are you sure you're okay?"

"Yeah. I had a flashback to some childhood issues. They bite me in the ass sometimes, even though I worked through them a long time ago."

"I understand."

"Do you?"

"Yes. Have I ever told you about my parents?"

My eyebrows drew together. "Um. No?"

He smoothed a nonexistent wrinkle from his bright green shirt. "A deity oversees each of the twelve kingdoms that make up the realm of the gods."

"Like the Firsts in this realm?"

"No. Your Firsts are lesser beings compared to the gods and certainly inferior to the Deity."

I smirked. "Of course."

"The Deity is neither male nor female. It is an overwhelming presence that is power-personified and all-knowing. I believe the Christian version of the Holy Trinity is the closest comparison." He shook his head. "The Deity's Chosen rule kingdoms of what you would equate to gods and angels, though there are other beings in the realm considered the servant class. My parents were rulers of the third kingdom. Part of the Chosen."

"So, you're a prince?"

"Yes. My sister is now the queen. Our parents were fair and just rulers who loved their children. They were also merciless when other Chosen encroached on their territory. My father had a lifetime dispute with a neighboring king and eventually started a war. Many beings lost their immortal lives, including the neighboring king, whom my father killed. The Deity was not pleased and appeared in person to ask about it. My parents lied and said it was an accident."

The pain in his voice almost buckled my knees. I took his hand. "I take it the lie didn't land?"

"The Deity knows everything, so lying is futile. There were no rules against wars, killing, or lying. But only because there had never been such an incident. The Deity was furious and sentenced my parents to death for their indiscretions, then ordered us to serve the other districts' leaders for one hundred years. It also removed our ability to lie. My parents' deaths were an example to the rest of us should we break the rules."

My heart ached for him. I couldn't imagine watching my adoptive parents die. "I'm sorry. That had to be devastating."

"Yes. My brother and sister had always envied the close relationship I had with my parents and alienated me after their deaths. They served in district two and shipped me to eleven. I did well in those hundred years without them. Thrived, even. I gained the respect of their royalty and had many followers. Until my sister took the throne. She ordered me back to her district and stripped me of my title and land. It hurt because I still hoped she loved me."

He opened the side door and took a moment to gather his thoughts as we stepped inside. "It did not have the effect she wished, but it still profoundly influenced me. I wondered aimlessly until anger set in. Anger so deep I almost drowned in it."

"But you didn't."

"Correct. I used it to fuel me. I built wealth and bought land no one wanted on the outskirts of her kingdom. She laughed as she allowed it, thinking the purchase would prove her right."

"I'm not following. Prove her right about what?"

"About my inferiority to other gods. I worked tirelessly to gain the trust of the lesser beings in the area. And fell in love with them. It became my own little kingdom, built out of spite and forged of love. I didn't care if it was legal because I was hyper-focused on proving my siblings wrong. On proving I belonged."

"Is that why you're so good at empire-building?"

He nodded as he placed a warm hand on my lower back and led me down a hall. "I have built four empires since then. The first is still the one I love most and live in when I visit the realm."

He considered our realm temporary. His home contained an entire empire he loved, so I didn't blame him. My heart still ached. I wondered if he would forget about the houses I helped him pick when he left. "You love it."

"Yes."

"So, what brought you here?"

"I lived happily there for a long time. Then, one day, my sister realized I'd gained too much influence and decided she had a use for me."

I winced. "Let me guess. She ruined it for you?"

"In a way. She had become very good at political maneuvering and skirting around the rules. But she needed someone to sell to a neighboring kingdom and betrothed me to a goddess I never met. It is unheard of in the kingdoms to become betrothed to anyone other than our soulmates, so I refused."

"Let me guess, she insisted."

"Correct. She restored my title and held me captive in a monotone room, trying to force me to believe the woman she betrothed me to was my soulmate."

I leaned into him to offer comfort. "You said she can't lie. That sounds like a whopper to me."

"It wasn't a direct lie, and she didn't physically hurt me. But the mental and emotional torture was..." He trailed off, then shook his head. "She was unaware I'd been having regular talks with the Deity to ensure I didn't overstep as I established myself. I'd gained the support of thousands of angels and many other gods from all districts. A decision I was grateful for when my sister deemed me sufficiently brainwashed and forced me in front of her court to declare my soulmate. The woman intended for me did not look like she cared about the lie."

"But you did," I mumbled.

"Yes. I gave my sister a chance to reconsider her actions. She had no intention of being honest, so I called the Deity and asked for a judgment. To my relief, it intervened on my behalf. It punished my sister by transferring some of her wealth and land to me and limiting her influence. Then, it declared me, my people, and my land sovereign. I am not a king, but with my title restored and the blessings of the Deity, I rule them. No other Chosen may interfere with me or my people."

My chest ached at the thought of him having so much to return home to. "That's good."

"Yes. My territory has prospered, and my people are happy. I was content to stay with them for the rest of my days. But the Deity appeared one day and handed me a key to the other realms. Then ordered me to travel to the ones with gods present. Because the fate of both my realm and the realm where my soulmate lives depends on me. This is my sixth one."

"So, you're on a treasure hunt?"

"No." His face grew stern. "I'm telling you this because the Deity does not believe in loopholes. It will give a Chosen enough room to make the right decision, but eventually, it will enforce the rules. I cannot lie. Even going by a shortened version of my name is walking a fine line. Should I cross it, there will be consequences."

"No way. That's..." I paused when a thought struck. "You said you needed to find your soulmate and help her realm."

"Correct."

"How long will you be here before you need to move on?"

He shot me a look I generally reserved for the person in an unnecessary meeting who would not stop asking dumb questions.

The answer smashed me in the face. "Sorry. Having a 'how stupid can I be' moment."

The room brightened with his smile. "Take your time."

"Are you telling me I could have been hitting that..." I motioned to his perfect body. "All this time, and you didn't bother to mention it?"

Cavil's sexy laugh turned my legs to jelly. "I do like how you worship my beauty. I hope to return the favor soon."

Lust exploded, and I yearned to jump him right there in the hallway. "Oh, you'll have your chance." I dialed it back when I realized my vampires probably noticed the heat coursing through me. "But not right now. I need to work out how to control the blood bonds so everyone in my house can't feel our sexy times. Alex would never let me live it down."

He bit back a laugh. "Very well. I shall wait for you to learn control." Cavil guided me into a sitting room.

Like the pocket, it looked like a crayon exploded inside it. Hot pink sofas faced each other in front of a fireplace made of pure white stone. Acacia floors with unique patterns peeked out underneath bright orange rugs. Electric blue dotted the room. The neon green walls had wooden chair rails that were far too sophisticated for all the bright colors. I didn't laugh, though. Or even react. For some reason, the bright, colorful room worked.

"Do you like it?" Cavil was so close his breath tickled my ear.

I shivered. "You keep doing that, and my vamps will get a peep show." I ran a hand over the back of one of the pink sofas. It was so soft I wanted to bury myself in it. Or break it in, I thought as I turned and met his eyes. "It's so you, I can't help but like it. Though I must admit, it gives me wicked thoughts." The room dimmed with my smile. It took me a moment to realize my magic leaked, and I cut it off.

In the silence that followed, I worked to work through my lust to assess how it happened and why he had such a potent effect on me. Cavil valued honesty, but I wasn't sure if the brutal type counted. I took the chance. "When I pulled you off that street and taught you about this realm, I didn't do it with an ulterior motive. I helped, so you had a chance to build a life. One that makes you happy. I'm grateful you like to keep me close. I feel drawn to you. It's why I brought Roman to you for negotiations. Your friendship has meant everything to me in the last few months. But we should step back before we do something we'll both regret."

"I will never regret spending time with you."

"Me, too. You're like this bright sunshine after a drenching rain. Everywhere you go, you light up the world. And I'm darkness personified. You saw what happened when I used my magic." I motioned toward the lights. "And you may not have noticed, but I'm kind of a smart ass, lazy about my magic, and aside from Alex, I don't really have any friends. Have you ever asked yourself why?"

"No. You have many people surrounding you."

"My family cares, yes. But making friends is difficult because people can sense the well of darkness inside me. I purposely do nothing to change their minds because no one needs the kind of destruction I'm capable of in their lives. If Alex would let me shake him loose, I'd do it." I shook my head. "Not the point. I kill without remorse when needed, poke at people relentlessly, and soak up drama every chance I get. The one value I have in common with you is that I appreciate honesty. But only because I was raised by a shifter who could both scent a lie and wipe me off the face of the planet if he wanted to." I realized I was rambling. Cavil made me do a lot of things I wouldn't normally do. "I would never forgive myself if I permanently dimmed your light."

He moved to the window and peered out. "You are not darkness personified, though your magic will always align with the night. You are more like a bright moon in a starry sky. Every time you enter a room, you light up the darkness like no one I've ever seen."

Before I could argue, he continued. "You save people for no reason other than wanting them to have a good life. You took in a foul-mouthed gnome with nowhere else to go and handed a couple of wayward vampires over to Ara instead of ejecting them from your vehicle. And even helped a God new to this realm. You have no obligation to your biological family. Yet, you tried to help a sister you never knew grow her confidence. And you came to her aid when she needed you most during the battle. You even try to be a friend to your grandmother."

"That's because I can relate to her lack of friends and dark spirit."

"I disagree. It's because you want to save her. Which most would consider ridiculous, considering her age and status. But not you. You see right through the façade and do everything you can to make sure she knows she has someone other than Tarquin who cares about her. In doing so, you have earned her respect. And you have come to love her as much as she loves you.

"Most of your biological family finds your attitude toward them refreshing." Cavil's strange accent thickened. "It's true that you are a dark creature by nature who belongs to the night. But, unlike other dark creatures, you somehow light it up. I am honored to know you and will not be reconsidering our relationship."

Tears burned my eyes. "Then why am I still terrified I'll ruin you if you stick around?"

"You can't. I was ruined a long time ago." He motioned for me to sit. "Take all the time you need to sort out your bonds." He moved toward the door and paused. "I will not let you go without a fight."

The tears I'd been holding back ran down my cheeks, and I swiped my sleeve across my face. I had no words.

Chapter Fourteen

It took me several hours and two phone conversations with Meemaw to work the bonds, find their differences, and learn the feel of each person. Although I managed to mute my feelings from each one individually, I struggled to keep all four closed on my end while still monitoring them. The privacy issue ate at me. When I complained to Meemaw, she laughed and told me to keep trying until I got it right.

Frustrated and exhausted, I continued with my plan to spy. Elsie took Spencer to the new town by the odd-shaped hill while I worked with Elizabeth.

As we reached the village, she jammed her fingers in her ears. "Too much noise."

I taught her how to mute it. "Work on it until you can tune out everything but one sound."

"How did you learn all this without other vampires to help you?"

An elemental-mage hybrid strolled down the main street, dissolving the snow and drying the road. Vehicles were too large to fit through the gates, so my parents created a hidden parking lot near their farm. I'd have to ask her to do the same at my place. "I've always known how to tune my hearing."

"Because you were born a vampire?"

"Either that or my biological mother taught me when I was too young to remember." She didn't want me listening in on her treasonous conversations, so probably the latter.

She pointed toward a group of people. "If I focus on them, can I hear what they're saying?"

"Yes. Tune everything else out, then turn up the volume. It takes concentration." When she figured it out, I motioned toward the center of town. "Let's walk around so you can practice."

Several hybrids lined up outside a massive dome two blocks off the main trapezoid, their heads ducked against the heavy snow. A wolf-witch hybrid marched out the door, followed by three teenagers with varying magics. Unlike in Allure, where paranormals felt free to shift whenever they wanted to, most hybrids stuck with their human forms. I wondered if they'd ever feel comfortable enough to be themselves after the years of pretending to be human. Those lessons were hard to shake. Each person who exited the building carried a bundle of supplies in bags and boxes I recognized from Maria's intake warehouse. I'd heard rumors she moved to the pocket to help hybrids settle, but hadn't checked on her.

"Are you in line?" A fairy-witch with skin a little too pink and a puffy coat rested a hand on Elizabeth's arm.

I whipped around so fast she hopped back a step. I held up both hands like a criminal, then lowered them. "You can go ahead." The long line shuffled forward as the next person entered the dome. I texted Elsie.

Lily

The hybrid intake warehouse needs volunteers.

Elsie

And…

Lily

Newbies can learn a lot about the community by helping.

Elsie

New vampires + the masses = disaster

Lily

How long before they can help?

Elsie

A year or two

Damn. I'd go insane hanging around the house for two years with all the big personalities invading my space. I sent a shit emoji and continued down the street toward a new three-story building next to the gate leading to Dale's bar. It was as odd as the ones Jen built, with its curved roofs and sharp angles. A sloppy smile spread across my face when I noticed the sign on the front. It mirrored Dale's smaller bar in the human world.

"A bar?" Elizabeth's hands shook as she adjusted her scarf.

I strode to the door. "Yes. Will you be okay if we pop inside for a minute?"

With a curt nod, she squared her shoulders. "Sure."

Where Hooves resembled a pub, the new place was modern, with a stage on one end for live music. The bar was still wooden but had clean, contemporary lines and intricate dwarven carvings. Several free-standing tables dotted the floor, with tan chairs stacked on top. It had at least three times the space of his other bar.

Darla burst from the back. "Hey, Lily."

"Hey. This is one of my new vampires, Elizabeth. You guys are opening a place here?"

"Nice to meet you, Elizabeth. We didn't intend to. But more hybrids have been migrating here since we found ourselves appointed leaders. Dale wants everyone inside before the government finds them."

"Nice. Can I help?" The thought of drinking so close to home thrilled me. Maybe Flintous and June would join me, and we could have fun without Deva interrupting us with her lectures.

"Help evacuate, or at the bar?"

"The bar. Though I'll help evacuate, too."

"We might need an extra server occasionally."

I worked as a server once. It was one of my fondest toxic workplaces. My coworkers were a bunch of drinkers, and the manager was a misogynistic ass who liked to grope the staff. The pay was so low I didn't have a clue how they made ends meet. I had to quit because I moved too fast when we got busy. It wouldn't be a problem inside a pocket. "Sure. I'll help when you need it."

Her eyes narrowed. "Still haven't accepted your title?"

"Nope. Don't plan to." If I kept making vampires, Meemaw would probably press the issue.

She snapped her fingers. "We need you to name the pocket for promotional spells."

"Why does everyone insist it's my responsibility?"

"Because it is."

I sighed. "I'll work on it. Any suggestions?"

"No. But something snappy would be best for our maginet ad campaign."

After one last look around, I moved toward the door. "I'll think of something. When are you opening?"

"In a few days."

I couldn't wait.

Ice pelted my face when we stepped outside. I motioned toward the winding road. "Watch this." I went fluid, stopped, and bounced back to Elizabeth. "When you first go fluid, objects will come at you fast. You can stop much faster than a human, so pay attention. Go ahead."

She bunched up as if getting ready for a race.

"Relax. It's a natural skill, so no need to concentrate."

"Got it." Elizabeth moved fast, but not as fast as if she went fluid. A foot slipped, and with a shriek, she skidded down the road on her ass.

"Are you okay?" I pressed my lips together to hide my laughter.

She burst out laughing as she took my hand to stand. "I see what you mean about paying attention."

I let my laugh escape as I helped dust her off. "You'll get better balance with practice." I pointed toward home. "Go fluid all the way home. Keep trying to go faster. Your speed will improve with age, so never stop pushing your limits. I'll stay behind you and catch you if you hit a patch of ice."

She improved as we raced home, staying on the road and laughing as we navigated the icy twists and turns. As soon as our feet touched the deck, I pulled her to a stop. "Nice work. Practice every day, but stay on the property.

"Sure." She took off. Slow at first, then increasing her speed as she gained confidence.

After ensuring she was okay, I blew through the back door and skidded across the floor. "June! Flint! I have great news."

June poked her head out of the hallway. "Flint's on patrol duty." She stepped closer. "What's up?"

"Dale's opening a bar in the pocket in a few days."

Her purple eyes glittered. "No kidding? Sign me up. This place is boring without a watering hole."

I rubbed my hands together in glee. "I can't wait to become regulars. And it's right down the street."

Elsie zipped into the kitchen and screeched to a halt. "Spencer did well. How about Elizabeth?"

"She did great." I motioned toward the back door. "I taught her how to go fluid. She's practicing."

"Good. I didn't want to mention it in front of them, but we need to talk about your lust."

My mood soured. "I'm working on it."

She crossed her arms. "The hot god's interest in you isn't exactly a secret. And none of us are prudes, so you can lust over him."

"I am," June said. When she had our attention, she bared her teeth. "Kidding. I'm a two-hundred-year-old dragon. We spend half our lives naked." She scooted into the room. "So, you and Cavil?"

I tried to hide my thundering heart as I shrugged. "He's convinced we're soulmates."

"Nice." June extended her fist.

I bumped it.

Elsie crossed her arms. "Are you avoiding sleeping with him because you think your lust will bother us?"

"It's not personal. I want privacy for my own selfish reasons. But it will happen, and you'll probably feel it." My stomach turned to jelly as I thought about the ways I'd ravish him. "Not to change the subject, but everyone insists I name this mess of a pocket. I need your help."

June jerked a thumb over her shoulder. "I'm on duty. Want to move to the new security office?"

"We have a new security office?" I trailed her down the hall.

Whereas our old office wasn't much more than a storage closet, the new one was spacious and had three monitoring stations. Cameras and spells covered every inch of both properties. They even showed the gate and the trail leading to it. Enormous screens and a giant hologram monitored the entire trail.

"Who came up with this?" I asked as I lowered myself into a chair.

June rolled to the controls and shrunk the hologram. "Me. It's important to monitor what's going on within a domain."

I leaned forward and examined the maze in the DMZ. "Wow. Did you tell the gnomes?"

"Sure. And it's less exciting than you'd think. All they do is work. The poor little guys."

"They love it." I tilted my head when Alex exited the garage on a four-wheeler and began plowing the driveway. "Let's come up with a couple of names, then let the hybrid community choose which one they like."

I suggested something snappy to appease Darla, but Elsie and June insisted on using fancy words. We settled on three options: Hermitage, Querencia, and Eldritch. The first two options mean sanctuary or haven. But I liked Eldritch, which meant strange. I didn't care which one the hybrids picked if it meant everyone quit hounding me about it.

Elsie posted a poll with the names on a community bulletin app the tech mages created for the leaders of each pocket. "I'll give them twenty-four hours to respond unless you want to drag it out?"

"Sounds good to me."

Elizabeth, Spencer, and I stood beside the frozen fountain in the town trapezoid. I monitored them while they practiced listening. I created a game where they had five minutes to find an interesting topic, and the one with the best gossip received a point. Whoever had the most points at the end of an hour didn't have to do chores the next day. It was the guidance I wished someone had given me as a kid. And it turned out to be fun as they found some interesting things. Like how a shifter-ogre hybrid's penis was too big for a regular-sized person. It wasn't only funny, but good to know. I wanted to take a peek.

Spencer drew in a breath.

"What do you have?" I gave a passing wolf the stink-eye.

He frantically scanned the street. "We need to leave. They're coming after us."

I zipped through conversations, trying to hear what he had picked up. Before I could catch it, the door to a building flew open, and several hybrids dressed in all black with their faces covered stepped out.

A woman shrieked. Hybrids pulled their kids away from the fountain and disappeared down the streets leading toward the square. A few took fighting stances and began circling around them.

One of the men in black raised a gun, and the others followed.

If my new vampires weren't with me, I would have fought them for fun. But they weren't ready for all that, so I shoved them toward an alley. "Move!"

They took off at a human pace, then sped up. As newbies, they weren't as fast as me, but they didn't need to be. They needed to be faster than the crowd chasing us. I stayed behind them, hoping to be a shield.

A bullet zinged past my ear as we stuck to the winding road. I wasn't too worried. Hitting a moving target with a bullet was hard. Hitting a target moving at vampire speeds was nearly impossible. Especially if they were the same guys who didn't bother to aim as they shot up the bar.

It was a misjudgment on my part as bullets from multiple shooters blanketed the area. We moved faster and pulled away. The number of gunshots increased. Elizabeth hit the ground, a plume of blood spreading from her right shoulder. "Oh, hell no. Keep moving, Spencer!" I threw her over my shoulders and went fluid to catch him. He went down just short of the wards. I threw Elizabeth through and dragged Spencer across the line. "Alex!" I waved at the monitoring spell.

The back door burst open. Purple and white blocked my vision as Glac and June launched into the air. Elsie burst out, examined me, threw Spencer over her shoulders, and disappeared inside. I followed with Elizabeth.

We set them on the floor, and I raced to the garage for blood. Alex appeared at the bottom of the stairs in his lion form, sniffed in my direction, and bolted out the back. Elsie and I shared a look. The two newbies were healing well, so we took off.

We made it to the wards and skidded to a stop.

A ring of fire surrounded the group of gun-wielding hybrids. Alex stood nearby, naked. The amber glow from his eyes turned the turquoise snow a sickly color. Glacintial perched behind him in his dragon form, his horned head lowered over my brother protectively, while June circled the area in the sky.

I crept forward to stand beside my brother as a gun went off, and the bullet disintegrated as it met dragon fire.

The hybrids were all dressed in black, just like the ones who shot up the bar. One pointed to me. "Lily First. If you don't rescind the hybrid induction into the coalition, we will kill you, your house, and every pureblood who tries to help you."

I eyed the bunch of idiots. There were only nine of them. Every single one had less than half of my power. "Oh yeah? You and what army?"

Alex elbowed me. "Stop it, Lily."

The man lowered his gun. "We have informed the humans about you and your vampire allies, and they will soon act. Unless you follow our instructions."

My heart skipped a beat. Those fuckers turned my uncle Roman in. "You guys are idiots if you think the humans will follow you."

His chest puffed out. "We have a contract. A little insurance from the Bellicose leaders if we lost the war."

I thew my hands in the air. "Humans can break contracts without repercussions! And if you think they'll leave you alone, you're sadly mistaken. That's not how they work."

"You know nothing about humans," he growled. "You have until noon tomorrow to convince your parents to rescind the agreement with the fake queen."

They flashed away.

I stormed back toward the house to check on my people. Alex trotted beside me. "They're delusional."

"Very. And they put Roman in danger after all he's done for the hybrids."

Elizabeth and Spencer healed within an hour of being shot. Much too fast for vampires so young. When they went to shower and sleep, I joined the dragons, Elsie, and Alex, in the dining room.

Glac tapped the table. "They are a puny group. Lily is correct that they are no match for her."

Alex sighed. "I know. She still didn't need to say it."

"Sure I did. They're idiots." I sipped the water June slid in front of me. "No one's answering Roman's phone. I need to warn him."

Glac nodded. "I am going to find Drake. Our queen may need to send more dragons to protect you."

I choked on my water. "Protect me, eh?"

"We know you don't need protection," June said. "But you're a royal, with very few allies, and our queen made an oath to Queen Jenella to protect her and her interests. If you're a target, we need more dragons."

It was news to me. "So, you lied about why you moved here?"

"No," Flintous said. "We came to do as we said. When you offered your home to us, you became ours to protect."

I didn't have the energy to argue, so I stood. "I'm going to Roman's. Who's going with me?"

Alex pulled his car into an empty parking spot on the street, slid out, and sniffed. "I'll never understand why Roman lives here. There's too much noise, and it stinks."

Elsie hopped out of the back without taking her attention away from a rental car with two men inside. "Yeah. He's not known for making sound decisions."

We took a lap around the block, scanning the area for other agents. It was risky going to visit my uncle with the feds watching us. We found him in the front yard, adding ice melt to the sidewalk. His heavy coat, snow boots, and jeans helped him blend in with his neighbors.

The bag thudded against the ground, and he moved toward us at a human pace. "Oh, my. This is a pleasant surprise." He swept me in a hug. "And you've brought a friend." Roman's demeanor was all off, which meant someone was listening.

"This is my friend, Elsie. How are you doing, Uncle Roman?"

"Hello, Elsie. I'm pleased to report we have a house full of sober people."

"Nice. Any trouble lately?" My eyes flicked to the car with federal agents inside.

"Oh, no. I believe this batch will do well in their new lives." A predatory grin ghosted across his face as several vampires I'd never seen piled into three transport vans down the street.

I almost asked him where he found the new vampires, but decided I didn't want to know, considering he tried to take good old Jed's entire squad of elites.

He led us up the stairs and motioned us inside. After removing his coat, he put his finger to his lips to keep us quiet and moved toward an office. A privacy spell snapped into place when we crossed the threshold. "Lily, I am sorry to say we can no longer live in this wonderful neighborhood. In all my many years, I have not once encroached on another vampire's territory. But I must make a special request in this situation, you see."

I tried not to tune him out. Roman was a bit long-winded. "Sure. That's what we came to talk to you about. We came across some hybrids who claimed they told the feds about you."

"Did they?" He waved a dismissive hand. "I already concluded that we must evacuate the premises. My house is in danger, and I cannot allow it to stand. Therefore, I would like to put in a special request to move my house to your pocket."

I blinked. "Why are you asking me?"

"Oh, my. I seem to have forgotten your lack of knowledge. It is your territory. Therefore, I must follow territory rules should I wish to reside within a certain distance of you."

"May I ask where you plan to build?" Elsie asked.

"Oh, yes. Of course. I understand the pocket is barren of population, so finding the ideal spot will not be an issue. The humans are causing us too much distress. Since the hybrids are responsible for the trouble, they are in danger of breaching their agreement with me. I must rely on my niece's generosity to right the situation, you see."

Alex lowered himself to a chair, but his muscles stayed bunched and ready to strike. "I picked up two agents across the street, but they were bored and having doubts about their assignment."

Roman crossed his arms. "Is that so? Huh. The day shift agents speculated on us being a shifter pack." He flipped his laptop around. "Three entire families disappeared from Southeast Boise yesterday."

My fists clenched so hard fingernails cut into my palms when I recognized two kids I'd helped save. "Are you sure they didn't move to the pocket? Several people were picking up supplies."

"I don't believe they left voluntarily. Someone breached their houses and left the doors open. This was before the human government put my house under surveillance. One must do what they can to protect their loved ones, even if it means requesting sanctuary from his sister's heir."

"You don't need my permission. Jen designed the pocket as a sanctuary for hybrids. You are part of the hybrid community."

"Don't I? Hmm." He waved a dismissive hand. "Please remember you said that. It is quite difficult for two house masters to share a single territory."

I bet it was, considering the enormous egos most of them had. "What do you know about the government's plans?"

"Nothing new. Which I can only interpret as meaning they are ready to strike. We must make haste." He plucked a set of keys off a peg with a grimace. "My house is ready to go. I only needed you to arrive with permission to move into your territory." He shoved the laptop under his arm. "This property will burn to the ground in three minutes. Good luck." Roman vanished.

Holy hell. If the feds across the street saw us come in, they'd think we set the fire. I latched onto Elsie and Alex's arms and bolted out the back.

Alex pointed down the alley. "Agents on the left. Go through the yards."

We hopped fences and kept to the shadows. A massive brown dog charged from the back deck at the third house and let out a deep bark. I grabbed Alex's arm and went fluid, dragging the shadows with me as we leaped over the fence seconds before his jowls closed on my leg. We veered around another yard with a dog and emerged behind a hedge near where we parked. I layered more shadows around us and scanned the area. "Anything?"

Elsie poked at the darkness. "Since when can you do shadow magic?"

"Gramps showed me a better way."

Alex shook his head. "I'm not picking up anything."

We jogged toward the car and jumped in. All three of us sat in silence, scanning the street. Alex stayed alert as he pulled out of the space, careful to drive the speed limit as he exited the neighborhood. As we turned on the main road, flames shot into the air from the direction of Roman's house, followed by a loud 'boom.'

My eyes grew wide when I realized it wasn't just a house fire, but an explosion. "What the hell was he thinking?"

"He's right to put his house first," Elsie said from the back seat.

"You think framing us is okay?"

"It is if it saves his own house, yes."

"That's bullshit." I spun back around and rubbed my eyes. It was a shitty thing to do, no matter the circumstances.

The freeway on-ramp was less than a block away when red and blue flashing lights lit up behind us.

Alex turned on his blinker, his eyes taking on a slight glow. "Don't say a word. And don't use persuasion. They're looking for it."

"Didn't plan to." I totally planned to if it meant avoiding arrest.

"I mean it, Lily. Don't do anything a human wouldn't do. These guys have a lot of information about us and are prepared to shoot if we do the slightest thing to raise suspicion. There's an entire army of federal agents and cops ready to flood the area if we try to use magic. Cooperate and hand over your ID when they request it. And keep your snarky replies to yourself. When they ask questions, demand a lawyer. Don't say a word other than you want a lawyer."

The hair on my arms stood at his warning, and my ego deflated. It wasn't like my brother to be so specific unless the situation was dire. "Sure."

Elsie checked her pockets. "Where did you learn about the human legal system?"

"We always knew this might happen one day, so I studied law on the internet and watched a bunch of TV shows. They might push or try to manipulate you. Give them nothing and keep demanding a lawyer." Alex rolled down his window.

I took out my phone and hit 'record.'

Several police cars came out of nowhere, surrounded us, and uniformed officers spilled out. Some pulled their guns while others moved to the back of their vehicles. More police cars filled the blank spaces around us. Blue and red lights swirled through the entire area, causing people passing to slow down and gawk.

Alex turned off the engine. "Stay calm. Do what you're told for once and don't move faster than you need to." His hands shook as he held them out the window. The terror in his eyes sent a spike of fear through me.

Clonk, clonk, clonk.

An officer knocked on my window. I jumped as I activated the privacy spell on my phone and set it in the console facing the door. My face reflected an innocent expression as I rolled the window down.

A bright flashlight hit my eyes, and I flinched. "Hands where I can see them!"

I raised my hands, palms out, and scanned the police. They were hyper-alert. Some had their hands on their weapons, while others pointed guns at us. There wasn't a single hybrid in the group. My parents had loaded the local and state government with them, so over half the police were hybrids. Since Jen made the pocket, many moved there to form an enforcer unit. But it was still strange not to sense one.

Alex opened his door, keeping his hands up. Once they cuffed him, flashlight guy shifted away. "Open the door and step out. Keep your hands visible."

How in the hell was I supposed to do that? I lowered my right hand and hit the latch, then raised it in slow-motion as I complied. An officer searched and cuffed me, then dug out my ID and led me to a police car while they did the same to Elsie.

A tingle in my chest lit up, and I scanned the street. Roman drove by, a smug smile on his face. He didn't spare me a glance. The asshole set us up.

Chapter Fifteen

Our arrest didn't go the way we hoped. The police didn't read us our rights or ask us a single question. I wanted to ask for a lawyer in a mic-drop moment, damn it. I tugged on the handcuffs to see how sturdy they were. It wouldn't take much to break them. But between Alex's warning and our parents instructing us to act human until they bailed us out if we ever found ourselves in trouble, I hesitated. If I hadn't trusted them so much or was alone, I'd have broken loose and disappeared long before we made it to the local police station.

Breaking out would have been the smarter option, I thought, as a guy shoved me up a set of stairs and onto a human plane. He kicked my knee, and I stumbled forward as another one grabbed my arm and slammed me into a seat across the aisle from Alex. Elsie came next, her eyes closed. After they shoved her in the seat beside me, she faced me and cracked them open. A red glow peeked through. I concentrated on her blood bond and found seething anger, so I sent an order to calm down. No way I'd let the assholes win so early in the game.

More than a dozen agents filtered in and filled the surrounding seats. I bit my tongue to stop my fangs from popping out. It struggled to heal because I kept having to bite it. The federal agents were a bunch of assholes.

Meanwhile, Alex lounged in his tiny window seat as if he wasn't concerned about our predicament. I supposed he wasn't, considering he could kill them with a thought.

Which we should have done the second they pulled us over. We could have killed them, fled to the pocket, and never looked back. But we didn't, so we needed to wait for our parents or someone else to come for us. Besides, I left my phone in the car recording. The spell I activated made it invisible to humans when not in my hand. The recording would give our parents some idea of what happened to us. In hindsight, I should have brought it with me.

Alex swung his head to peer out the window, breaking my train of thought. A hint of a smile crossed his face. I wondered what he picked up from the agents to cause the expression. None of us had made so much as a peep since our arrest, so I didn't ask.

The plane ride sucked. It baffled me how humans enjoyed being hurled through the sky in a tin can. It was two levels beyond the amount of trust I wanted to give an inanimate object. The seats were uncomfortable, and there was no magic to protect us if we fell out of the sky. I latched onto an armrest with white knuckles for a long time. The tension in my muscles didn't loosen until we touched down several hours later. The agents herded us into a van parked inside a hangar, and we spent the next hour in traffic.

From the murmurings of the agents, we were somewhere around Washington, D.C. Being a couple thousand miles away from home sucked. Even if we freed ourselves, we were too far away from our support network.

The van stopped inside an underground parking garage, and the agents pulled us out and shoved us toward a door. Elsie's anger spiked, so I reinforced my order. Her anger was justified, but if Alex hadn't acted, he had a good reason. He probably wanted to gather as much information as possible before we escaped.

The number of guards multiplied as they led us down a bland hall to an elevator with unmarked buttons. By the motion, we were going down. Interesting.

When the doors opened, they shoved us into a hallway full of steel bars. A woman behind plexiglass scanned us, and the steel groaned as the door rolled open. A weak spell in the metal proved they knew about magic and used it. It was so weak that I didn't sense the magic until they shoved us through.

My heart pounded as they dragged Alex down the hallway on the left. His eyes flashed a warning as they shoved Elsie and me into a room on the right. A hard-faced woman motioned for me to step forward. The male guards pushed Elsie onto a bench while she removed my restraints. "Strip. And don't try anything, or you're dead." Two men pulled weapons and pointed them at me.

I tried not to meet Elsie's eyes or show amusement at her statement. It wouldn't be us who died if we chose not to comply. Especially if I used my magic. I peeled off my clothes and folded them, moving super slow to push the woman's buttons. After I set them on the bench, I smoothed out the wrinkles and faced her.

The fuckers did cavity searches. Then threw us in a shower room and ordered us to scrub ourselves with the smelliest soap on the planet. Elsie clutched her phone in her hand the entire time. Not a single agent picked up on it.

When we were done, they gave us khaki jumpsuits to wear. My hair was going to be a rat's nest when it dried, I thought, as they led me into a tiny interrogation room. Two large men strode through the door, both human. They stared me down, trying to look intimidating, as they took the chairs across the table.

The silver-haired man with a ruddy complexion opened a file. "It says here your name is Liliana First. No middle name, is that correct?"

The handcuffs clinked as I rested my hands on the table. "I want a lawyer."

His muddy brown eyes met mine. "Confirm your name."

"I'll give my name to a lawyer."

The younger man on the left examined me with sharp blue eyes. "Is that so?"

I stayed silent.

He leaned forward. "Only American citizens have the right to a lawyer. And you aren't one, are you?"

"I'll be glad to work that out with my attorney."

They kept me there for hours as they accused me of everything from kidnapping to arson. They even tried to intimidate me into talking by saying I committed an act of terrorism. When it didn't work, they tried to manipulate me into turning on Alex and Elsie by informing me my brother had already spilled the entire story. I didn't budge, so they suggested I was the leader of a terrorist organization. Alex was probably having fun plucking information out of their heads. Based on the feeling emanating from Elsie, she also enjoyed herself as she messed with them.

Their last tactic was to make snide comments designed to anger me. All it did was encourage me to find new and exciting ways to request a lawyer.

The two agents who showed up at my house came in when they gave up. Agent Harper ignored the coffee stain on his shirt as he set a file down and scooted his chair forward. "Are you tired, Miss First?"

I gave him a flat stare.

"Hungry?" He pulled a soggy sandwich out of his bag, unwrapped it, and savored a bite.

I remained completely still as I suppressed a gag. The guy chewed with his mouth open, and I had to tune out the noise when my stomach churned. Not a single muscle twitched as I kept a flat stare on my face.

Agent Davis took a long drink of water and pushed it to the middle of the table. "I bet you're getting thirsty." When I didn't respond, he sighed. "Look. I'm going to level with you." He raised an eyebrow.

"You can level with my lawyer."

A predatory smirk formed on his face. "We already know you're some kind of witch. We suspect you have your brother and friend under some sort of silence spell."

I clenched my jaw, so I didn't laugh at the thought of controlling Alex.

Agent Harper wrapped up his mutilated sandwich and left it on the table. "I'll tell you what. If you show us how you do your spells, we'll bring you any meal you want." He raised an eyebrow.

I made a show of eyeing his nasty food as a thousand snarky comments ran through my mind. I leaned forward and met his eyes. "The only thing I want is a lawyer."

They exchanged a look, and Agent Harper stood. "We'll see how tough you are after we leave you to rot for a few days without food or water."

I stood with a sigh. "Fine." I waited for a reaction. After a few seconds, Agent Davis raised an eyebrow. "It will give my lawyer a reason to sue you."

He latched onto my elbow too hard as they towed me down the hall and through more steel bars. Agent Harper shoved me into a cell, took a key, and wiggled it. "Last chance to answer our questions."

"My lawyer can answer your questions."

He shook his head and removed my cuffs before slamming the door in my face. I examined the tiny room. There wasn't much to it. On one side was a cot. The other side had a small sink and toilet. There wasn't so much as a cup to drink out of or soap to wash my hands. I scrubbed them with water before using them as a cup. My face puckered at the rusty taste. It was a good thing I wasn't human, or I'd get sick from drinking it.

I paused when I heard voices and tuned my hearing to them. Agents made lewd comments from somewhere nearby. One laughed at my thirst. Interesting, I thought as I moved to the bed and settled in. They had my cell wired with small cameras. I could hear the buzz of electricity where they peeked out from opposite corners. Once I found them, I stared at the ceiling and focused on the conversation down the corridor.

"These prisoners are going to sue."

"Naw. Harper's sure they're supers."

"That idiot. If they could use magic on us, they would have by now."

I almost laughed. If only they knew how rigid the rules around revealing ourselves were. Well, unless your name was Jenella. Then you can declare war in a subdivision and leave the rest of us to deal with it. I shoved that thought away. She'd be here in a second if she knew where we were.

"These three didn't cause the explosion. The local authorities are saying it's a gas leak."

"It doesn't matter. Harper's been watching the dark-haired woman and the man for a while now and is sure he's right."

"Did they do something suspicious on camera?"

"No. They haven't done a single thing. Not unless you consider scaring a snoopy vlogger suspicious."

"Vlogger?"

"Some ditzy woman convinced they're vampires. But that idiot Harper hates to be wrong, so he used the explosion as an excuse to detain them. If our special unit determines they're human, they'll dispose of them. No harm, no foul."

The conversation turned to sports, so I tuned them out. The idiots wanted so badly to prove us magical that they were willing to break their own laws to do it. And what kind of special unit were they yapping about? I expected them to run blood tests. When those came back normal, which they would, they'd move on to torture. Elsie and I would use persuasion to make them think they completed their task. Alex would simply mess with their heads. He rarely used the ability, but he was good at it. It was the only thing that kept him alive before our parents took him in.

But if they had a special unit and already knew about the paranormal community, we were in deep shit. And I needed to plan our escape. Alex and I could also use magic to fry their cameras if needed. Mine would probably attract more government officials to me. Because if anyone qualified as crazy enough to become a blood source, it was those people. It was a chance I was willing to take.

A door slamming down the hall caught my attention. I moved to the tiny window and peered out. Two men dragged a shackled prisoner to a nearby cell. I sensed Elsie's feelings on the matter were as indifferent as my own.

Good. I settled back onto my bed and started considering how to break out.

Time moved like molasses inside the tiny cell. I spent my time working out, finger-combing the tangles out of my greasy hair, and drinking the nasty water. Occasionally, I'd pretend to sleep. It felt like I'd been there for a decade, though it was probably a couple of days. True to their word, no one brought me food or water.

I was deep in thought when a bright light flashed inside my cell. The fingers I'd been drumming on my stomach for what seemed like forever froze. Goosebumps broke out when the scent of sunshine after a long rain filled my cell. "Hey, you sexy beast. There are cameras in every corner."

"I've looped the feed." Cavil leaned against the door. "What are you doing?"

"Being unlawfully arrested and held without food, water, or the lawyer I've demanded multiple times. How about you?"

"Jonas found your video and went on a tirade. And Glacintial is a very good tracker."

"Nice."

"Are you ready to leave?"

"We can't leave. If we disappear, they'll have proof of our existence. There's still a chance they'll let us go. If not, we'll escape."

"They do not let people go from this facility. Ever."

"Who told you that?"

"Research."

"Great." I closed my eyes. "Does Jen know we're here?"

"Most likely, since your parents are ready to start a war to save you."

"Then text her. If she's willing to risk outing us, I'll go with you and never look back. But it's her call whether this is how we confirm our existence."

"It won't be a problem."

My eyes trailed over him. Cavil's eyes were darker than usual, and his face strained. A faint glow emanated from his entire body. "Alex read something when the cops surrounded us and told me to play along. He would have given me a signal if he thought it was time to escape."

His head dropped, and the light surrounding him dimmed. "I would contact Jenella, but I didn't bring my phone. Please come with me, Lily."

"I can't. I don't want to be the reason the humans attack us." My voice was too rough.

He motioned toward the cot. "Scoot over. I will stay with you until a guard appears."

"And just where am I supposed to scoot?"

Cavil's grin made my heart skip a beat. He reached down and pulled me to my feet. His massive body dwarfed the cot, and I stifled a laugh. He wiggled down and let his feet hang over the edge. Without warning, he snatched my wrist and pulled.

My laugh escaped as I settled on his chest. "Did you put a privacy spell on the room?"

"A ward, yes." His voice rumbled under my ear.

I raised my head to meet his eyes. "Roman framed us. He used us to evacuate his house and take over what he called my territory."

"Ara will not approve of his actions."

No, she wouldn't. And my new, too-bright house in the crazy pocket was growing on me. I didn't want to give it up. It wasn't a today problem, so I focused on soaking up Cavil's warmth.

After a few minutes of companionable silence, he shifted. "Do you need blood, Lily?"

Lightning zinged through my body. My stomach ached, and heat pooled in my core. The sensory overload made me wiggle to keep from exploding. I'd experienced lust plenty of times, but never to the degree his simple question spurred. It wasn't until my traitorous fangs popped out that I realized I was on the edge of losing control.

I took a few deep breaths and rested my forehead on his shoulder. "Not a good idea."

"Tarquin is wrong about my blood." Cavil ignored the near attack. "It will not harm or enslave you. You are a descendent of a sister realm to the gods, so it will nourish you and help you thrive should you filter out the magic."

"I'll manage."

"Not without food, water, and blood, you won't."

Burning lust lit inside me, and I fought to wrangle it under control. I lifted my head and met his eyes to reveal the glow. "Not a good idea right now."

A sexy smirk formed on his face. "I think it's a great idea."

"You like that, eh?"

He pulled me tighter. "It is...invigorating when you burn for me. It will be fine if you don't begin acting a fool from magic poisoning."

With a chuckle, I rested my head on his massive chest.

He tapped my back. "Feed, Lily. You'll need the extra strength and energy my blood provides to deal with these depraved creatures. Be sure to expel the magic."

"I'm very turned on right now. What if I can't stop?"

His chest bounced with laughter, causing me to shift, so his hardness was between my legs. His laughter cut off, and he sucked air between his teeth.

I groaned.

"It would take a lot more than a tiny bite to kill me." Cavil's voice was too rough.

I moved my hips against him. "Tiny, eh?"

"You're killing me, Lily. Feed."

I readjusted before we both exploded and tried to hide my panting. "Do what you need to do if I take too long."

"Anything I need to do?"

My face flushed. Cavil made me act like a swooning idiot. I met his eyes and gave a slight nod, my stomach doing all kinds of flip-flops as my fangs extended, and I struck.

I didn't bother to control my pheromones. His amazing blood hit my tongue, and I moaned. He wrapped his arms around me and pulled me closer as he rubbed his hard length against my core. My brain shorted out. Until I remembered where we were. There was no way our first time would be in a prison cell. I wrangled my thoughts around to concentrate on filtering out magic from his blood. A tough task, considering my body ached for him so hard. After I drank my fill, I released his neck, took a couple of deep breaths, and raised my head. "Thank..."

Before I could finish my sentence, I found myself under him and pinned to the thin mattress. Cavil's mouth found mine, his soft lips pressing down, his tongue a feather-light touch. The warmth of his hand slid down my body, his thumbs pausing briefly beside my nipples. Electric currents shot through me. I slid my hands under his shirt and ran them over the muscles of his back and sides, wrapping my legs around him. The kiss deepened, and I lost myself, the aching need overriding my reservations.

He broke the kiss and rested his hand on my hip. "I must go before we lose control."

Fire shot up my spine. "Yeah. This isn't the time or place." I didn't budge.

"You said they had no reason to arrest you?"

The question was equivalent to throwing a bucket of cold water over me. My lust died as I thought back to the moments leading up to our arrest. Cavil pulled me with him as he climbed to his feet. His size made the cell shrink by half. "No. Rogue hybrids chased us and said they turned my pureblood allies in. When Roman didn't answer his phone, we went to warn him. He made a territory truce contract with me, then informed us his house was about to explode. He even drove by with a smug look while we got arrested."

"You think he did it on purpose?"

"Yep. He already evacuated his people and waited for us to show up."

"Interesting. The utility company confirmed it was a gas leak not long after your arrest. They most likely moved you when they found out."

"Sounds about right. They've been trying to piss us off enough to expose our magic. These idiots underestimate what we're capable of. We're still here because Alex read something that spooked him. If they can't prove we're magical, they plan to kill us."

A hard expression rolled across his face. "After how long?"

"My best guess is after they do some medical tests. They might even try to torture us." I squared my shoulders. "I'll kill everyone before I let them lay a finger on Alex or Elsie. You should warn Jen."

"Your parents plan to send an entire legal team should you refuse to leave with me." He leaned in. "If you are still here in two days, I will be back to retrieve you, and I won't give you a choice."

My heart soared at his declaration, even as my aura ramped up. "I don't know whether to kiss you or punch you for suggesting I can't save myself."

His sunny smile brightened the room. "Should you need to leave before I return, move to a clearing so the dragons can whisk you to safety."

A clink down the hall interrupted our conversation. "We aren't ever together."

Cavil pulled me to him and rested his cheek on my head. "Come with me now. I will gather Elsie and Alex, and we will make our escape. You can stay inside the pockets."

I stepped back and shook my head. "Alex said to cooperate, so I'm going to. If we disappear, it will spook them, and they'll come after us. We'll never be able to go home and a lot of hybrids still live in the city. When they can't find us, they'll find and eliminate them."

Cavil picked up one of my gnarly curls and ran it through his fingers. "Very well. But promise me you will not let them hurt you."

"You forget I have some mad skills." My attempt to smile failed. "Like I said, if they hurt Alex or Elsie, then we're out of here, and I'll deal with the consequences."

Heavy footsteps drew closer.

Cavil glanced toward the door. "I better go. Your parents' legal team will descend on this building soon."

I brushed my lips against his and settled in the exact position on the cot where he found me. He kissed my forehead, met my eyes, and flashed away. A pop and the scent of ozone from spent magic told me he released the privacy bubble and the camera loop.

Chapter Sixteen

Time continued to crawl. The cold would have soaked into my bones if I hadn't been able to control my body temperature. I reminded myself to shiver as I worked with my blood bonds. I figured out how to block my end while monitoring all four vampires and couldn't wait to test it. Elizabeth was content. Happy, even. Pascal still held a ball of resentment, but a hint of intrigue peeked through. Spencer remained focused and determined. Elsie, like me, had accepted her fate.

Even if we managed to escape, we'd need to trek across the country in the middle of winter to get home. We could always flee to a nearby pocket. If Anitta's lessons were accurate, there were several on the east coast. But I forgot where. Maybe those dragons Cavil mentioned would help.

After what seemed like days, footsteps pounded outside, and the door to my cell squealed, revealing four guards. One stepped forward. "Stand and hold your arms out."

I complied, moving at the slowest pace possible. He yanked my arms way too hard and slapped cuffs on me, then shoved me toward the door. Another guard grabbed my ass as he pushed me down the hall toward the exit. I slammed my mouth shut when my fangs extended. I had to concentrate hard to retract them when the groping guard smirked beside me.

The place was a labyrinth, and it took forever to get to the elevators. I counted steps and committed the direction they took me to memory. When the elevator spit us out onto a floor containing offices, I caught a glimpse outside. We were on the third or fourth floor in a city. Several heavy safety doors stood open. Conversations confirmed it was an office area. They shoved me inside a room and slammed the door.

Alex and Elsie sat on one side of a table. Two women and a man on the other. A woman with long black hair stood. "You must be Lily. Please, have a seat."

The man cleared his throat and offered a plastic smile. "Hello, Lily. We are your new legal counsel." He introduced himself and the two women.

They weren't our parents' lawyers because they'd never trust humans with our fate. Especially not humans with New York accents. If their accents weren't enough evidence of how we were being played, then their fast heartbeats gave them away. They were nervous. Or excited to trick us. By the blank looks on Elsie and Alex's faces, they weren't buying it, either. I shuffled over to an empty chair and sat without saying a word.

The third person's dark brown eyes settled on Elsie. "I see here you're being held on federal charges of terrorism."

Elsie said nothing.

The two women took turns asking questions while we stayed blank-faced and silent.

The man leaned back in his chair, his arms and legs spread wide, demanding half the table. As if the two women were insignificant. I'd witnessed the same body language in several toxic workplaces and always found it interesting. He flattened his hand on the table. "Look. We can't help you if you don't help us."

I laced my fingers together to keep myself from throat-punching him. "We'll be glad to talk to real lawyers."

He froze. Ha! Didn't expect that, did you, Mr. Big Ego?

He leaned forward, his cheap suit bunching at the shoulders. "What makes you think we're not real lawyers, Lily?" My name sounded forced.

I raised an eyebrow.

His face flushed with anger, and his jaw clenched. Temper, temper.

The woman with black hair shifted in her seat. "If you don't trust us, that's fine. But we are here to help you."

"We want the lawyers our family hired," Alex said in a monotone voice.

The man stood. "They lack clearance to enter this facility. If you want to play it this way, then what happens next is on you." He stormed out of the room.

The two women shared a look and followed. They left us alone on purpose. The idiots were hoping we'd talk amongst ourselves in full view of their cameras. I suspected most people probably took the opportunity. But most people weren't raised by Jonas and Ann Marie First. Nor did they spend most of their life in a vampire house like Elsie. When surrounded by people capable of reading every nuance of your body language and vital signs, you learn to control them.

It didn't take long before two men in black suits strolled in. Their magic slammed into me and rolled off. Alex's chair clanged as he fell to the floor with a growl.

The second man's eyes lit with interest as they settled on me. "Ah. Vampires, then." He moved toward Alex as he scrambled to his feet and sniffed him. "And a shifter. It's rather odd for families to contain multiple factions."

They weren't the most powerful paranormals, but their magic felt off. I stood and faced the guy who stayed by the door. When our eyes met, he made a strange noise. It wasn't a laugh or even a giggle. It sounded like he said the words 'ha ha ha.' "Did you buy that laugh? Because there's no way it's real."

He launched himself at me.

Unfortunately, his buddy caught him. "You will regret your taunting, Miss First."

I doubted it. I folded my hands and stayed silent.

He wrenched the door open. "Take them to the hole."

Prison guards dragged us out of the room and shoved us into the elevator.

The guys with magic were way too confident based on their power level. They were mid-level at best. Which meant they should have noticed how powerful we were. But they didn't. I wasn't sure if it was because we were in a secure federal prison, so they assumed they held the upper hand, or they couldn't read us.

The ride took us deeper into the underground portion of the facility. They herded us down a hallway with cheap white tiles on the floors and walls. The scent of disinfectants and blood clogged my nose as we passed a few of our fellow prisoners in chairs along the wall in the hallway. All humans.

"Second room on the left." A guard groped my boob as I shuffled through the door.

I had to fake a stumble to keep up appearances. When the door closed, separating me from Alex and Elsie, I scanned the room to see what they had in store for us. A vinyl bed sat in the center, and a small counter with a sink on the right. An X-ray machine, like the ones in human dental offices, hung over the bed.

A man with light brown hair came through a door. His cold brown eyes scanned me from head-to-toe. "On the table."

My heart pounded when more strange magic glided over my skin and dissipated.

The odd magic sparked my interest, so I let my eyes go glassy and complied.

He leaned in and poked my bottom eyelid. "Interesting eye color you have there, Liliana. May I call you Miss Umbra, or do you prefer First?"

"You can call me by either name. But only if I can call you Dickwad."

The punch landed on my jaw, even though I saw it coming from a mile away.

I spit blood into a bowl sitting on a tray beside the bed.

By his predatory grin, I assumed he was some kind of shifter, though the magic wasn't right. "The government is aware of your identity and your capabilities. We will use any means necessary to confirm it."

Impossible. The only people who knew my full capabilities were my parents. Not even Alex had seen them. If they knew, they would have been much more careful with me.

A silver instrument gleamed in the light as he raised it. "Not talking is perhaps the smartest move you've made in the last few months." He picked up a pair of pliers and squeezed them twice. "Of course, it won't do you any good now. These contain a spell. It comes in handy when trying to extract fangs." He leaned in so close his putrid garlic breath blasted me in the face. "And I will take great delight in removing yours while you scream."

Playtime over. I ran every scenario through my head as fast as my brain would work. The guy knew my title, sure. But not my abilities. And he was mid-level and something close to a shifter, but not quite. Even with his odd magic, I'd win in a fight.

Before I decided what to do, magic restraints latched onto my arms and legs. A band slid around my forehead. A zing shot from them and rattled through my bones. Before it dissolved, the guy latched onto my head with unnatural strength, and more magic surged through my body.

His lips quirked up. "Relax."

My fangs popped out at the thought of slaughtering him. It would have to wait, though. Another wave of magic smashed through me, so I didn't notice the pliers closed around my bottom right fang.

The guy yanked, and a searing pain started in my mouth and radiated across my jaw. The wave of magic eased as he held up the pliers. His laugh was as fake as his kind demeanor. "See, that was easy. Only three more to go."

Fiery anger lit inside my chest, causing my eyes to glow a sickly reddish gold. It was almost as bad as when good ole Jed sent his vampires to rape and kill me. If they couldn't stop me, there wasn't a chance in hell a weak shifter with strange magic would. As another wave of magic rolled through the restraints, I tamped down the anger. I needed to see how the torture scenario played out. But no way was he taking another fang.

The guy set the pliers down with my fang still attached. "Tell me about your little gated communities."

I blinked. I'd never met a paranormal unfamiliar with the pockets. "Can't help you there."

"I see. You still think you will live through this. Perhaps you even believe you can escape." Another fake laugh echoed through the room. "You won't. But I'll be glad to provide you with a little motivation." He swung the door open, and Alex and Elsie stumbled in.

Blood ran down Alex's temple, and his eyes were too glassy. Gashes covered Elsie's face and arms.

I lost my shit.

White-hot rage ignited so fast my control slipped. Using my full strength, I ripped myself free of the restraints and launched toward the guy. Pain zipped through my elbow and hip as we smashed into a wall. We separated and traded punches. A loud clang caused me to twist in the opposite direction as his torture tray hit the floor. The distraction allowed him to charge.

As he hit, I let my body go limp. Something stuck in my ankle while something else dug into my back. I extended my claws, kicked my foot out, and slammed them into his sides. Warm blood flowed over my hands. I used my superior strength and jerked him to his feet.

He hopped away a second before Elsie slammed him against the tiny counter. My mouth dropped open when he morphed into his second form. The guy looked like an experiment gone wrong. Or a lab-grown shifter. His eyebrows were extra bushy, and his teeth a jagged mess. Patches of hair dotted his right cheek just under his eye. Another ran across his forehead. Even his knuckles were dotted with the wiry shit. He had a single claw on the thumb of his right hand, resembling a cat shifter. Thicker claws extended from the middle and ring finger of his left.

"What in the holy living fuck?"

A feral smile formed on his face. "You do not know what you're up against. After I bleed you until you're near death, I'm going to cut off the man's balls and fuck your friend while you watch."

The guy's ego-power ratio was off. "You think you're all that, eh?"

His chest puffed out. "Get back in the chair before I show you what I can do, bitch."

I glanced at Alex, but he still stood near the door, his eyes unfocused. I leaned forward. "Make me."

His snarl bounced off the walls as he shoved Elsie aside and launched himself at me.

I raised my arm and went fluid, elbow out. As soon as it smashed into his chest, I used my full strength to knee him in the balls. Faster than the blink of an eye, I snatched the pliers off the floor and tossed them to Elsie. I shoved the guy against the wall so hard that dust rained down on us.

He grabbed some kind of medical instrument and stabbed me twice before I let go and stepped back. "Fuck you, bitch! You're never getting out of here. You and your freak friends are government property now."

"No shit?" I shuffled closer to Alex.

"You aren't going anywhere, so you might as well cooperate. If not, I'll carve you up piece by piece and cum while you scream." He launched at Alex. A second before the stab landed, he collapsed on the floor, blood running from his nose.

I went fluid and slammed my claws into his chest. He gurgled as he went limp. I pulled the fire alarm, latched onto Alex, and blew out the door. The humans didn't realize anyone was there until I chucked the guy's heart at one of the more handsy guards.

I linked arms with Elsie and increased my speed, knocking people over, slamming guards and prisoners through the walls, and tearing up the floor in my wake. As we shot up the stairs, someone shouted, and several footsteps thundered above us.

I slowed as several people descended on us from both directions. An agent tried to pull Alex from my grasp.

Elsie's feral growl raised the hairs on my arms as she kicked him.

Alex shook his head, fighting to bring himself out of the stupor they put him in. The people closest to us collapsed.

It gave us some breathing room. Some agents pulled guns, while others stood poised to fight. Several had the strange magic, though I didn't sense a high-level paranormal in the group. The consequences of what I was about to do flitted through my mind. I'd have to worry about those later because saving Alex and Elsie was the priority. Besides, if we didn't take the opportunity to escape, we'd never get another chance. I was sure of it. For the first time in years, I activated my mage abilities and flashed away.

Unlike when other mages transported me, there was no flash of light or disorientation. Where they flashed blind and sometimes smashed into obstacles, I saw where I was going. It was a handy skill that allowed me to change directions as needed and as destructive as my mage magic. I had to wind through several hallways before I found the exit. As we flew through the indoor maze, I cast power out in front of us, and the steel bars and doors blocking our path disintegrated. In my wake, blood-red vapor drifted through the air and coated everything with a thick oil-like substance.

A comforting warmth of satisfaction spread through my chest when the screaming began. Somewhere, deep inside, I shuddered at the darkness clouding my judgment. But I didn't contain it as we shot up four flights of stairs, through several hallways, out an exit door, and through the underground parking garage. I spotted a side exit, and we spilled out into the street. I didn't fear my darkness, nor did I hold it back. Sheer exhilaration spread through me when the building shook.

A gigantic hand coiled around me, and the smell of dragon fire doused some of my glee. As we lifted off the ground, a smile spread across my face as the sprawling building imploded. When the dust from the collapse settled, a massive plume of golden fire shot into the sky. The screams of the people inside soothed my soul.

Chapter Seventeen

A HEAVY FEELING IN my chest replaced the rage by the time the dragon released his grip. A massive silver head appeared in front of my face, and familiar fiery silver eyes assessed me. *Are you good now?*

"I'm fine, Lyran. Thanks." My tongue ran along the hole my fang left. A tsunami of guilt crashed over me. I killed a lot of people. Sure, the agents were pricks, and the guards were pervs. But there were plenty of people inside the building who didn't deserve to die. Still, the darkness radiated a satisfied strength that caused me to pull my shoulders back. I blinked and fought to regain my balance. Something inside me had fundamentally shifted, causing the dark and light to blur. A gray haze clouded my vision. Giving into my darkness was a mistake I fought my whole life to avoid. And now that I had, it wasn't going away.

"What the hell did you do, Lily?" Alex stomped toward me, an amber glow lighting his sharp eyes.

I pulled him into a hug. "You good now?"

"Yeah. They drugged me with narcotics and a tranquilizer dart. It clouded my mind for a while."

I stepped back and bared my teeth. "The asshole ripped out a fang."

Elsie flinched and held up the pliers, the tooth still caught in its grips. "They have spelled instruments."

Something in her tone made me pause. "You've seen those before." It wasn't a question.

"Housemasters used to use them to control vampires suffering from bloodlust. Mistress Ara ended the practice over a hundred years ago."

The last remnants of salty blood coated my tongue. "Will it grow back?"

Her eyes filled with pure hatred. "Sure. It took mine about a year."

Alex squeezed my arm. "Where are we?"

Good question. I spun in a slow circle. Glacintial and my new drinking buddy, Lyran, stood nearby in their dragon forms.

We are in the pocket of Domerage, which is close to the human city of Washington, D.C. Glacintial's conversational tone made me pause.

"You're not mad at me, Glac?"

No. Humans try to dominate and eliminate that which they do not understand. This was inevitable after we waged a battle in their domain. Had you not escaped, they would have experimented on you until they found answers, or you died.

Several of them were excited about the prospect, Lyran added.

I swallowed back a bitter comment. "How do we get home?"

Elsie motioned toward a town. "There's a transport station in this pocket. Let's grab something to eat and head there."

Alex held up his phone. "I recorded a bunch of stuff and made notes about what I learned. I've been texting them to Mom and Dad."

My heart skipped a beat at the mention of our parents. I hoped they didn't disown me for killing all those people. "Good. Which way is the station?"

The town wasn't as small as the village Jen created in our pocket. Tall buildings crowded the downtown area, and several suburbs surrounded it. Holograms hovered above their boundaries, showing which pureblood faction lived there. The dragons circled downtown, then landed in a marked field before shifting into their human forms.

We strolled through, stopping to buy food and a few blood bags from a vendor. Unlike Allure, where the crowds of different paranormals mixed, the ones in Domerage kept to their own factions. Holograms hovered above the intersections, flashing warnings like, 'fairies only beyond this point.' And 'Shifter territory. All others will be mauled.' We stayed on the public trails leading toward the transport station and ignored the judgmental looks of the locals.

Elsie, Alex, and I still wore the khaki clothes they put us in at the prison. My snazzy spelled boots were gone, replaced by uncomfortable, thin white sandals. My big toe hung over the edge of the shredded plastic soles.

A vampire appeared in front of us a block from the station. She scanned the group, and her focus landed on me. "Good afternoon."

Why do people always talk right when I take a bite? I finished chewing, careful not to let too much food touch the gaping hole in my mouth. After I finished, I met the woman's navy blue eyes. "Whazzup?"

"Master Emil has requested an audience with the rogue vampires spotted in town."

"We haven't spotted any rogue vampires." I swung my head toward Elsie. "Have you noticed any rogues?"

A warning flashed through her eyes. "No, Mistress."

I turned my attention back to the woman. "Sorry, we can't help you." I took another bite.

Alex tucked his phone away and cleared his throat. Another warning.

The woman clenched her fists. "Master Emil does not allow strange vampires to wonder through his territory."

"No shit? Smart." Especially after Roman framed us. I should have told him to find his own damn pocket when he asked to share mine. "We're just passing through." I waved a hand toward the transport station. "We'll be out of his territory in a few minutes."

Her eyes scanned the dragons looming behind us, pretending to ignore the conversation. "Your shifter and dragon friends can stay here."

"Not a chance," Alex said. "If Lily needs to check in with this so-called master, then we all go."

"Master Emil will not be pleased." She motioned toward a street marked 'Vampires Only. No fangs, no entry.' "This way, please."

I stared longingly toward the station as she led us in the opposite direction. We were so close to making our escape. I considered making a run for it, but the guilt from what I'd just done pressed down on me, and I didn't want to kill anyone else.

Elsie linked her arm with mine without saying a word. The dragons and Alex hung back far enough to appear polite.

The wards surrounding the gothic-style mansion weren't very strong. Vampires of all shapes and sizes lined the sidewalk leading to the black front door. A man wearing a crisp white dress shirt and black pants stood on the raised porch. His eyes locked with mine and widened.

We continued to the bottom of the steps before Elsie released my arm and stepped behind me. Two vampires stood on the steps, blocking us. I focused on the Master. His icy blue eyes bore into me, but he didn't speak.

I ramped up my aura. A couple of vampires who lined the sidewalk took an involuntary step back. Neat trick, that. I'd have to thank Gramps. My gaze swept across the stereotypical gothic-style vampire house and settled on Emil. "Are you standing up there to compensate for your height or your tiny dick?"

His eyes flashed red. "Good afternoon. I don't believe I've made your acquaintance."

"Your vampire said you wanted to see us." I skipped the pleasantries.

He came down two steps, so we were at eye level, and his minions scrambled to reposition themselves. "I've had reports of a powerful rogue in town."

"Can't help you with that." I motioned toward our drab clothes. "As you can see, we have enough problems of our own."

"You are the rogue they referred to." The guy missed my sarcasm.

"Sorry to disappoint."

He raised a hand in a slow, deliberate motion. "You must be a rogue. Because why else would you encroach on *my* territory?"

Ah. There was the bruised ego. Heat radiated across my back from Elsie as she stepped closer and tapped me in warning. "Encroached, eh? According to rule nine fifty-six of the Compact of Umbra, a vampire may cross through an established territory without checking in with the house master if she doesn't stay for over twenty-four hours. We've been here less than an hour."

Several vampires gasped at my recital of the laws. Or my flippant attitude. I wasn't sure which.

His eyes flashed red again. "Unless the vampire is a rogue. Then I may kill her. And everyone knows better than to enter this pocket as a multi-faction group unless they wish to die."

I put my aura on blast. "You think you can take me, Emil?" When his brow furrowed, I continued. "Because I should warn you, I've had a bad day. So, if you want your house slaughtered and your head on a spike, then bring it on. Otherwise, we'll be on our way." I turned my back to him and shoved Elsie down the sidewalk as I walked away.

I sensed him coming before I took two steps. For a housemaster, he didn't move very fast. The claws on my right hand flipped out. I spun, slammed them into his throat, kneed him in the stomach, and elbowed his temple with my left arm. All in one move.

He hit the ground with a 'thud.'

I pinned him with my knee and leaned over so I was inches from his face. "Did you have a question?"

A few of his vampires took a step forward when he gurgled.

"Order your vampires to attack and see what happens." I released him and walked away without looking back.

The woman who led us to the house stood, blocking the dragons from entering the wards. "We will report this to the queen. What house are you from?"

Power swirled in my eyes as I glared at her.

She lowered her head. "For the official record, Mistress."

We didn't have a house name because I never wanted to establish one. So, I said the first thing that popped into my head. "The house of Lilith."

She stumbled back and her eyes darted toward something behind me. "You're the heir," she croaked.

Not bothering to answer, I picked up my pace just enough to hurry without looking scared and high-tailed it to the transport station.

We had time before the transport to Allure arrived, so we bought new clothes. Alex bought a cleanup spell, but they wouldn't work on us, so Elsie and I rented showers. I found some nice hiking boots but needed an extra trip to Allure to have them spelled for my toe claws.

A flock of fairies swooped over our heads as we left the shower room. A minotaur clomped by with two calves trotting to keep up. The station wasn't too busy, but it was just as jarring as Allure to see paranormals in their natural form. I hoped one day the hybrids would feel as free.

Alex lounged in a chair in the waiting area, his phone in his hand. He held it up when I took the seat beside him. "I texted Mom and Dad to let them know we escaped."

"You didn't call them?"

His eyes narrowed. "No. I sent them a text."

"So, you chickened out."

"I didn't chicken out. They're busy."

"Brock brock."

He wagged his phone at me. "Knock it off, Lily. We're in serious trouble."

I leaned back and rubbed my eyes. "Yeah, no shit. What did they say?"

His phone rang. "I guess we'll see." He hit the answer button. "Hey, Dad."

My hearing tuned to his phone in time to hear Dad chew him out for texting. I chuckled, then focused on my vampires. Other than Elsie, anticipation radiated from them, and I wondered if they already knew we were free.

Alex groaned and closed his eyes. "She did more than escape. She blew up the building."

"Jen's gonna kick my ass for losing my temper."

He handed me the phone. "Dad wants to talk to you."

I flinched as I took the phone. "Hey, Dad."

"Tell me about these government agents."

"Not much to tell other than the guy who tried to torture us wasn't human. He registered as a shifter but shifted into some kind of mutant. It looked grotesque, and his magic felt off. Almost as if the natural magic in the air flipped inside out. Does that make sense?"

"No." Dad's voice sounded strained. "Get your ass on the transport and call either me or your mom if you run into more trouble."

I waved a hand. "Alex is too chicken to call people, but he'll be glad to text."

"Stop it, Lily. I'll call you," Alex said from beside me.

"Stop arguing," Dad growled. "And the next time Drake orders you to stay in the pocket, you stay. Are we clear?"

I swallowed. I completely forgot Drake told us to stay put. "Crystal."

He hung up.

Chapter Eighteen

Shouting near the entrance drew my attention as the transport's door opened for boarding. I stood on my tip-toes but couldn't see the commotion. Two enforcers raced by, one shifted into a tiger, and his clothes scattered across the floor. A spell activated, folding them and placing them in a bin. Neat.

Pop! Pop! Pop!

Everyone waiting for the transport to Allure rushed toward the doors at the sound of gunshots. I latched onto Alex and went fluid, ducking inside ahead of the crowd. As soon as Elsie caught up, we crawled under the massive windows, raising our heads to peer out. White scales blocked the view. The gunshots seemed to continue for hours.

Go! Glacintial's voice boomed through my head as he launched himself into the air. The scene came into view. Some paranormals scrambled away from the gunshots, but most moved toward the attackers. Glacintial swooped over the entrance, leading the charge. Lyran, still in human form, snuck around the back of the crowd, flanking the group.

"Purebloods are nuts," I said as the crowd cleared enough to see the shooters. Several men poured into the station, their magic type not registering. I flipped on my rarely used magic sight and gasped. "How did humans get in here?"

Alex's face screwed up in concentration. "They're spelled. Can't you see that pinkish-orange glow?"

Sure enough. It was faint, but their black clothes had a slight pink tinge. "What is that?"

"Not sure. But it won't matter in a few seconds when those purebloods kill them."

The words barely left Alex's mouth when a mage threw a magic ball, and a spelled human slumped to the floor. A magical shield appeared around the group. But not before at least two launched something toward the transport across from ours.

"Grenade!" I yelled and jammed my fingers in my ears. The doors to the transport slammed shut, and it zipped down the tunnel and hurled into the sky. A massive explosion roared through the station a mere second after we launched. We clutched each other to keep from slamming against the wall as the transport rocketed out of the pocket.

Elsie uncurled, rubbed her head, and moved to a row of empty seats with window views. "Can they enter every pocket with that spell?"

"Not ours. Anyone entering needs permission." And I doubted they'd make it through the gates of Allure since they had so many talented and high-powered gate guards.

"From who?"

"Jen, our parents, Cavil, Alex, or me. Maybe Dale."

"We need to alert the other pockets."

"You're right. Hey, Alex? Want to text Jen with this very important information so we can avoid her reaction?"

"We'll probably end up in another jail inside Allure after this, so you can tell her yourself when she visits to kick your ass."

I bit back a laugh as I leaned my head back and closed my eyes to listen. Everyone chattered about the shooting, but no one had any information, so I turned my thoughts to Cavil. I should have let him rescue us. Our disappearance wouldn't have been as easy to trace or prove as blowing up a federal facility. Plus, I'd have spent a glorious night thanking him. My daydream barely began when the transport shuttered. My eyes flew open, and I jumped out of my seat.

Several people around us also stood. Alex took my hand and motioned Elsie to his other side. "Hang on to me, and don't let go. The transport's magic will flash us to the ground if this thing goes down. If it fails, I'll do it without blowing anything up."

I laced my fingers with his. "Is that a jab at me? Because I feel like it is."

Boom!

The transport tilted sideways, and my feet went out from under me. A sharp pain radiated through my shoulder when an ogre smashed into my side. The motion wrenched our arms, and I fought to let go of Alex, so I didn't hurt him. He tightened his grip, and I hurled in the opposite direction. The window came into view a second before blinding pain blasted my face.

Blood exploded from my nose and clouded my vision. I swiped my free arm over my eyes and screeched as the ground came straight for me. A light flickered, and I landed in a heap in the center row of a frozen, dead cornfield. A piece of metal zipped past my head, and I smashed my throbbing face into the dirt. Wide-eyed purebloods began popping in around us. The massive disc smashed into the ground a few yards away, tumbled through the field, and exploded into a fireball. Chunks of spelled metal rained down on us.

A self-destruct spell ignited, I thought as I climbed to my feet. A tug on my hand brought me back to the present, and I released my grip. The blood bond practice paid off, and I sensed Elsie without trying, so I slogged in her direction. She popped through a row of corn at the same time I did, and we assessed each other. She cradled her left arm against her side and the left side of her face was black from a bruise.

Alex stepped through behind me and wiped his hands on his filthy jeans. "We need to move."

Gunshots exploded from somewhere nearby. I linked my arm through Alex's and went fluid. Not stopping until we reached a road. Ears on full alert, I lowered myself to the ground and crawled on my stomach to peer out.

Police cars lined the street. Several unmarked SUVs screeched to a halt beyond them, and humans in suits and uniforms spilled out and flooded the area. Our corner only had a few officers guarding it, but by the sirens, more were on the way. My heart pounded as I flipped on my magic sight.

"I can flash us down the road a couple of miles." Alex's voice was barely audible.

"Stay low and off the roads. I think they're looking for us."

"They are," Elsie murmured from his other side.

"Flash us, then I'll go fluid before anyone spots us. Elsie?"

"I'll help you drag Alex so we can move faster."

Alex took our hands, and we landed at the edge of a harvested field on our stomachs. We were on our feet and moving before a full second ticked by. Our speed increased with both of us going fluid, and I had a hard time focusing on our surroundings.

Luckily, the land was so flat there weren't many obstacles, and the roads seemed to go on forever. Fat gray clouds moved in, and the temperature dropped as we ran. We made it about ten miles, and Alex flashed us again.

He pointed toward a grove of trees. "We can hide there."

"No." Elsie's eyes cast a red glow on the ground as they scanned the area. "Not there. We need to hide and rest, but not on private property or in the most obvious place."

She was right. We didn't need some farmer with an itchy trigger finger finding us camping on his property. And if the feds checked the area, the trees would be the first place they looked.

Alex pulled out his phone and accessed the location app. Unlike humans, our phones didn't track us, even with GPS on. Tech magic allowed them to accept incoming location services but block outgoing ones. "We're close to Des Moines, Iowa. There's a pocket to the west of it."

"How far?"

"Around fifty miles."

We'd pass out from exhaustion before we went fluid and flashed for fifty miles. With the flat land, they would spot us if we walked. "Let's find somewhere to rest until dark. Then we can hide in the shadows and walk." I glanced toward the flashing lights. They were mere dots on the horizon. "We need to keep moving until we can't see the lights."

We made it a few more miles before collapsing from exhaustion. I struggled to swallow because my mouth was dry, and sweat soaked our clothes. Without water and rest, we'd never make it to the pocket.

Elsie pulled out the blood she bought at the transport station and handed one to me.

"Thanks." For the first time since I started drinking it, I didn't complain.

Tiny snowflakes drifted down from the sky as Alex curled between us. The sound of tires on asphalt made us duck down and fall silent. We stayed there long after the police car passed. Good thing, too. Because it looped back.

Elsie closed her eyes. "Are they looking for us, Alex?"

"They're not after us specifically. They didn't catch any paranormals from the transport and hope to spot one."

"We won't make it if we don't replenish our energy. And we can't stay out here in the snow. Suggestions?"

He popped his head up and scanned the area. "Let's rest in that group of overgrown hedges. I'll text Glacintial. If he doesn't find us by the time it gets dark, we'll move on."

The prickly hedges stabbed me in several places as we wiggled through them to where the shadows were thickest. Alex stripped, shifted into his lion form, curled against me, and fell asleep. We only had a couple of hours until dark. As we waited, the snowfall increased by the minute and soaked us to the bone. Regulating our body temperatures made us waste valuable energy.

I checked Alex's phone every few minutes to see if the dragons responded, but they hadn't. My eyes drooped as I watched over the other two. The exhaustion was bone-deep, and I considered checking us into a human hotel and taking our chances. But we didn't have our IDs or money. Inside the pockets, we used our magic to buy things and identify ourselves. As much as I hated the purebloods they housed, I couldn't wait to find one.

Snow blanketed the ground by the time the sun sank low enough to use the shadows. Alex shifted back into his human form, and we trudged to the edge of the field. I glanced back and discovered another problem. Footprints. The last thing we needed was to draw the police right to us. And with the snow falling, it wasn't as dark as we'd hoped. Alex didn't have enough magic left to cover them as we walked, and I didn't dare use mine. "Those are going to be a problem."

Elsie pointed toward an empty drainage ditch. "Let's walk in there."

They'd help hide our footprints but also slow us down. I scanned the area for a better option but didn't find one. "Okay."

We settled into an even pace as we skirted around the city and turned south, adding a few miles to our walk. Alex shivered uncontrollably, and my protective instincts kicked in. "You should shift."

"I'm fine for now. If it gets colder, I will."

I kept my eye on him but didn't comment. He never took my suggestions, and I trusted him to care for himself. But I couldn't help but worry.

We had to stop a few times and crouch down when cars passed. None of them were police cars. Though I heard helicopters searching to our east.

When we reached a freeway, Elsie pointed. "The gate is in that recreational area."

I watched the cars zipping by and frowned. "Are you sure?" Considering the sheer number of humans around, it seemed like an odd place for a gate to me.

"Positive. I came here with Mistress Ara twice to check on the local house."

I wondered why. But after meeting the last housemaster, combined with Roman's betrayal, I didn't care. Besides Meemaw, not a single housemaster proved themselves worthy of my thoughts. They were all awful. I threw it out of my head and focused on trudging down a drainage ditch. If I had to kiss the ass of some whacky power-hungry asshat to find a warm place where Alex and Elsie could rest, I'd do it. "Let's go fluid and make a run for it."

Chapter Nineteen

An audible gasp escaped as Alex's icy hand slid into mine. Elsie and I shared a look. My brother wouldn't last much longer unless he shifted. As one, we took off across the freeway, down the road, and into the preserve.

I flipped on my magic sight and spotted the gate a hundred yards away. With our energy drained, the shadows surrounding us weren't very thick.

Elsie stumbled, caught herself, and continued, her breathing too labored.

"We're almost there." When I pulled my attention away from the road to scan the surrounding trees, I slammed through a knee-high branch, and a loud 'crack' filled the night.

We froze.

A mass of humans poured out of the trees between us and the gate, guns raised. They moved into a sloppy formation, their heads swiveling. "Did you hear it?" A middle-aged man with a long, unkempt beard and a beer belly asked.

Elsie dragged us into the trees, and we worked together to strengthen the shadows.

"Something triggered trap number two," another man said.

They fell silent. After a few seconds, one moved in our direction, not even trying to silence his footsteps. He lifted his rifle and aimed it down the trail we'd left in the snow. "You see this, Jim?"

The guy, Jim, I supposed, lowered himself into a crouch. "What did this?"

The older man spat on the ground. "Looks like a large snail trail. Might be one of them aliens."

A younger man whisper whooped. "We got one! I told you they were in the preserve."

A heavy-set man with yet another unkempt beard lifted his hunting rifle and peered in our general direction through the scope. "We know you're there. Come on out."

They fell silent. After a few seconds, the first bearded guy lifted his rifle to his shoulder. "Screw it. Let's shoot it up."

I layered more shadows as we lowered ourselves to the ground and scooted behind a tree, moving slow enough not to catch their eye. We huddled together, knowing the tree wasn't thick enough to stop the bullets.

"Should we run for the gate?" Alex whispered in my ear.

I shook my head and projected images of the guys shooting at anything that moved.

As soon as the men opened fire, Alex flashed us to the left, closer to the gate.

Sirens sounded in the distance.

"We need to go now!" Elsie's urgent plea was barely audible.

As one, we darted toward the gate. Gunfire drowned out the men's shouts as bullets rained down around us. A pinch of pain in my elbow almost made me lose my grip on Alex.

He latched onto my arm above the wound. "Fuck this!"

Elsie stumbled and landed on her face, causing a chain reaction. Alex tried to keep his balance, then let himself fall, dragging me with him and covering us with his body.

The guns fell silent, and I swung my head in their direction. The entire group lay scattered on the ground like a bunch of camouflaged turds. "What did you do?" I squirmed out from underneath him.

Something huge landed on top of us, and muscular arms squeezed my ribs so tight I heard a 'crack.' I bit my tongue to keep from squawking.

A flash of light blinded me, and for the third time that day, my face planted against something hard. Throbbing radiated in my jaw as I sat up and pried my swollen eyes open. A massive gate with three guards loomed in front of us.

"I hate it when mages appear like that," a shifter guard growled.

The arms released me. "I am a god." Cavil's face was hard as he offered me a hand. He pulled Alex to his feet and threw Elsie over his shoulder as if she weighed nothing.

"You're going to find this hard to believe, but I don't care." The guy held out a magical scanner. "Scan in."

Alex ran his magical ID through it. "Have you had any trouble besides the trigger-happy humans?"

"No. But they're trouble enough. We're stranded until they give up."

I scanned my magic and followed him through. "Has this happened before?"

"The local militia gets restless and hunts us sometimes, but it's never this bad." His eyes widened when he read my credentials.

Alex nodded. "They might need a healer." He tapped his temple. "Brain injury."

"We saw in the monitoring spell." He motioned toward a coven of witches racing toward the exit.

After Cavil and Elsie scanned in, I turned to the shifter. "You might want to put the pocket on high alert. The humans shot down our transport near here. And some idiot figured out how to coat humans in a spell and send them into pockets to die."

He inclined his head. "I'll mention it to my supervisor."

The pocket wasn't as big as the last one we fled to, but there was a smattering of businesses. We bought more fresh clothes and a few hygiene spells, while Cavil checked us into a hotel. I watched the skies, hoping to spot a dragon. "Have you heard from Glacintial and Lyran?"

"No," Alex said. "But they're dragons, so I'm sure they're fine."

I limped toward the hotel's entrance. "Where have I heard that before?" I snapped my fingers. "I know. It was when you got kidnapped, and everyone insisted you'd be fine because Glac guarded you."

"I *was* fine for a while. My cockiness exposed Glac. I won't make the same mistake again."

I believed him. Alex had a very analytical mind, so he'd probably assessed it from every angle.

The hotel only had one room available, so the four of us piled into it, and I made Alex take the first shower. He couldn't regulate his body temperature without shifting and needed the heat more than us. I was proven right when he emerged from the bathroom as a lion. His massive mouth opened in a yawn, revealing razor-sharp teeth as he curled up on the bed Elsie had claimed. She watched him out of the corner of her eye as she sipped blood to heal from three gunshot wounds. As soon as he settled, I sent her to shower and assessed my own injuries. A bullet had grazed my thigh, but it was already healing. The second wound felt much worse. "Hey, Cavil, will you look at this? I can't see it."

He leaned down and poked at my elbow. "There's some kind of metal in it." I gritted my teeth against the pain as heat warmed the area. The bullet clonked off the cheap dresser, and the pain eased.

I bent over and picked it up. It wasn't a regular bullet, but a chunk of silver. I held it up. "They wasted a lot of money on this ammo."

Cavil lowered himself to the bed. "Is it not a normal projectile?"

"Humans think silver bullets will kill werewolves. They must have been hunting shifters."

He took the chunk of silver from my hand. "So, it's a myth?"

"Yeah. But I couldn't tell you where it came from." I planned to find out as soon as we made it home. Well, made it home *and* kicked Roman's ass out of my pocket.

When I finished showering, I cracked the bathroom door open. My knees almost buckled, and my stomach growled when the scent of food drifted through the door. I threw on a pair of yoga pants and a sweatshirt and raced out the door.

Cavil handed me a burger and fries. "Eat first, then sleep. I'll flash you home tomorrow." He marched into the bathroom and shut the door.

Elsie scarfed her burger down without taking time to breathe.

I grinned as I lowered myself to the bed. "Hungry?"

She paused. "Famished. I haven't starved in ages and am no longer used to it."

"Yeah. Me too." I tore into my food.

Elsie disposed of her plate and plopped onto the bed face first. "Scoot over, sleepyhead." She shoved at Alex. "Get some sleep, Lily. We can't solve any problems until we're rested."

Cavil came out of the bathroom looking sinful in his hot pink sweats and bright blue T-shirt. His damp hair stuck up in different directions, making him look so fuckable my entire body lit on fire. Until I noticed the dark circles under his eyes. I was too tired to flirt or sneak a quickie in, so I threw my plate away and slid into bed. Sleep took me as his arm slid around my waist.

A soft kiss on my forehead roused me out of a deep sleep. I snuggled deeper into the covers, too warm and comfortable to wake up.

"Lily, we need to go." The sexy, smooth voice made me shiver.

"She doesn't sleep much, but it's hard to wake her when she does."

I pried my eyes open. Electric blue jewels floated a few inches away. The sunny smile attached to them brought me out of my stupor. "Hey, Cavil." I sat up and fought to orient myself. Elsie devoured a breakfast burrito and sipped a blood bag on the other bed. Alex lounged beside her, his face buried in his phone. I stumbled toward the magichef for coffee. "How long was I asleep?"

Cavil stood and stretched, revealing his perfect abs. "A little over twelve hours."

"No problem," Elsie said between bites. "We just woke up a few minutes ago."

"As soon as you're ready, I'll flash you home or to Allure." Cavil pulled out his phone. "Jenella has grounded all transports after yesterday's incident."

"No shit? Huh." I sipped my coffee. "How did you find us?"

"I made a magical contract to help you when you need it. It allows me to find your location."

A deep frown formed on my face. I was grateful he showed up, but wasn't sure what I thought about someone always being able to find me. "How does that work, exactly?"

"I feel a pinch in my chest when you're in danger. If it becomes too uncomfortable, I can flash to your location."

I sipped my coffee and thought about how he showed up in my cell. "Handy." It still made me uncomfortable, but I let it go.

Alex wiggled his own phone. "Between the transport and the building collapse, they have enough evidence to confirm our existence."

"So we played right into the hands of the people responsible for the strange magic."

Cavil nodded. "Correct. Jenella prepared for humans to learn about us, but not like this."

Yeah. Jen didn't go into the fight blind. My actions only moved up the timeline. I downed the rest of my coffee. "Then let's go home. I need to check on my vampires."

Alex shook his head. "Not yet. Let's go to Allure and fill them in before more hybrids disappear."

My face screwed up. "I'd rather go home."

"Then let's take a vote. All in favor of going to Allure before returning home, raise your hand."

Chapter Twenty

The gates to Allure buzzed with activity. Several purebloods stood in line outside. I even spotted a few hybrids. I jerked my arm out of Cavil's grip. "You're supposed to be on my side."

He slung his newly freed arm around me. "Always."

"This is the right thing to do, and you know it," Alex said as he examined the line. "Besides, if we didn't go to them, they'd come to us, and our house is already full."

My brother was almost always right. "Whatever."

Elsie tried to brush the wrinkles out of her cheap T-shirt. "You're mad because you want to resolve your territory dispute."

"Yeah. That crusty old fuck will pay for this. But I also want to check on Spencer and Elizabeth. And Pascal is making progress." I bared my teeth when the witch coven turned to stare.

Cavil cleared his throat. "You will have your chance."

The line moved forward, and relief flooded me when I spotted Meemaw and Jen waiting on the Allure side of the gate. "Who tattled?"

"I informed your grandmother of your return," Cavil answered.

Alex pointed at the landing area to our right. "Look."

Glacintial and Lyran appeared out of nowhere, melted into their human forms, and sauntered in our direction.

"Hey, no cutting the line," someone behind us said.

As one, we turned toward the voice. A group of beaver shifters flinched like they shared a brain.

"You can go ahead of us." Alex motioned toward the line.

They muttered a thank you as they scrambled forward.

The gate guards in Allure were fast and efficient. I'd never noticed because when I showed up to release my magic, I was too busy coming up with ways to counter their harassment.

Instead of their usual disdain, they practically ignored us as they gazed adoringly at Cavil. I would have laughed on any other day. But I was still tired and sore and wanted to go home, so I kept my mouth shut and tried not to glare when they rubbed themselves against him.

One of Meemaw's stealth hugs wrapped around me the minute I stepped through. "I'm so glad you're back."

"Me too." I pulled away from her. "Roman framed us."

She patted my arm. "We will discuss his involvement later."

The dragons had a brief conversation with Alex and flew off toward Dragon Headquarters.

Jen didn't spare them a glance or bother hugging me. Instead, she slammed her fists on her hips. "What did the humans do to make you blow up their building?"

My mouth opened, and I tapped my lip. "They tore out a fang."

Meemaw's elites gasped.

"I restrained myself at first. Then they drugged, tortured, and threatened Alex and Elsie, and I lost my shit."

Jen's brow furrowed. "Holy hell. Why did you let them close enough to take your fang?"

"Humans aren't acting alone. Several men were there with some kind of odd magic, including the guy with the spelled pliers. When we escaped, they sent humans coated in magic into a nearby pocket to shoot up the transport station."

"I heard. Did you read their magic?"

"Yeah. Sort of."

Jen inclined her head and scanned our group. "Let's go somewhere more private to go over the details."

No one argued as she led us to the flashing circle.

The palace was the fanciest place I'd ever seen. The high ceilings and expensive finishings always made me want to prance around using a snooty accent. It seemed like an alternate reality as Jen led us into an elevator. "Why didn't I know about this elevator?"

A smile lit her face. "Verity doesn't use it. But Helen has a strict no flashing in the palace rule. She even throws visitors out for breaking it. Mat had elevators installed because he hated climbing stairs a hundred times a day. There's one in each wing."

"Huh." I clasped my hands in front of me. "So, how much trouble am I in?"

Her head whipped toward me. "Trouble?"

"Yeah. For exposing us to humans. Last I checked, it's against coalition law."

Jen opened her mouth to answer, but the elevator beeped, so she motioned toward her office.

Verity sat at the half-moon desk out front and scanned our group. "Need me for anything?"

"No," Jen said as we passed. "Unless you want to know what the humans are doing?"

"I do." She stood, picked up a tablet, and followed us in.

Jen motioned toward a seating area on the far end. "Have a seat."

My stomach growled when I spotted the food covering every inch of the massive coffee table as I plopped down on a sofa. Cavil and Alex flanked me. Elsie stood beside the windows near where I sensed Gramps. Meemaw, Jen, and Verity sat across from us.

"To answer your question, you're not in much trouble. It was my decision to expose us to humans, and Roman chose to blow up his house when he knew they were watching. You did what you needed to do."

"And you did it spectacularly." Meemaw beamed with pride. "Now, tell me. How did you end up in a federal facility?"

We took turns explaining. When we were done, Alex tapped his phone. "We have recordings. I entertained myself by scanning their minds. Our parents have my notes, but they're not coherent. I'll clean them up and send them to you."

"I'll also send my recordings." Elsie pulled her phone out.

"That reminds me. I left my phone in Alex's car."

Jen nodded. "Glacintial saw the whole incident. Jonas recovered Alex's car and your phone." Her fingers tapped her leg. "What did they do to your magic?"

I shrugged as guilt washed over me for how I reacted. "Other than ripping my fang out by the root and collecting some spit full of blood, they didn't do anything. I got the fang back."

Ara leaned forward. "Our blood registers as human."

"The magic on the guy who took it felt inverted, and he looked grotesque when he shifted."

Cavil leaned an elbow on the arm of the sofa. "It may be from the realm of Gartolia. They are a warring realm that enjoys taking over lesser realms. Your description is in line with one of their weaker factions."

Drake stormed through the adjoining door. "What did you say about Gartolia?"

Cavil pulled what looked like a stack of poker chips from his pocket and held them out. "I took these from the facility."

Drake picked one up and examined it, swore under his breath, and handed it to Jen. "What did you learn, Alex?"

My brother closed his eyes. "The humans have some interesting ideas about us. They've confirmed we exist and even have a few paranormals who served the Bellicose, giving them information. But they're wrong about who we are and our numbers. They have the locations of nine gates, including the one at the bar. It's almost like they're being fed false information on purpose."

Drake lowered himself into a chair. "We haven't heard from our contacts. Was there any sign of them?"

"No. A few guys in the lower level were pondering the mechanics of magic scanning devices. Others were thinking about a few of your people who work in the government. They were arrested but disappeared when the guards left them alone."

Cavil nodded. "I rescued them. I offered to do the same for Lily, but she declined because she worried about exposing her magic."

My head swung his way so fast I got whiplash. "Why didn't you tell me others had disappeared? If I'd known, I would have left with you in a second."

He shrugged. "I tried to tell you, but you said Alex had a plan. No one expected you to destroy the entire building."

I blinked. "Yeah. I lost my temper." And something inside me shifted when I did. But I wasn't airing my laundry in front of everyone.

Alex cleared his throat. "When they arrested us, I had a plan. Once they transferred us, it wasn't an option. I knew Glacintial followed us when we were on that airplane. If Lily didn't destroy the building, the dragons would have. He was waiting for permission from Deva."

Jen hadn't taken her eyes off me. "I gave her the green light to get you out after they turned Ann Marie's lawyers away." Her brow creased as she leaned forward. "Why does your magic feel different?"

So much for keeping that nugget to myself. "None of your business."

A smile ghosted across her face. "You accepted your darker side."

"I don't have a dark side."

"Do, too."

"What are we, twelve? No, I don't."

Alex kicked my ankle. "Don't mind Lily. She's used to being the one who makes childish arguments."

"I do not."

"Do too," he and Jen said in unison.

A laugh burst out of me, and I rubbed my temples. "When I lost my temper, I forgot to be careful with my magic, and it did something."

Cavil took my hand. "There was never anything wrong with it. You are a dark goddess who embraced her night magic for the first time. Now you can choose which nasty surprises you cast."

I had zero desire to be a dark goddess. Which was on par with my thoughts about being a housemaster or a princess. "When can we go home?"

Jen always appreciated a change of subject, so she went with it. "You can go as soon as we're done here. A group of agents has already raided your human house. Ann Marie removed or warded everything, so they didn't find a single piece of evidence you're anything other than human."

"Did she save my work laptop and gaming system?" Alex asked.

"I don't know what that is. She moved your office."

He sighed in relief. "I'll clean up the notes and send them to you. Does anyone know why they abducted us? Not a single one thought about it."

Abducted was the right word. No one read us our rights, so it wasn't an arrest. If we were humans, we would sue, though we'd probably lose, considering they marked us as terrorists.

"Your failure to follow my orders and stay in the pocket caused this incident. Had you listened, none of this would have happened." Drake growled.

"I forgot you said that." I met his hard green eyes. "A group of hybrids attacked us when I was training Elizabeth and Spencer. When the dragons surrounded them, they said they wanted the agreement with the coalition revoked. They've been talking to the feds, and they said they told them about Roman's house. He didn't answer the phone, so we went to warn him. It was supposed to be a quick trip."

"Is that so?"

"Yeah. Dale knows about the rogue hybrids. They're the same group who shot up his bar. But he might need your help with them." A thought popped into my head. "Why did Roman frame us, Meemaw?"

"He claims you simply arrived at an inopportune time."

I snorted. "And you believe him?"

"Of course not, dear. I believe Roman used your visit as an opportunity. He did not intentionally set you up."

Sure, he didn't. And I'd never forgive him. It stung because, out of all my new blood relations, I thought Roman was the nicest. I'd forgotten an important lesson I'd learned at an early age. I can't trust my biological family. Falling for their lies and deception was on me. "You said I'm your heir, right?"

Meemaw's intelligent eyes narrowed. "Yes."

"Does that mean I outrank Roman?"

"You outrank everyone except me and your grandfather." Her eyes sparked with interest, and she leaned forward. "Why?"

"Because Jen made the pocket for us, not the purebloods. And I wanted to warn you I'm going to revoke his permission and banish his house from it. They are no longer welcome in my territory."

I expected some sort of objection. Instead, Meemaw leaned back, her eyes shining with pride. After a few seconds, her shoulders shook, followed by a tinkering laugh. "Do you understand the implications of such a drastic action?"

"Yes." I'd studied vampire behaviors and laws for years, trying to understand more about myself. The only person able to revoke access on a large scale was Meemaw. But with the power of Lilith, I could control other vampires. One of the few times Meemaw used the rule was to give humans the right to allow vampires into their homes. If a human refused or revoked their permission, the compulsion made it so the offending vampire couldn't so much as set foot inside. It was one legend the humans got right about us.

Gramps made an appearance and put a hand on Meemaw's shaking shoulder. "You are not as ignorant as you led us to believe."

"Oh, no. Ignorant is my middle name. But I've known you were my grandparents for most of my life, and my mom has an extensive library. I researched your abilities after I escaped from Jed's clutches. Until recently, I didn't know I'd inherited them. Then I didn't want to step on any toes." I met his eyes. "If there's one thing this family has taught me, it's how I can't trust any of you. So I don't give a shit about your toes anymore."

Jen's mouth did one of those fish-flap things. "Um."

Gramps's hand tightened on Meemaw's shoulder, and he leaned forward. "And what have I or your grandmother done to prove ourselves untrustworthy?"

"You haven't given me a single reason not to trust you. But then, neither did Roman until he fed us to the humans to save his own ass." I crossed my arms. "My adopted family would never consider throwing me under the bus like that. I have their support, so I don't need yours. Especially if you plan to stab me in the back."

Drake leaned forward, his green eyes like lasers as they focused on me. "I swear I will never betray you, Alex, or anyone you consider family."

The magical contract zinged through my head, and I squawked.

Jen grinned and repeated his words. Meemaw followed. Gramps examined me with a fierceness I'd only seen in battle. "You will need to learn to trust me."

My mouth quirked up. "Fair enough." The tension in my shoulders drained with their oaths. But I doubted Jen or Drake had it in them to betray me like Roman did. And being cagey wasn't my grandparents' style. If Gramps wanted to throw me under the bus, he'd make a sarcastic comment as the wheels smashed me into the road. And Meemaw would just shred me without bothering to find a bus. Neither would be as sneaky about it as Roman. I needed to stop holding them accountable for the actions of my biological parents. I said as much.

Meemaw waved a hand. "It is of no consequence, dear. We love having a spirited granddaughter. Your ability to create and enforce boundaries in violent ways is a breath of fresh air."

Chapter Twenty-One

We landed outside our pocket house. Entire subdivisions were popping up around the original village. Apparently, the hybrids were content to stick with the odd-shaped architecture Jen created because many of the new houses copied it. There were ten times more than Jen made, but it still wasn't enough to account for the area's hybrid population. I scanned the road to see if I could spot Roman's vampires.

"Why the fuck did you land on the damn lawn?" Flemming's voice came from the pink shrubs beside the back deck.

I bit back a smile as my muscles relaxed. "Hey, Flemming. Sorry." I stepped onto the fresh path leading around the house. "Better?"

He raised his middle finger and lowered it when the back door opened. "Pay attention next time." He stepped back into the shrub, and it transformed into a perfect cube.

Mom stepped out onto the back deck. "What did you do?"

I led our group down the trail and up the stairs. "Long story."

She pulled me and Alex into a group hug. "I bet."

Cavil inclined his head. "Hello, Ann Marie."

Flintous stepped out the door behind her. His red eyes settled on Alex. "You look much healthier than I expected."

I patted his arm as I passed. "We've had time to recover. Jen's griffins wouldn't let us leave until we were fat and happy."

He trailed me through the kitchen. "Sounds boring."

An ear-to-ear grin spread across my face. "It was a snooze fest."

"Your new vampires are quite handy in a crisis. They even impressed Mistress Ara with their control."

"Nice."

Inside, Dad leaned a shoulder against the wall as he examined us. After we met his inspection, he moved toward Cavil and shook his hand. "Our deal is complete. You have my blessing."

Cavil inclined his head.

My stomach fell. "What in the hell is that about?"

Dad's eyes twinkled with mischief. "Cavil believes you are his soulmate and asked for my blessing. I told him he had to prove himself worthy. He has."

Mom moved to his side. "And what am I, chopped liver? I don't remember anyone asking for my blessing."

Cavil flinched. "I apologize. Alienating you wasn't my intention. Jonas cornered me, and we came to an agreement."

My face flushed with anger. "What is this, the middle ages? You can't just sell your daughter to the first god who shows up in the realm."

"Sure, I can." Dad patted my head like I was still a kid. "Especially if it gets under your skin or keeps those tears from falling."

"Button pushing is my job." My voice cracked, and I wrapped my arms around him, unable to hold the tears back. "I thought we were going to die, Dad."

He hugged me back, his comforting warmth grounding me. "I didn't doubt you for a minute. You two are survivors and stronger than you think." He kept his hands on my shoulders as he met my eyes. "Now that I've sold you to a god for a favor, you'll need those skills."

A teary laugh escaped. "Yeah. Cavil's awful."

Said god cleared his throat. "I swear I will always care for Lily to the best of my ability."

The contract zinged through my skull. "Damnit, Cavil!" I rubbed my eyes. "Has Roman tried anything?"

Mom and Dad exchanged a look. "He is claiming this pocket as his own," Mom said.

Oh, hell no. "How can he do that when he isn't even a hybrid?"

Dad leaned forward. "He claims he has rights since I contracted him in as part of the hybrid community."

"And what does Meemaw say about it? When I asked her in Allure, she didn't say much."

"It's not her responsibility to fight your battles for you. Nor is it ours." Dad moved to the magichef. "This is a problem you'll need to solve."

I closed my eyes. "If I kick his entire house out, then what?"

"Can you? Kick his house out?" Elsie asked.

I inclined my head. "If I use my magic, maybe. But it will be bloody. What will it say to the vampire community? Will the other masters see me as soft and declare open season on Lily? Or will they think I'm fair and lenient?"

Elsie averted her eyes. "Roman is the oldest vampire in the world. He's stronger than you, and he knows it. If he's challenging you for territory, you only win by taking his house."

Thick silence blanketed the room.

Mom cleared her throat. "Roman has nearly forty vampires."

I flinched. I didn't want the four I had, let alone forty more. "Are you sure there isn't something else I can do? Because we don't have room for forty vampires."

Dad leaned forward. "Roman built a mansion in the hills big enough to house them. If you win, it's yours."

Alex shook his head. "So, the only way to solve this is for Lily to move into his house?"

"It's customary when housemasters fight for territory," Elsie said.

When his wide eyes turned to me, he resembled the broken little kid I fell in love with. I blinked back more tears. "You can move in with me."

"You know I can't. Not until I learn how to block out thoughts. Deva thinks it will take at least a year."

"Yeah. But Elsie's right. I'm too powerful, and now that everyone knows about me, other masters will keep challenging me if I don't do something drastic."

My brother's eyes watered. "We've never lived apart."

The tears I held back spilled down my face. "Yeah. This whole situation is shitty."

Glac rested a hand on Alex's shoulder. "If I may impart some wisdom?"

My throat was too tight to speak, so I nodded.

"You two are extremely powerful together, and I believe you will always remain close."

"But?" Alex growled.

"But you are also individually powerful and from different factions. You must each find your place amongst your own kind. If you don't, you will never grow."

"I agree," Dad said. When my head whipped toward him, his lips tugged down. "You were stagnant in your lives before we sent you to Allure. It's time to spread your wings and grow. Just remember who your family is."

My heart shattered into pieces at the resigned look in Alex's eyes, so I focused on Elsie. "So, should I wait until he shows up here and challenges me? Or march in and take over? How does it work?"

Mom patted Alex's arm. "His place is only three or four miles away."

Elsie nodded in agreement. "We'll still be close enough so you and Alex can have your childish arguments. It's your territory, so it's up to you where you fight."

Roman's compound sat on a hill a couple of miles outside the village on a massive plot of land. The wall surrounding it went on for miles and resembled the ones around the upscale houses in my grandparents' neighborhood. It kept with the odd theme of the pocket in front, with circular and triangular shapes poking out in every direction. The sprawling, modern mansion behind the facade reminded me of something you'd find a celebrity or a billionaire living in. The entire thing was white, with clean lines and pristine landscaping. Everything about it screamed 'king of the pocket.' If I doubted Roman removed me from the equation as a power play, seeing how he established himself inside my territory confirmed it.

Elsie's whistle tore me out of my thoughts. "This is a statement. He's insulting you in front of everyone."

"Yep." I scanned the vampires on the wall. When I first met Roman, his second, Folomi, was his only vampire. It didn't take him long to recruit more. Most were high-powered, and all were smart and competent. My stomach soured as doubt crept into my head about whether I'd win. "You should stand back."

She dropped her hands to her sides, and her posture relaxed. "Not a chance."

My lips twitched. "This might suck. Roman's a lot older than me."

"True. Use your mage skills and don't hold back. Vampires are ruthless, so be more ruthless than him. If you can make a bloody statement and assert dominance, other house masters will think twice before messing with you."

Several scenarios ran through my head. Meemaw would handle it by using her persuasion, followed by torture and violence. But I didn't have the time or patience to go that route. Gramps would slaughter everyone before they realized he was there. Neither method was dramatic enough to make a statement. Fortunately, I had a lot of experience with drama, so I'd need to do it my way. "Stay with me and out of the firing lane."

"The what?"

I turned my head toward her. Power swirled in my eyes, casting a dusty golden-red glow. I drank Cavil's blood to be at maximum power for my showdown with Roman. Dressed in black leather from head to toe and my hair flowing free, the glowing eyes maximized my badass look.

Elsie flinched. "Got it."

I squared my shoulders to hide my nerves and strolled toward the gates. A vampire I'd never met stepped into my path. I flicked my wrist. Dark power streamed from my fingers, and the gate crashed open, sending the vampire flying. As I breached the wards, bright multicolored sparks shot into the air, resembling fireworks.

Several more vampires poured out of the mansion and went fluid, racing toward us. I threw up a wall in front of them. Blood-red magic leaked down their side and formed into whips. A series of cracks drowned out the sounds of their war cries. A few stopped just out of the firing line, while others veered in a new direction.

A cannon-like sound boomed through the compound when my wall exploded. Lancing pain stabbed through my head as I tried to focus on how to make the dark twist restrain the vampires without killing them. Black arrows exploded from it and chased down the retreating vampires, slammed into them, and pinned them to the ground. With a flick of my other wrist, the ones trying to flank us smashed into a new wall.

I stopped at the base of the curved marble steps leading to the double front doors. "*Roman! You will report to me now!*" The persuasion in my voice echoed through the surrounding hills.

The door creaked as it opened, and Roman, Senga, and Folomi glided out and stopped on the porch. Several emotions ghosted across Roman's face before he focused on his feet. His red face screwed up in concentration as he fought my compulsion. When he beat it, he gave me a triumphant smirk. "Hello Niece. I hope you enjoyed your vacation. As you can see, I have claimed this territory. I will allow you time to relocate, of course. But it's mine now, and I do not intend to let it go."

I used my mage skills and flashed to him. A red mist spread over the blue lawn, giving it a purple sheen before fading to black and wrapping his vampires in a tight ball. My teeth were in Roman's throat before he registered my movement. As soon as his blood touched my tongue, I slammed my pre-cut finger into his mouth and returned to my spot on the sidewalk.

Dark spots blinded me as the new blood bonds crashed through my head. I fought to blink them away and control them for a second too long.

Pain exploded as something hard smashed into my face. I dug my fingers into Roman's side and extended my claws. Using the trick I'd seen Mat do with his swords, I fired up my dark mage magic and ran them down my claws.

Roman's shrill scream made my teeth ache. An elbow landed right between my boobs, and I dug my claws in deeper as we tumbled down the steps. *"You will stop this coup right now, Liliana Umbra."*

I shook off his compulsion and retracted my claws, then jammed them into him several times in rapid succession. Pinches of pain ran down my back and sides when he did the same.

We rolled down the sidewalk so fast that we smashed into a few vampires racing toward us before they realized we were there. My head was still fuzzy from bonding Roman's house, so I had lost my concentration as I let out another wave of my nasty magic. I felt it smash into them as the sickening sound of my ribs cracking from Roman's punch stole my focus. The guy was too strong for me to fight physically. I sent another stream of magic through him.

We let go of each other, hopped to our feet, and separated. I wheezed as my ribs knitted themselves back together.

"You think you can fight me, niece? I've been dominating housemasters since the beginning of time. And you are merely a babe. Powerful, yes. But barely a vampire, let alone a master. I should have killed you on that rooftop while pretending to mentor you."

Red clouded my vision, and I fought to clear it. "Mentoring, eh? Is that what you call droning on about shit I already knew? If I remember right, *I* almost killed *you* with an air conditioner. And it wasn't even difficult."

Roman's shoulder punched into my stomach. The air left my lungs, and I wheezed. His fangs snapped in my face, and pain radiated from my chest where he dug for my heart. The salty scent of blood clogged my nose.

I was going to die. He was too strong and the impact of so many bonds distracted me. I once again scrambled to throw them to the back of my mind. No way I'd go out without a fight, and if I kept worry about them, it was over. I released them, and let them wander through my head, and instead focused on my magic. I let it fly unrestrained. A wall swirling with black and red power formed between us, and I didn't care if it killed him.

He was gone before it rose, so I dissipated it. The stabbing in my chest told me he maneuvered behind me, so I went fluid as I spun, ducked, and threw another wall at him as I charged. Our bodies collided with a sickening 'thud.' We flew a few feet and landed in a heap. I had my claws out, ready to strike.

Intense pain pounded through my head, and I lost my train of thought.

Roman rolled me over, and his face stretched into a feral grin. A milky sheen coated his irises. "I may regret this one day, but I somehow doubt it." His claws descended toward me.

I flashed a few feet away, keeping my grip on him. An orange dust cloud shot into the air as I flashed again to reverse our positions. My claws slammed into his chest below his throat before he oriented himself. I swung my leg up and threatened his balls with toe claws. The magic running through them made contact, and a deafening screech ripped from his throat. Spots still danced across my vision but cleared enough to see his eyes grow as big as saucers and his face pinch with pain. I increased the magic.

Roman released his grip on me, and silence fell over us. The only sound was our ragged breathing.

I made sure my claws would cause maximum damage if he tried to move as I leaned down. "Say uncle."

A puzzled look ghosted across his face before the blood bond with him, and by default, his vampires finally settled in my head. Someone stirred nearby. Right. Time to be overdramatic. "Roman Umbra. You have broken our alliance contract and abused my generosity. Payment for the violation is your house."

His eyes flipped toward Folomi, who stood a few steps away, wrapped like a mummy in latex-like black magic. "You have done well, Lily. But I cannot surrender my entire house."

I sorted through the new bonds as I stared him down and found nothing but love radiating from Roman. My eyebrows drew together. "Because I'm not a complete dick like you, I'll allow you to keep Folomi. But I will not break the blood bond." I needed to keep my eye on him so he didn't pull more bullshit in the future.

He sighed in relief. "Thank you."

I removed my claws and stepped back. "Don't thank me. I revoke your permission to stay in my pocket. Take Folomi and don't fuck with me again." I released the magic holding his vampires.

After he inspected Folomi, he paused. "For what it's worth, I'm proud of you, niece. I did not expect you to take your place so soon. And I'm pleased it worked out this way." They vanished.

I spun in a slow circle to inspect his people. Or mine, I supposed. When I spotted my two newbies among them, I almost lost my shit. I'd told them to stay home.

Elizabeth stood over a vampire, her hyena teeth inches away from the face of a woman hundreds of years older than her. Muscles she didn't have bulged from her arms and legs. Red, knife-like claws sunk into the woman's stomach just under her ribs. The form was both beautiful and grotesque.

Near her, Spencer stood over another bloody vampire. His back hunched unnaturally, the bulging muscles straining against his T-shirt.

The same knives extended from his fingers and dripped blood. My baby vampires were as beautiful in their full form as they were freaky.

"Spencer, Elizabeth. Let them go," I managed to sound casual.

They stepped back and resumed their human forms.

One of Roman's vampires tore her eyes away from Spencer and stepped forward. "Who are you to remove our master?"

"I didn't take your master. I replaced him. Elsie?"

"Yes, Mistress?"

Blood gushed from several wounds, and a massive black bruise covered her face. Her eyes were slits from the swelling. She'd live. "Round up our new vampires."

Her swollen lips twitched. "On it."

I glanced toward the ruined wards and grimaced. Alex stood inside the wall, his eyes so sad my chest ached. The dragons flanked him. At the gate, a crowd of hybrids fought for position to see what was going on. Mom and Dad held them back, their eyes full of pride. Near them, an entire area lit up from Cavil's smile.

"Got 'em," Elsie said from behind me.

I pried my eyes away from my family to focus on the sea of vampires. My mouth felt like cotton, and I swallowed as I ramped up my aura to put on the show. "I'm Princess Lily, Daughter of Jonas the First and the Sorceress Ann Marie."

"Princess?" someone whispered.

"Correct." My hands curled into fists. "I am also the Granddaughter of the First Queen of Ahl and Heir to the Throne of Umbra. Welcome to the House of Lilith. Elsie is my second. Treat her orders as if they're mine. Belonging to my house is a privilege. Break my rules or disrespect the hybrids, and you'll die. I don't have the patience for your bullshit, so don't test me. Elsie, read them the rules and check out our new home."

"Yes, Mistress."

I paused as I limped toward the gate. "Call me Lily. And I don't want Roman's rooms, so figure something else out."

She bit her lip to keep from laughing as she nodded.

I went fluid and wrapped Alex in a hug. "I'm sorry." There were no other words. When Elsie explained what I needed to do, it didn't occur to me how much not having Alex around would hurt. But I also didn't want to spend the rest of my life worrying about other masters waging war against us. The best way to protect him was to establish myself, even if it hurt. He didn't agree. Not even when our parents encouraged me. Alex begged me to think of a different way, but I didn't.

He shoved me away. "You're always sorry after you make decisions that screw up your life. After you conveniently forget to ask what I want. Fuck you, Lily." Alex switched into his lion form and fled.

When I moved to follow, June blocked my path. "Give him some space."

"I will watch over him and protect him with my life. I swear it." Glacintial launched into the air as the contract settled over me.

Cavil's arm wrapped around me. "You won."

I tore my eyes away from Alex. "I'm pretty sure Roman let me win, but yeah." My eyes stung with tears as I tugged him toward a multi-colored tree and extracted a gift. "I didn't want to give it to you before in case...." I trailed off and held up the gold chain. Dangling from the end of it was my fang.

His face stayed neutral as he took it from me and examined it.

I swallowed at his lack of reaction. What was I thinking? He was a god with a massive following. He probably thought my little tooth necklace was gross. Most people didn't have darkness clouding their vision like me. Especially not a god who could create sunshine. "You don't have to wear it if you don't want to."

"No one has ever given me such a gift." His fists closed around the necklace possessively as he slipped it over his head.

"Yeah. Kinda like how no one has ever given me such mixed signals."

He spun me around, and his lips trailed down my temple to my ear. "I meant it is heartfelt. I will never take it off."

Shivers ran down my spine. "That's kind of unhygienic. But maybe take it out once in a while and think of me?"

His laugh rattled my bones. "I am a god. I can keep my most prized possession clean." His lips touched mine. "You've left me speechless, Lily. Thank you. I will treasure it always."

A throat cleared behind us, and I pulled away. "Thank you. For saving our asses and...everything. I need to stay here for a few days while we work out how this will go."

Cavil ran a finger down my cheek. "I must return to Allure. I will text you." He disappeared.

Chapter Twenty-Two

I barely toured the common areas when Senga appeared. "You have a visitor."

Something in her tone made me pause before I answered. "Who?"

"The hybrid leader, Dale. In the sitting room."

I didn't know where the sitting room was, but assumed I'd find it near the main entrance. Dale lounged on a fussy blue chair in a pristine white room. "How's it hanging, Dale?"

Amusement sparked in his eyes. "What in the ever-loving hell are you doing now?"

I sighed. "Apparently, I'm a housemaster now."

Rumbling laughter echoed through the room. "You, who refused to acknowledge your bloodline, not only beat the oldest vampire but took his house? You?" More laughter. "I cannot fucking believe it."

I slammed my hands on my hips. "Roman set me up and almost got Alex killed. What was I supposed to do?"

His enormous head shook. "I don't care. It's just fucking funny."

It was, I supposed. Especially considering it was the last thing I wanted.

He rubbed his eyes. "You are single-handedly my favorite entertainment. I can never predict what mess you'll find." His face sobered and his eyes sharpened. "I'm glad you took over. The pureblood master made the hybrids nervous."

I winced. "He didn't cause too much trouble, did he?"

"None. But everyone was on edge. They're elated that one of their own took the house." He examined the room. "Are you going to live here?"

I shrugged. "For now." I couldn't help but think being forced to live in the pristine mansion was payback for making fun of my parents' house in Allure. "Are you here for PR, or is there a point to your visit?"

He rubbed his chin. "I came to request help from the vampires. Maria can't keep up with supplies. And we need people to knock on doors and convince hybrids to take shelter here before the feds figure out what they are."

"How many?"

"About a quarter of the hybrids will not evacuate, including Sheila. She's convinced humans will become accustomed to us if we stay."

"Sheila won't listen to me, but we'll help knock on doors. I'll also assign ten vampires to help Maria with supplies." They needed something to do since I didn't own businesses and couldn't provide them with jobs.

"Maria will be thrilled."

I bet. She hated purebloods more than most. If it were up to me, I'd let Sheila and her loyalists take their chances. But Dale was the hybrid leader, so I supposed he had to help them. "Have you found the guys who shot up your bar?"

"They're no longer an issue."

"Good. Are dragons still patrolling the area?"

"Yes. The consort doesn't want to force them to move because he's worried about how people will perceive the queen."

Drake was a good guy. Between him and Jen, they could have coerced everyone to hide in the pockets. But they were trying to build trust. I liked how respectful they were to the hybrids. Though, I had to admit I'd become biased. "I'll take a team out and see what we can do."

He gave us the locations of the holdouts.

I assigned Elsie to lead the group at Maria's. A third of the vampires stayed at the mansion with strict instructions to watch over my newbies. My group was divided into pairs, and I took Senga with me. I thought about making her my third, but I wanted to see how well we worked together first. Her intense personality sometimes rubbed me the wrong way, and I didn't trust any of Roman's vampires enough to hand them a position of power.

We headed toward the bench where three families still lingered.

The first one wouldn't answer the door, so we left a coded note and moved to the second. It was a small house a block from my former coworker, Susan's place. An ancient leopard shifter I didn't recognize opened the door, and his eyebrows drew together. "The blood bar is closed."

I shifted my weight. "Funny. We're here to encourage you to take shelter inside a pocket because the human government is hunting us."

"Are you?"

Senga's hand landed on my arm. "The Queen of Ahl has built a pocket we named Eldritch for hybrids. They will welcome you."

His eyes lit with interest. "As you can see, I'm not a hybrid. Nor do I support their cause. I will not be going with you."

I examined his face. His magic registered as a regular shifter, but something about him made me uneasy. "Okay. Self-appointed militias are also hunting paranormals, so be careful." I moved back down his driveway and hid in the shadows.

The guy stood in his doorway for a full minute before closing it.

Senga shifted beside me. "He's an ancient cat shifter. They're solitary creatures."

Her words punched me in the gut. Alex wasn't a solitary creature. And I missed him so much I couldn't think about him without drowning in despair. We might have been codependents or something. I threw it out of my head and moved toward Susan's house.

"Where are you going?" Senga asked.

"To check on a friend."

Susan didn't answer her door until I texted to tell her it was me. She wore a pair of yoga pants and a faded T-shirt. Her hair was piled on her head, and the lines on her face were more prominent than I'd ever seen. "Lily. Senga. I'm so glad you're here. Roman's not answering his phone, and I need help."

A floor-to-ceiling pile of boxes lined one side of the small room. I frowned when I spotted them. "Are you moving?"

"That's what I need help with." She bit her lip. "These guys in black suits showed up and questioned me about my medium abilities. They found my streaming channel and monitored it for a while. A ghost told me they're up to something. Ashley doesn't have anyone else, so I need to hide." Ashley was her teenage daughter.

I pulled my phone out. "You can come to the pocket."

Her head shook before I finished speaking. "Ashley is human."

"I can let her in. And we have people to move your stuff. You can stay with us until the architecture mages build you a house."

Tears streaked down her face. "Can we go tonight?"

Five vampires arrived and cleared her house in an hour, then loaded Susan and Ashley into a truck to take back to Eldritch. My mom agreed to meet them and give them permission to access the pocket. We stopped by a few more hybrid houses, but they wouldn't leave, so we gave them our dire warning. At the end of the night, we only convinced a handful to evacuate.

The privacy bubble had shrunk again and only covered one block. Relief flooded me as we entered it, and I saw how much progress the mages had made. I scanned all the new bonds one at a time. Something felt off about five of them, including Senga's. It was almost as if there was an echo in them. I delved deeper into one, and a familiar energy washed over me.

My skin broke into goosebumps at the discovery, but I kept my breathing even and didn't react as I held the door to Hooves open for Senga. I filled Dale in on our lack of progress as we waited for the rest of our team.

When we reached the mansion, my mind reeled about what to do. I thought about calling Meemaw, but Dad had a point about fighting my own battles. It was something I needed to figure out myself.

The next day, I trekked to the other end of the mansion to check on Susan and Ashley. I gave them a three-bedroom apartment at the far end, so they had a piece of the expansive yard to themselves. They loved it and were excited to start their new lives.

As I left, I texted Elsie to call a house meeting and pulled Spencer and Elizabeth into a vacant room to explain my plan.

The room I chose was large enough to accommodate a house twice the size of my new group. Chairs lined up in perfectly straight rows, and several sat empty. I watched as the vampires formed small clusters as they took a seat. Spencer and Elizabeth zipped around the room, delivering small cups to them.

When I sensed unease roll through the blood bonds, I motioned for Elsie to stay by the door. Many of my new vampires weren't loyal to any housemaster, but understood the reasons for them. Others hated being part of such a large house or small house. They were a diverse group. The five with echoes gave me nothing.

After everyone settled, my eyes landed on Senga. "The drink in your hand is my blood. *Drink it.*" I used persuasion.

All but the five traitors did as they were told. A few of the younger ones collapsed. I motioned toward one. "We lift each other up in this house. It's your duty to watch over each other and have each other's backs. If one of your brothers or sisters falls, it's your responsibility to pick them up." Several vampires followed my orders.

I dropped my arms and refocused on Senga's group. *"Drink."*

The small glass hit me square in the chest as she launched out of her seat. "We aren't tying ourselves to an abomination! I refuse and request an immediate transfer."

I raised an eyebrow. "After a hostile takeover, vampires are required to give the new master five years. It's up to you how you spend them." I held out a fresh cup. "Either you drink willingly, or I'll make you. Your choice."

She eyed it with a skeptical look. "Are you implying I'm not loyal?"

"No. I'm implying you weren't loyal to Roman, and you sure as hell aren't loyal to me." I leaned forward. "How did you and Jed fool Roman?"

Her face scrunched. "It wasn't difficult. Roman lost his mind a long time ago."

My uncle wasn't nearly as crazy as he pretended. But it wasn't my place to say anything, so I nodded. *"Explain."* I used extra persuasion.

Several vampires gasped.

Senga blocked the blood bond. I bonded with their master instead of creating a direct one, so it wasn't as strong. Had I not been monitoring her, the attempt might have worked.

I went fluid, forced her mouth open, and poured. When my eyes landed on the other traitors, they drank. Their bonds flared as I returned to the front of the room. I'd not only put my blood in the cups, but added venom with my unique blend of the vampire virus. Meemaw said venom was more potent than blood bonds, so it was worth a try. So far, no one had hyena teeth, but the ones who already drank felt as strong as the vampires I made. When Senga quit convulsing, my attention returned to her. *"Explain."*

She launched out of her chair. "You can't do this to your father! He loves you, and you have done nothing but hurt him."

My laugh was a little too ragged. "That motherfucker has no love for anyone but himself." My fists clenched and unclenched. Thinking about good ole Jed enraged me. I fought the urge to let my dark magic wipe out every vampire in the room.

"You don't know him like I do." Senga's calculating eyes swung around the room. "Master Jedediah is twice the master you'll ever be."

Elsie's laughter rang out. Good ole Jed was her original master, and she hated him almost as much as me. "Master Jedediah is a monster and a child abuser. The queen herself has removed his power. So you can fuck right off with that sales pitch."

I blinked. It wasn't like her to drop protocol. "Agreed."

Senga stepped toward me but halted. It was impossible for a vampire to attack their master. "Why couldn't you just die at the hands of the humans like you were supposed to?" She dug into the bond, attempting to break it.

Jed's echo faded as I pressed my will, but it was still there, so I delved deeper. The magic in his bond was unmistakably my mother's. The realization caused my iron-like grip on Senga's bond to slip.

"Jedediah will kill you for this," she growled.

I leaned forward until we were eye-to-eye. "No, he won't. I am the heir and have the power of Lilith, while he's a coward who needs his mommy to spank his ass. Or did you not hear about the last time he tried to kill me?" She was strong. So strong, it took everything I had to keep control. Right before she won the tug-of-war, I sent a wave of magic down the bond.

Light exploded in the room, and the scent of ozone clogged the air. The five vampires' eyes went glassy.

I took advantage of the situation. "Why did Jed send you to Roman? And what did he plan to do to me?"

"Master Jedediah knew Roman guarded you. He planted me to report back with inside information."

What an ass. "And did you?"

"Yes. Until Mistress Ara tried to break his bonds. She's stupid if she thinks it worked."

My fangs extended. "Do. Not. Insult. My. Meemaw."

A wave of vacant nods spread through the room.

"Continue."

"He instructed me to leak information to the Bellicose about his father's whereabouts so they'd kill him. He had strong ties to their leadership. When I failed, I tried to make up for it by planting seeds within the hybrids about you and the coalition. We didn't expect the human government to intervene, but we took the opportunity when presented. We told them all about you and that lion you call a brother. Roman was too stupid to pick up on our ruse and went along with framing Sheila and displacing you."

Me. I was his strong ties to the Bellicose. My mother, with whom Jed shared a child, started their resurgence. He probably thought he could leverage that. The manipulative prick. My eyes closed as I thought it through. Right before the fight, someone exposed the entire battle plan. Jen and Mat were pissed and ordered the traitors exposed. They didn't check on the vampires because Ara usually monitored them. "Did you give the battle plan to the Bellicose?"

"Yes. Among other things." Her smile was pure evil.

Holy shit. It felt like a ton of bricks crashed on my head. Senga, and by association, Jed, had got so many people killed to what? Take out Quin? Or Jen? The sheer shock paralyzed me for a touch too long. I raised my eyes and met Senga's. "You are so fucked."

Roman had an entire prison under the house, so I stashed Jed's vampires inside separate cells and texted Drake. I considered texting Jen, but he usually handled hybrid relations. I wanted to keep what I learned quiet if they were working with others.

Elsie and I stood at the front entrance as Drake descended on us in his massive dragon form. He was larger and more regal than any other dragon I'd seen. Well, except for Deva and Bastien. They rivaled his regalness. Or whatever.

He touched down and shifted into a fully clothed version of his human form. His lips twitched. "Nice house."

I raised my middle finger and pretended to scratch my nose.

Drake threw his head back and laughed. "You said you had an urgent matter."

"Yeah. Remember how someone kept leaking high-level battle plans to the Bellicose?"

Flames lit in his eyes. "Yes."

"I found our traitor."

Roman's house sucked, I thought as I sprawled across a wicker sofa in an unnecessary sunroom. My eyes stayed glued to a gnarled oak-like tree in the backyard while I tried to count the number of colors on the branch for the millionth time. My heart ached from missing Alex, and Cavil had to go to Allure to meet with Jen and her advisors about the traitor issue. Drake and a few other dragons dragged Jed's group to Allure, but I still felt their bonds. They weren't having fun. I buried them in the back of my head with a sigh.

The other new vampires didn't cause problems. They were all older and well-behaved. So much so, it only took me a day or so to sort through their bonds and decide who to check on. My newbies still needed guidance, so I monitored them closely.

The mansion was all marble and shine. The rooms Elsie gave me were cold and impersonal, and the rest of the house was far too sophisticated to be comfortable. I was lonely and bored and longed to go back and make a different choice.

Movement in the doorway pulled my attention away from the tree. "Yes?"

"You have visitors." Susan fought to keep the concern out of her voice. "I settled them in the kitchen."

I rubbed my face with both hands. "Thanks." When my feet touched the ground, I wobbled. How long had I been on the sofa? I'd lost track of time and didn't know if it had been hours or weeks. My legs were tight, and I couldn't remember which direction to go.

Susan extended an arm and pointed. "That way. Are you okay?"

"Yeah. Thanks."

A jolt went through me when I reached the kitchen. Alex sat at the table, munching on a sandwich. Beside him, Glacintial sipped a beer. A thrill shot through me at the sight of them. I clutched the door frame to keep from racing across the room and hugging my brother.

Alex set his sandwich down and raised his head. "You look like shit."

My lips twitched. "Gee, thanks."

He blinked. "Ha! You missed me! I knew it."

I moved further into the room. "Stay out of my head."

"Not a chance." He waved a hand. "So, how's mausoleum living going for you? Have you pretended to be Mom or Lady of the Manor yet?"

I perched on a chair. "I hadn't thought about acting like Mom, no. And I hate it here. But it *was* necessary."

He nodded. "Glac and I have talked. I still don't believe living here is in your best interest. Not only because you suck at life without me keeping you reasonable, but because a depressed Lily is dangerous."

My ears perked up. "Oh?"

He waved a hand. "This house was designed for royalty."

"True."

"And you hate being royalty."

"Also true."

"We came up with a solution."

My eyes narrowed. "Who's we?"

"Everyone who cares about you."

I took a deep breath and bit my tongue. I hated it when other people decided things for me. It reminded me of how my biological mother controlled me. "Who? Because I thought you hated me now."

He raised a finger. "Hate is a strong word. I'm pissed at you and will continue to be for a long time."

"Fair. But there wasn't any other way."

Alex stood, a small smile ghosting across his face. "Come with me before I change my mind."

I followed him out the ridiculously oversized door, a silent Glac trailing behind. Alex laced his arms with ours and flashed.

We landed on the lawn of what used to be our bright blue house. A tan one that reflected our house in the human world greeted me. Only it was twice the size. Where the DMZ and Cavil's mansion used to be was a street with houses lining each side, all in the same style as ours but much smaller.

I craned my neck toward the gate to see if there were other changes but didn't spot any, so I returned my gaze to the houses. "Where's Cavil's house?"

Alex shoved me toward the back door. "Let's go inside."

The conversation died, and several stabbing sensations dug into my chest as I entered the room. I blinked at the crowd gathered around a massive table.

Cavil stood and moved to me. "Hello, Lily."

"Hey, Your Hotness. What's all this about?"

Everyone was there. Mom and Dad sat at a square table across from Drake and Jen, Flintous and June beside them. Emine and her brother Rayar sat on the other side. Emine's eyes were so sad it was hard to focus on them. Meemaw and Gramps took up the third side. She motioned me over. "You may sit here, Lily."

Alex shoved me in her direction. He and Glac took seats on the fourth side.

I lowered myself into the chair beside Meemaw and waited for Cavil to settle. "What's going on?"

Jen leaned her elbows on the table. "You look like shit."

I sighed. "So I've heard."

She chuckled. "We've figured out a way for your vampire house to live here without causing Alex pain."

My stunned gaze snapped to my brother. "The houses?"

He shrugged. "Deva's been helping me to block thoughts. It won't be long before I can tune them all out."

"Your vampires will be good practice for him, love," Deva said from somewhere deeper in the house. She appeared in the doorway. Jen's friend,

Tracy, and the dragon prince, Bastien, stood behind her. Tracy gave me a pinky wave.

Mom nodded. "Hopefully, this solution will stop you two from moping around."

My eyes burned with tears. Alex and I were too attached to each other. We had been since he was six and I was twelve. We were each other's BFF and support. And without him around, I felt like someone carved my heart out and left me hollow. Not that I'd admit it. "So, what's the catch?"

Meemaw's tinkering laugh filled the dining room. "No catch, dear. We simply wish you to be happy."

I focused on Alex. "Are you sure you're okay with this?"

He nodded. "Your four original vampires can live here. Deva agreed to allow the dragons to stay and sent two more to help tutor me."

Deva's predatory grin sent chills down my spine. "It is a hybrid pocket, so I don't see the harm in mixing factions."

"I agree," Meemaw said. "And it will deter future incidents."

Relief flooded me, and a spark of happiness lit in my chest. I turned to Cavil. "What about you? Are you moving to Allure?"

His sunny smile held a tinge of mischief. "Did you forget about how Jonas sold you to me for a favor? I will live here. I've chosen a room so you don't feel rushed. In exchange, I have prepared a room in my house in Allure for you."

Lust exploded inside me as everything we could do to each other raced through my mind. "And your bear shifters?"

"They will remain. I assigned them three of the new houses."

A genuine smile formed as I thought about all those straight-laced, rule-following vampires adjusting to such a weird house. "This will be interesting."

Alex nodded. "The drama will keep you out of trouble."

It would. The hope I thought was gone forever ignited inside me. My eyes brimmed with tears of relief. I blinked them back. "Okay. Let's break the news to my house."

Jen raised her hand. "Before you go, I have a request."

"Of course you do."

"I need your help with handling the human government."

My spine straightened, and my eyes filled with power. "I'm in."

The end (for now).

One More Thing

THANK YOU SO MUCH for reading to the end.

If you haven't already done so, please take a moment to leave a few stars.

Lily and Cavil will continue their romance in the final book of the series, The Queen of Ahl (Book 4). It's still scheduled to be released at the end of April. Jenella is forced to deal with the fallout from Lily destroying a federal prison facility, her grief, her past, her future, and, worse, government officials.

Later this year, the first book or two of a new series in a new world will be released. You can find the full description on the series page on my website at. While you're there, sign up for my newsletter at www.mlconklin.com to stay updated on upcoming releases.

Thanks again to everyone who helped me with this book. The editors, proofreaders, beta readers, and ARC readers were all amazing to work with and continue to make me a better writer, one criticism at a time. The cover designers at getcovers.com do a great job with the covers.

I'd thank my furry assistants, but Callie, one of my feline assistants, stuck her tongue out at me for five minutes straight when I suggested it. My other feline assistant, Gracie, slept on my head last night and is now curled up in my spot in the warm bed. I'm jealous. I will thank my canine assistant, Zorro because he'll give me those sad puppy-dog eyes if I don't.

Like most authors, I thank my readers in every newsletter and at the end of every book. So much so it becomes routine. But my appreciation couldn't be more sincere. I wrote this series in 2019, and it took me years to work up the courage to publish it. I'm glad I didn't give up because I have met some of the best people and received the kindest emails and comments. You are what keeps me going.

Thank you.
ML Conklin

Email: mlconklin@mlconklin.com

Here's my socials:
I'm most active on:
Threads: https://www.threads.com/authormlconklin
Facebook: https://www.facebook.com/author.mlconklin
Instagram: https://www.instagram.com/authormlconklin
I also have accounts on:
Bluesky: https://bsky.app/profile/authormlconklin.bsky.social
TikTok: https://www.tiktok.com/@authormlconklin
X (Twitter): https://www.twitter.com/authormlconklin

Series Info.

The Paranormals of Ahl series:

The Dragon Problem (Book 1)
Bug Magic (Book 2)
The Mage Vampire Hybrid (Book 2.5) – Lily's POV
Crowns and Curses (Book 3)
The Hybrid Heir (Book 3.5) – Lily's POV
The Queen of Ahl (Book 4) – Coming Soon

Printed in Dunstable, United Kingdom

67898069R00143